Rowena Portch

*May the Spirit
bless you with
abundant love*
Ro

THE
PROTECTED

BOOK I

of the Spirian Series

Outskirts Press, Inc.
Denver, Colorado

The Protected
Book I of the Spirian Series
All Rights Reserved.
Copyright © 2010 Rowena Portch
v2.0

Outskirts Press, Inc.
http://www.outskirtspress.com

ISBN: 978-1-4327-5866-0

Outskirts Press and the "OP" logo are trademarks belonging to Outskirts Press, Inc.

PRINTED IN THE UNITED STATES OF AMERICA

Acknowledgements

My most sincere gratitude is extended to my fabulous husband, Gregg, who never gave up on me, and who offered generous encouragement to tell my story. The many hours he donated toward my writing time is appreciated and will hopefully be reciprocated with the success of this series.

I also want to thank my children, Erika, Nick, Andrew, and Zach, for their encouragement and valuable feedback. The same holds true for my mother and father, and my friends, Denise, Georgian, and Esther, who endured several revisions of this story.

A special thanks is also extended to my editor, Mead Hunter, who laboriously polished each word to make this entire story shine.

I am very blessed to be surrounded by so many true souls who share their gifts willingly for the price of a smile. God bless you all.

Those who are gifted are called Spirians,
a race that is not quite human, but not quite spirit either.
They are caught between the physical and spiritual realms
where anything is possible.

Chapter 1

*A*world of duality has many names: yin and yang, good and evil, light and dark. When one overshadows the other, a paradigm shift occurs to restore balance; such is the law of all life.

Some people discover their life's purpose early on in life. I discovered mine when I thought my life was over.

I awoke to the constant beeps of monitors and the smell of alcohol and bleach. The nightmares were becoming more real and demented. In my previous dreams, I was merely an observer. This one was different. I was involved, but as a man, not a woman. Who was I in this dream? In this shadowy realm, I peered into a mirror, but the man who stared back at me was unfamiliar. One thing for sure——I felt his pain as if it were my own.

Prior to my relentless nightmares, the last thing I remembered was Sam's car spinning out of control and my head slamming into a hard, sharp object.

Sam and I were technical writers for a software firm in Seattle. We were on our way back from the annual company conference held at Safeco field. After the event coordinators got through with it, the baseball field resembled a rock star stage gone technical. Big screen projectors lined the outfield. The turf was covered in cloth and a wooden podium towered out of an impressive stage made to look like marble.

Sam was trying to guess what the theme would be for next year when his cell phone rang. He never got a chance to answer it. A car had swerved into our lane, its tail lights flashed brightly. Sam slammed on his brakes, the rear end of the car slid sideways slamming into a truck. That's when I hit my head. I didn't remember anything after that.

There was a good-sized bump on my scalp and my head felt like it was stuck in a vice. A stabbing pain bit through my right leg. I reached for it and tried to sit up. The room spun around me. My head felt heavy and thick. Though I was mostly blind, I saw, in great clarity, green ooze seeping through the walls.

Someone entered my room. Given the weight of the sound, the person couldn't weigh more than 90 pounds—hardly a threat. Three years ago, I began feeling a bit paranoid as if people were watching me. It was unjustified, but I kept my distance from others except for Sam. For some reason, he seemed safe—perhaps because he was gay and had some oddities to his character that made mine pale in comparison.

"You're awake," she said. I could only see her shape and the faded hue of her smock. She was a tiny bit of goods, standing at about 5 foot 2 inches tall.

"Yeah," I replied, so groggy that my voice hardly sounded

like my own. "Where am I?" My throat was dry and raw.

She fumbled with the IV tubes and pressed a button on my monitor. "Harborview Medical Center." Her tiny hand pressed against my forehead. Her skin felt cool against mine. "You're a bit warm. How do you feel?"

I winced from the pain engulfing my leg. "Like I've been recruited for a horror movie," I said.

She laughed in response. "Would you like something for the pain?"

I shook my head. Drugs were definitely on my "things to avoid" list, since I witnessed their effects on my late husband, Derrick. "Are you aware that green ooze is seeping out of the walls?"

She was silent for a second then chuckled. "You've been on morphine for three days. It can make you see things."

Yeah, I thought. It spawned some rather convincing dreams as well. It proved my theory that drugs are evil.

The girl was still and silent for a moment as if she were studying me. "Your friend said that you're blind."

I smiled, grateful to know that Sam was alive and well enough to tell people about me. "I am," I said. "Mostly, anyway."

Her silence and posture indicated that she wanted to ask more but was not comfortable doing so. I was grateful. My blindness was not something I enjoyed talking about, especially to strangers.

"I'm Katie," she said. A pleasant aroma of lilac permeated the air around her as she moved.

I knew that she already knew more about me than I would have voluntarily revealed, but I answered her sweet introduction as she may have expected. "I'm Skye." My head pounded and felt far too heavy for my neck to support. "How's Sam?"

I listened to her babble on about his animated personality. He had suffered a concussion and a broken tibia. His spleen was also enlarged, so they were keeping him for observation.

"There was also a dog in the car," I said. "Maiyun, my service dog. Is she…"

Katie remained silent and my chest constricted around my heart.

"I didn't hear about a dog," she said, probably noticing the tears that welled in my eyes.

She placed her hand on my arm, offering reassurance. "I'll ask the paramedics who brought you in. Perhaps they know what happened to her."

I forced a smile. "I'd appreciate that." In my heart, I knew that Maiyun was okay. She and I had a bond that I never had with my other service dogs. I had trained her myself with the gracious help from my retired dog, Nika. She passed away when Maiyun was eight months old. Somehow, Maiyun knew her job was important and she took it seriously.

"Tell me about her," said Katie as she removed the items that cluttered my bed tray.

The smell of food wafted in from the hallway; it had

to be mealtime. The smell of sirloin steak and rich gravy caused my mouth to water with anticipation. My stomach growled with eager anticipation.

Maiyun's grey-masked face entered my thoughts and I began to smile. "She'll be two this year," I said.

"Wow, she's young."

I smiled and nodded. "Yeah."

"Is she a Lab?" asked Katie.

I shook my head. "No, she is three-quarter Malamute, and one-quarter Siberian Husky."

Katie was quiet for a moment. "I thought those dogs were used to pull sleds?"

"They are," I said. "Typically. She was a gift from a friend."

"She must be very special," said Katie. "I'll try to find her for you."

A young man entered the room with a tray of food. It didn't smell like sirloin steak. Katie lifted the lids and identified the contents. "Beef broth, two saltine crackers, cherry Jell-O, and a hot cup of tea."

My stomach growled again, this time in protest. "Am I on a diet?"

Katie shook her head. "Unfortunately, we need to start you with simple foods to give your system time to adjust. You haven't eaten anything for three days."

"Good," I said. "Maybe I lost a pound or two."

"Doesn't look like you really need to," she said sweetly.

My expression reflected the doubt I felt in her words.

When I was 37, I stood at 5 foot 7 and weighed 138 pounds. Now, I'm 45, one inch shorter, and 55 pounds heavier. Most people didn't notice the added years and weight, but I did.

Katie finished arranging the food, and then pushed the tray toward me. "Bon appétit" she said.

"I don't suppose there is any chance of me getting a one-pump mocha with cinnamon powder and whole milk?" I asked.

She laughed. "Not tonight." She checked the equipment one last time before leaving. "I'll see you tomorrow, Skye."

"Bye, Katie. Thanks for the company."

The room was silent again, filled only with the rhythmic beeping of the monitors, some conversation in the next room, and a TV show from down the hall. The bed beside me was empty.

I took my time enjoying the food, allowing each flavor and texture to dance on my tongue along with the steak and veggies I conjured with my imagination. The meal was sparse, but satisfying.

A tall, stocky man entered the room, followed by a dark, younger man. Without full-spectrum light, I could not see their faces.

"Good evening, Miss Taylor. I'm Doctor Jigante and this is Doctor Mel. How are you feeling?"

"Like I've been run over by a truck."

He chuckled.

The tall one lifted my chart from the end of my bed and flipped through the pages. "Well, your last pain shot was eight hours ago. You can have another."

"No thank you," I said. "The green ooze coming through the walls is a strong deterrent."

"Yes," he mused. "Morphine can have that effect. I can give you something else, if you prefer?"

I shook my head. "No, my imagination needs no assistance. It's scary enough the way it is, thank you."

He put the chart down then proceeded to shine a bright light into my eyes. "Your chart indicates that you're blind."

I blinked a few times, trying to clear the spots from my limited field of vision. "Well, I am now."

"Is your blindness due to an injury?" he asked.

I shook my head. "No. I have Retinitis Pigmentosa."

"When were you diagnosed?"

"When I was 20. The doctor claimed I would be completely blind by the time was 30."

"And are you?" he asked.

"Am I 30, no. Am I blind—partially. I see shapes and shadows for the most part. If the light is bright enough, I can see detail."

"Hmm." His reply dripped with doubt.

I received that response a lot. The doctor at the University of Washington, locally known as the U-Dub, had the nerve to tell me my eyes could not see anything. It didn't matter that I could tell him how many fingers he held up. He attributed it to some uncanny ability to use other senses. Hogwash.

Dr. Jigante lifted the covers off my right leg. It looked

as large as a tree trunk and felt just as heavy. His touch on my skin felt cold and empty. No compassion or empathy at all, strictly business.

He rambled off some instructions to Dr. Mel that sounded like another language. Dr. Mel left quickly.

"Am I going to live?" I asked jokingly, trying to lighten his dark mood.

"You have an infection," he said. "Dr. Mel has left to get you antibiotics."

What I needed was a good acupuncturist and some herbs. Fat chance I'd find them here, though.

Dr. Mel returned with a syringe and small bottles. He filled the syringe, and then injected its contents into my IV tube.

Dr. Jigante finished changing my dressing, and then re-covered my leg. "You suffered a minor concussion and multiple fractures to your femur, Miss Taylor. We had to install a titanium rod to hold your bone together. You also tore the PCL in your right knee."

I pursed my lips. "Well, that doesn't sound too bad," I said jokingly. "When can I go home?"

He scribbled something on my chart. "When your blood count is normal and you are able to get around."

"How soon can I try?"

He made a gruff sound that reminded me of an old man in pain. "Maybe tomorrow." He put my chart back and touched my foot. "I'll see you then."

The two men talked among themselves as they left the

room. Again, it seemed to be in a different language.

I couldn't read the clock on the wall, but given the darkening light, I gauged it to be around seven or eight in the evening. I needed rest, but I wasn't the least bit tired, nor was I too eager to have another nightmare.

I sighed and tried to move my tree trunk of a leg. Pain ripped through me like a blazing hot knife, tearing through my flesh, followed by a muscle cramp from hell. I must have cried out loud because two nurses ran into my room. I didn't have the capacity to tell them I was all right. The pain gripped me and restricted my breath.

Sweat dripped down my forehead. The shorter nurse pried up my eyelids and stared into my eyes, while the taller one grabbed my chart. "Why has she gone so long without pain meds?"

I shook my head.

The short nurse patted my arm. "It will help, honey." She nodded to the taller nurse, who dashed out of the room.

"No pain meds," I strained to say. "Please?" Another pain gripped my leg. I could feel the spasms run up and down my thigh. I tried to stifle my groan, but it escaped my throat.

The taller nurse returned and confidently injected my IV with morphine.

The familiar heavy fog engulfed my brain and eased away the pain.

The shorter nurse patted my hand. "There now,

better?"

I wanted to rip the IV out of my arm and wrap the cord around her neck, but my reprieve from the intense pain called for gratitude instead. "Yes, thank you."

If I was ever going to escape the onslaught of drugs, I needed to control the pain. My limbs began to feel heavy and my eyes could no longer distinguish between illusion and reality.

The nightmare returned.

A redheaded woman stared at me with wide green eyes. Her body was tall and sleek. Copper hair fell in disarray about her shoulders. The bedroom smelled of sex and sweat where the man and woman laid in bed. The man glanced up at me, a devious smile stretched over his perfect teeth.

My hands reached out but they were not my own. They were the hands of a man. Thoughts swam through my head like hordes of sharks in a feeding frenzy. Some of the thoughts were the woman's, others belonged to the man she laid with, few were my own. Their union was complete and my body felt hollow. I couldn't breathe without pain.

The woman approached me. I knew her—intimately. She raised her fist and produced a knife. I turned to escape and felt the sharp steel pierce my flesh and cut through my ribs. When I faced her, I saw no remorse. Her lover laughed. His strong, chiseled face was evenly tanned and flawlessly groomed.

The woman fell at my feet, her life suddenly and inexplicably spent. Mine, too, felt spent, though I continued to breathe. My heart pumped blood through my veins, but it was void of life and void of love. I looked in the mirror across the room. Hazel eyes shone back at me. The face in the reflection was eerily similar to that of the woman's lover, though the eyes were more golden than green. Like the hands, the reflection staring back at me was not my own.

From the bed, the woman's lover reached out to me. My world turned black.

Chapter 2

In a world where everything exists and nothing exists at the same time, it is difficult to distinguish reality from illusion.

I felt my skin tingle. I opened my eyes to find a man standing beside me. Oddly, despite the lack of light, I could see him in brilliant detail. He wore faded blue jeans and a black brushed-cotton shirt with long sleeves. The white collar that distinguished him as a holy man shone brightly. He stood tall and in proportion to his stocky build. I noticed his trimmed silver hair, but what really stood out, were his eyes— Caribbean blue with flecks of silver. At first glance, he looked to be about 50 years old, but his face was not wrinkled and he moved too gracefully for a man that age.

He smiled, displaying a perfect set of brilliant teeth. They had to be fake, I was certain.

"I'm Reverend Mark," he said.

I blinked my eyes a few times, half expecting this illusion to fade; the walls' green ooze still looked comparatively real. Not wanting to appear rude, even to an illusion, I answered his greeting accordingly. "I'm Skye."

A lump formed in my throat. Had God sent an angel? It certainly would explain the intense vibration of color that surrounded his being. I had never seen anything like it. The color permeated his torso and surrounded him in a brilliant array of color.

"Am I dead?" I asked, sounding a bit foolish. "Have you come to take me home?"

He lifted his brow. "Are you ready?"

I hesitantly nodded my head, and swallowed against the constricting lump. My heart beat so hard in my chest, I found it hard to believe I was really dead. The man in my dream must have killed me, I thought, just as swiftly as he had killed the redheaded woman.

"Stand up, then, and I'll take you home."

My eyes grew wide. I wasn't too eager to repeat my last mistake. My leg felt heavy, too heavy to move. "I can't," I barely whispered.

His smile broadened. "Perhaps another day, then." It was more of a statement than a question.

He certainly was an odd man. I determined that I was not dead and he was not an angel sent to bring me home. Part of me was relieved. Another part was fascinated.

"Is there anything else I can do for you?" he asked.

"Take away this pain," I groaned.

"Pain is nothing more than illusion," he said. His eyes seemed to glow.

"It seems quite real on my end."

He placed his hands on my injured leg. Everything

tingled and felt very warm beneath his touch. The tingle changed to a buzz, and then I felt that buzz throughout my entire body. I saw a blue mist rise from his hands. Now I knew I was dreaming.

The dull pain slowly eased away. My eyes fluttered, and then suddenly felt heavy. I couldn't keep them open. The blissful darkness consumed me and allowed me to sleep in peace this time.

Something soft brushed against my nose. My eyes snapped open to find a large purple object in front of my face.

"Well, it's about time you woke up," a familiar voice said.

Sam held a huge purple bear with a big black nose up to my eyes. It was ironic how he and the bear shared the same round shape.

He wiggled the bear in front of me. "I brought you a soft and fuzzy," he said. "and it's purple!"

I squinted against the sunlight streaming in through the window. "Yes, I see that." For some reason, Sam thought that the closer an object was, the better I could see it. I tried correcting him many times, but he rarely listened.

He sat the bear down next to me. "You look like hell, Skye. How are you feeling?"

"Better, now that you're here," I said, emphasizing the sarcasm. Sam never was delicate with his choice of words, but he was always honest and had a great sense of humor. It really was refreshing to see him again.

He helped me sit up. His short, stubby hands matched the rest of his physique. At 5 foot 2 inches tall, he resembled a cuddly bear, round face and all, though not purple. Instead he wore his green plaid kilt and a black t-shirt with "Geek" written across the front in bold white letters. His fuzzy crewcut hair shone like bronze in the morning light. A rainbow-colored cast covered his left leg up to his thigh. How fitting, I thought. "Nice choice," I said, looking at the colorful ensemble.

He laughed and clumsily strutted his kilt and rainbow cast. "Do you think they clash?"

"Oh no," I said. "They scream, 'bold, daring, and take me now!'"

The rise of his bushy brow and smirking grin reflected my sarcasm. "Great, I'm asking a blind person for fashion advice."

I heard the breakfast cart in the hallway. Fat chance there was bacon, eggs, and toast on it for me. "Have you eaten?"

"No, they discharged me today. I'm just waiting for Karin to pick me up."

"How's your car?"

"I figure it will be melted down and turned into 420 cans of Red Bull before the turn of the week. It's totaled."

I frowned. "And Maiyun?"

His cherub face turned pale. "I don't know. I passed out." He reached over and grabbed my arm. "Oh, Skye, I'm so sorry."

I covered his hand with mine. "I'm sure she's fine."

The pain in his puppy eyes was too much. He always did have a flair for drama.

"Hey," I added. "She's fine. I know it."

He nodded, then backed away. "I should probably get back to my room before Karin comes."

I frowned. It wasn't like Sam to shut down like this. "You okay?"

"Yeah, I'll swing by tomorrow."

"Okay." I grabbed the bear and gave it a hug. "Hey, thanks for Mr. Fuzzy," I said, as Sam hobbled toward the door.

He glanced back with an evil grin and said, "Enjoy him, but not too much."

I was relieved to see his normal sense of humor return. Sam and I had been friends for seven years, back when his name was Samantha. I remembered his battle with the transgender process. It was a two-year ordeal and a very emotional one at that.

The testosterone shots made him intense and angry. He was miserable up to the day when he returned from San Francisco after his sex-change operation. He was several pounds lighter and happier than I had ever seen him.

Sam called himself queer. He enjoyed dating men and women, and prided himself on being polygamous. I didn't understand his sexual preferences, nor did he understand my choice of abstinence after my husband died. Our not understanding yet accepting one another's preferences was one of the reasons we were such good friends.

I attended Sam and Karin's hand-tying ceremony last year. Since polygamy is illegal in Washington, this ceremony provided a means for two or more people to be united in one relationship.

Sam had another wife in Colorado, and a husband in California. His lifestyle was odd to me, but I was sure mine would bore him to tears. I didn't have long to ponder our differences before the breakfast cart stopped in front of my door. I recognized Katie as she lifted a tray and carried it into my room. My mouth watered in anticipation.

"Good morning," she said cheerfully.

She was beautiful, and much younger than her brisk manner conveyed. Her blonde hair was held up by a yellow scrunchy and her green eyes were shining. Something had her in a good mood this morning.

She lowered my breakfast tray, and then set a steaming cup of coffee right beside it. "One pump mocha with cinnamon powder and whole milk?" Her brow lifted as if looking for confirmation.

My eyes widened and matched the enthusiasm in my smile. "Oh, you're an angel in the flesh." I picked up the ceramic mug and took a long, slow sip. I allowed the creamy liquid to linger on my tongue for a moment, enjoying the subtle hint of cocoa before swallowing. "It's perfect."

Katie lifted the tray cover and identified the contents for me. "Wheat toast, cream of wheat with all the trimmings, and canned peaches."

"Yes, it looks lovely."

She looked at me speculatively, her thin brows arched to a sharp peak. "You can see it?"

I glanced at the window. "Sunlight. If it's bright enough, I can see fairly well."

She looked as if she had more questions than she was allowed to ask.

"I'll tell you about it, sometime."

Her smirk turned into a smile. "You're very perceptive."

She had no idea, I thought. Since I was young, I could read people's intentions, which also led to knowing about their lies. It was a convenient gift at times, but could also be quite disturbing. The bright-colored vibration of energy that surrounded all life was easy for me to see and was always present.

My abilities disturbed my late husband, Derrick, so I learned to keep them suppressed. He was a religious man, whereas I was more spiritual. On many occasions, we simply agreed to disagree. There were times when I felt as if I was not really part of this world, just trapped in it for a while. There was more to this life, I knew it, I just couldn't quite touch it.

"I'll leave you to eat, and then I'll come back to check on you," said Katie.

I raised my coffee cup and smiled. "Thank you," I called out to her.

She turned and beamed a smile. "You're welcome."

My next few sips of coffee were pure heaven. I closed my eyes and gave silent thanks to our Father.

I did not consider myself a devout Christian as much as I was a spiritual one. I did not belong to a church, nor did I attend many services.

Derrick gave me a Bible one year for my birthday. He said that I often quoted the words of Jesus when I spoke. I was curious. After reading the New Testament, Jesus' wisdom touched me so deeply that I felt He was my blood brother. From then on, I vowed to follow His example. It was a poor attempt but an earnest one.

The cream of wheat looked half decent, not too sticky and not too runny. It had a bit of a malt fragrance to it. In surrounding bowls, there was some brown sugar, raisins, and a small pitcher of skim milk.

Not being a huge fan of either skim milk or sugar, I emptied the bowl of peaches into my cereal and stirred it up. Raisins were okay, but peaches sounded much better this morning. I took my time eating, savoring every morsel. Food was such a gift in life, one of my favorites. That probably explained why I couldn't lose weight.

Katie came back with a wheelchair, and a smile still beaming across her face.

"Are you up for a little stroll?" she asked.

I smiled back at her, grateful for any chance to escape this bed.

She checked my chart and furrowed her thin brows. "Did you want a pain shot first?"

My eyes narrowed as I said, "No!"

She put the chart back. "I didn't think so, but I noticed they gave you one at 11 last night."

"Yeah, well, it certainly wasn't my idea."

She pulled the wheelchair up beside my bed and locked the brakes. "Are you ready for this?" she asked.

"Ready as I'll ever be."

She removed my covers and then scooped her arm around my legs. "Okay," she said. "I'm going to swing your body over so that your legs are off the bed."

I took a deep breath, and then whispered, "Okay."

She positioned her other arm under my shoulders. With what seemed to be minimal effort, she had me sitting upright with my legs off the bed. She supported my right leg so it wouldn't bend. "You okay?"

I nodded, still holding my breath.

"I'm going to lower your right leg very slowly. It might be uncomfortable but just breathe through it, okay?"

Again, I nodded.

I heard someone say, "Skye, breathe." But I did not know if it was her, or just myself bracing for the pain that was to come.

I forced myself to take a breath. A quiet voice inside my head said, "Pain is just an illusion." I felt the blood drain from my face.

"Keep breathing, Skye. You look pale." She held my leg. "Are you sure you're up for this?"

"Yes, I'm fine." I took a deep breath. "Okay, go ahead."

Katie slowly lowered my right leg. My knee burned as if it were on fire. My flesh felt like it was tearing. Tears began to well in my eyes.

"Keep breathing," she said.

I breathed deep and tried to relax my leg. My thigh threatened to spasm. Again, the voice whispered, "Pain is just an illusion."

As the pain increased with each agonizing degree of flexion, I imagined my leg was whole and well. There was nothing wrong with it and there was no need for pain. Instinctively, I placed my right hand over my right knee and imagined the blue mist I had seen rise from Reverend Mark's hands.

No pain, I thought.

"Almost there," said Katie.

No pain, I opened my eyes and saw a film of blue mist rise from my hand. My eyes widened.

"You did it." Katie glanced up at me and smiled. "Well done."

I looked at my hand in amazement. Katie obviously did not see what I had seen.

"How do you feel?" she asked.

"Great." I felt more than great, to be exact. I was elated and perhaps a bit scared. What had just happened? Was it real or just another by-product of the morphine?

Katie had an expression of concern. "No pain?"

I shook my head. "No, not now."

She laughed. "Wow, you're doing great." She shifted her

hip against my thigh. "Ready to stand?"

"Yep."

"Only on your left leg." She scooted me off the bed and supported my weight until I found my balance. She then helped me pivot and expertly guided me into the chair.

"Voilà!" she said. "Success."

She lifted my feet onto the foot rests. "How are you doing?"

I nodded and smiled. "Better than expected." That was certainly no exaggeration of that truth by any measure.

"Amen to that," she added. "You're gonna like this," she sang, releasing the brakes. She grabbed the blanket from my bed and draped it over my legs. "Ready?"

I nodded. "Yes, I am."

The hall was buzzing with people. It must have been visiting hour or something. There was no sign of Reverend Mark.

Katie backed me into the elevator and pressed the lobby button.

"I had a visit from the Reverend last night," I said.

"The Reverend?"

"Yeah, Reverend Mark." I described him to her and explained enough about what he had done without sounding crazy.

She laughed. "Must have been the morphine," she said. "We don't have anyone like that on this floor."

It did seem rather odd how I could see him in such vivid detail, I thought. And the energy that surrounded him was too surreal. Perhaps it was just an illusion.

She pushed me past the latte stand and gift shop. We turned the corner and headed toward a door with a large blue sign that I couldn't read. She pressed her badge to the black reader and the doors swung open.

Cold air greeted us. At the end of the long hallway, I could hear some laughter.

"Okay, close your eyes," said Katie.

Even though I couldn't see much in this dim lighting, I did as she asked.

She pushed me into the room where I heard the laughter. Everyone was silent.

"You can open your eyes now."

It was too dark for me to see any detail, but one figure stood out from all the others.

My beautiful Maiyun walked slowly toward me and placed her large head on my lap. Tears welled in my eyes and were soon streaming down my face as I looked up and thanked God for keeping her safe.

I bent down to kiss the bridge of her nose. Her musty scent brought me comfort that can only come from familiarity.

She hobbled, clearly favoring her right hind leg.

"Oh, Maiyun, you're hurt." I glanced around the room, hoping to hear an explanation.

A middle-aged man with light-colored hair spoke up. "She was injured in the accident. Her right hip was dislocated. It took the vet three hours to reset it."

I reached over to give Maiyun a hug. I then looked at the room of people through teary eyes. "Thank you for taking care of her."

Maiyun pressed her right hip against my hand. Her fur felt cool to my palm. I imagined blue smoke rising up through my hand, in hopes of removing her pain as it had mine. She licked my other hand, encouraging me to continue. The increasing heat in my hand traveled up my arm. Blue mist rose from my hand, but no one else noticed.

"I'm Dan," the older man said. He gestured to a man on his left. "This is Craig." He then pointed to the woman to his right. "And this is Linda."

"We were the ones who brought you and your friend in after the accident," said Craig. "Your dog is an absolute delight to care for."

I smiled. Maiyun had the gift to charm everyone. The folks at work called her the office tramp because of her insatiable appetite for attention. She was definitely not shy about it, either.

"Yes," I admitted. "She most definitely is. Thank you all for your help."

Maiyun moved away from my hand. She was no longer limping.

"Wow!" said Craig. "What did you do?"

How would I explain something I didn't quite believe myself? "Acupressure," I said. "It works wonders for pain."

The silence that followed was a bit unnerving. "What vet did you bring her to?" I said, trying to distract their curious thoughts. "I would like to pay for their services."

It was Dan who answered. "Hometown Vet in Belfair. They were the only ones who would take a service dog."

"Why?" I asked.

"No one else wanted the liability."

I frowned. "You can't refuse to treat a service dog."

Dan shrugged. "Well, they did."

Linda spoke for the first time. There was something different about her. She radiated with shades of grey and spoke as if she were shy. I felt a chill down my spine and shivered from it.

"Does your acupressure work on humans?" she asked.

She stood and projected her energy toward me. It felt like steely probes. I drew the blanket up close to my chest.

"I injured my wrist last week and the pain is fairly intense. Can you help me?"

Everything about her warned me to back away. Something wasn't right. She wasn't telling the truth.

She held her arm out to me. I reached out and held her wrist. There was no injury, nor was there any pain. I pressed some points around her wrist but kept my intention in check.

I released her wrist. "There, better?"

She looked at me for a moment, bewildered. "Yes, thank you." She pulled her energy back and sat down. The chill I felt earlier was gone.

Everyone else in the room seemed oblivious to what had just happened.

Katie looked at my face. "You look a bit pale, Skye. Are you feeling all right?"

"A bit tired is all."

"Let's get you back to your room then," she said.

Maiyun stood and moved to my side as Katie released the brakes.

Dan walked toward Maiyun. "I'll keep an eye on her until you're released."

Maiyun pressed her chin on my leg. She didn't much care for our separation any more than I did.

Dan snapped the leash to her collar but she didn't move from my side.

I kissed her head. "Go with Dan," I whispered. "We'll be together soon."

She stepped away and watched as Katie backed me out of the tiny room. When we turned the corner, Maiyun howled.

Chapter 3

Humans are a mystery—particles assembled into a biological phenomenon. They are a puzzle begging to be solved, but the pieces are constantly changing.

I had returned to work just in time to be granted an RIF notice. "Reduction in force" is a polite way to say your services are no longer needed. As of next week, I was officially unemployed, sentenced to join the other 70 percent of the population who were also out of a job.

These days, there wasn't much need for a blind, dyslexic technical writer. In truth, I was ready to ditch the technical path and pursue my true passion as a body worker.

For the past 10 years, I practiced massage part time, mostly to retain some semblance of sanity. After having written technical manuals for a total of 30 years, it was time to hang up my keyboard.

I eagerly packed my work computer and Braille display for the last time, and handed everything to my manager. There was an odd sense of freedom that came with it. I had more than enough money packed away to not have to worry about my next paycheck, so there was no urgency in finding another job. On top of that, I was offered a generous nine-month severance with one year of medical benefits. This was a perfect opportunity to see more of Washington and I was told the peninsula was a great place to start.

The small town of Belfair, I soon learned, was a lovely vacation spot. After making quite a few phone calls, I managed to rent a quaint cabin on South Shore Road along the Hood Canal. My one-month stay was sure to provide endless opportunities for hikes, kayaking, and just plain relaxing.

Of course I also planned to pay Hometown Vets a visit and thank them for taking care of Maiyun. When I called several weeks ago, they said not to worry about paying for their services, but I still felt obligated to at least stop in and offer my gratitude.

I left early the following morning while it was bright enough for me to see. Technically, I shouldn't be driving, but I could not give up my independence just yet. So long as the sun was out, I didn't have many issues—that I knew of.

Maiyun rode in the rear seat of the cab of my Dakota. I flipped the seats up to give her plenty of room to view the sites or take a nap. The old black truck was paid for and still ran like a champ. We merged onto I-5 heading south.

Two hours later, we rolled into Belfair. I was surprised to see such a development in a small town that was just shy of nowhere. In the short two-mile span, there was a McDonald's, Rite-Aid, Safeway, and QFC Grocers, all of which were packed with clientele.

I saw the oval wooden sign for Hometown Vets and turned into the parking lot. A car honked loudly as I pulled into a space. I hardly noticed, really. It seemed that folks were increasingly liberal with their horns these days. I had grown numb to it over the years.

I let Maiyun out of the back and clipped her leash onto her collar. I left her service vest in the truck. She was tall enough where I could hold her collar and she could guide me over curbs and such.

We entered the clinic and was greeted by a tall, thin gal with short dark hair.

"Can I help you?"

"Yes, I would like to pay for services rendered to my dog, Maiyun. She was brought in by a paramedic several weeks ago. I believe his name was Dan."

"Do you know his last name?"

I frowned. "No."

She typed on the computer, and then shook her head. I don't have any records for Maiyun."

"She's a service dog," I offered, hoping to spark some memory. "She came in with a dislocated hip."

A young man with sand-colored hair walked around the corner. Maiyun seemed to instantly recognize him. Her tail wagged and she nudged my leg.

Another man entered the clinic with an unruly hound. It struggled against the leash to reach Maiyun. Maiyun sat beside me and nudged my hand.

The man approached me. "Are you aware that you pulled out right in front of me?"

I shook my head. "No."

"You must be blind then."

"Actually, I am," I replied.

The man had no response. He merely shook his head, and then turned toward the receptionist. "I have an appointment to see Dr. Ian."

The young woman looked at me apologetically. I smiled to assure her I was in no hurry.

"Sign in here, please." She pointed to a book on the counter.

The man Maiyun recognized came to greet us. "Ah," he said. "The service dog has returned, has she?" His faded Irish accent was charming.

I offered my hand. "I'm Skye, Maiyun's owner. Are you the doctor who fixed her hip?"

The young man shook my hand and stared much too intensely into my eyes. "Yes, I'm doctor Ian O'Dougherty." He looked down at Maiyun, and then knelt to her level to offer some attention. He examined her hip and looked up at me, fairly surprised. "I expected her to have a hitch to her step for a bit."

"I guess you did a better job than you thought," I explained. "I would like to pay for your services."

"No need," he said. "She's a service dog. There is no charge."

I had never heard of such a thing, but I didn't want to

question a blessing. "Well, please except my most sincere gratitude, then," I said. "This dog is everything to me."

"Yes," he said. "She feels the same about you." He scratched Maiyun's ear. He then turned to the man with the hound.

"Hi Mr. Green. I'm Doctor Ian." He bent down to greet the hound. "This must be Teddy?"

The hound lunged toward the doctor and bit down on his arm. Ian pulled back, but the dog held his grip. Blood began to stain the doctor's white sleeve. The dog released his hold, and then quickly lunged to get a better one despite his owner's feeble attempt to keep him under control. Ian jumped back out of the dog's reach and gripped his bloodied arm.

"Uh, sorry Doc. Teddy doesn't like strangers." His voice was barely audible over the hound's choked barks and slipping claws against the slick vinyl floor.

Without thinking, I reached over and grabbed the doctor's arm. He tried to pull it back, but my grip held firm as if I had no control over it. After a moment, he softened.

"Follow me," he said, leading me toward a back room. Maiyun trotted behind us.

My face was red with embarrassment, yet still, I could not leave his injury unattended. "I'm sorry," I whispered. I held his blood-soaked sleeve. The blue mist involuntarily rose from my hand. There was no stopping it, nor could I bring myself to let go.

The warmth of his blood ceased beneath my hand. His flesh felt cool to my touch. I slowly let go. My hand was shaking. "I shouldn't have done that."

The dim lights in the room prevented me from seeing Ian's face.

He rolled up his sleeve. "The bleeding has stopped," he said. I saw his head turn toward me. "The wound is almost healed."

I felt sick. I dropped to my knees and Maiyun pressed her body against me, as if to offer support. I'm a freak, I thought. It wasn't just the morphine. Something is wrong with me.

Ian helped me stand. "Thank you," he said. "I guess this makes us even, eh?"

There was no shock in his voice, nor did he think me crazy. "Yeah," I said. "We're even." I grabbed Maiyun's collar and headed for the door. I heard Ian chuckle behind me. He did not try to stop me from leaving.

What had just happened? I wondered, staring down at my bloodstained hand. It felt as if it were on fire. I needed to find some water. I remembered seeing the familiar Starbucks logo on the next corner. I could get cleaned up there and grab a much-needed cup of coffee. My hand was still burning and it shook as I turned the key.

Busy parking lots were always a nightmare for me to negotiate. There was too much activity and cars came at me from all angles. I always parked as far from buildings as possible; that way, I didn't have to squeeze into a space between two cars. Since I had no depth perception, it was impossible to tell how far away the other cars were. I learned to use some tricks that enabled me to function without hitting anything, but sometimes those tricks didn't work. It was better to be safe and just park where there were fewer cars.

I clipped Maiyun's service vest on, and headed for Starbucks across the lot. She was great at keeping me safe around cars and had learned to stay near the edge and not in the middle of the drive. Since I had no peripheral vision, it was hard to negotiate through crowds without bumping into people. Maiyun helped a lot with that, and kept me from falling off curbs or running into low-hanging branches and other objects.

I pulled the sleeve of my white sweater down over my bloody hand, still shaking and burning. My vision suddenly grew dark. I looked up and noticed the clouds moving in. That always made driving more difficult. Things appeared grey now and I had lost the ability to see detail.

We entered the crowded coffee shop. I politely asked the first person I met where the bathrooms were, and then headed straight toward them. A woman exited a door and held it open for me. "Thank you," I said.

I carefully pushed up my sweater sleeve and began cooling my hand under cold water. It was a good thing that I was not sickened by blood. There seemed to be quite a bit of it. I could feel the stickiness on my skin as I rubbed my hands and arms under the cool stream.

The fire was gone from my hand and the shaking had stopped as well. I still had no idea what possessed me to grab that man's arm and not let go, but I was sure I could never face him again. His reaction to it all was rather odd. He had said we were even, but he never questioned what happened, nor did he act surprised. I wondered why.

A hot cup of coffee sounded perfect. I got in line to place my order. The man in front of me ordered two drinks and two breakfast sandwiches. He was talking with the gal taking the order as if he knew her. She mentioned something about a massage. He stepped away, and Maiyun led me up to the counter.

"Hi, can I get something started for you?" The cashier asked.

"Yes, I'll have a grande one-pump mocha with whole milk and cinnamon powder, and one of those breakfast sandwiches that the other man ordered."

"Very good. For here or to go?"

"For here," I said. It was difficult enough driving as it was, let alone with something in my hands. I figured it would be safer for everyone if I were to enjoy my breakfast first, and then drive.

"That'll be $7.50."

I handed her my Starbucks card.

"Okay, you have $23 dollars left," she said, handing me back my card.

"I heard you mention something about massage to that

man. Is there a place around here that offers massage?" I asked.

"His name is Gregg," she said. "He and his wife run a health clinic. If you want a massage, that's the place to go."

I smiled. "Thank you."

There was no rush to find a job, so why was I so intrigued with this impromptu opportunity to work at a medical clinic? The answer eluded me as I made my way toward the pickup counter.

It was too dark to identify one man over another, so I walked toward someone who looked to be the same height as the man called Gregg.

"Excuse me," I said. "Are you Gregg?"

The man turned toward me and shook his head. "No, I'm sorry."

"I'm Gregg," the man behind him said. His fit and agile physique did not seem to match the wisdom in his tone.

I could feel the heat rise in my face. It was very inconvenient not being able to see clearly and embarrassing at times. I cleared my throat. "The lady at the counter said that you and your wife run a health clinic?"

"Uh, oh," he said, nodding at the woman who took our order. "What did I do this time?"

I liked his voice, and strangely felt comfortable talking to him. "She said that your health clinic offers massage?"

"Yeah, it's just down the street, right across from the vet clinic."

My stomach sank. I wondered if he knew the doctor

who worked there. I had a hard time getting the words out of my throat.

"Are you okay?" he asked.

I nodded. "I'm fine."

"Vente latte with two raw sugars, and a grande white chocolate latte," the barista called out.

Gregg turned to get his drinks. "Are you looking for a massage?"

I took a deep breath. "Actually, I'm looking for a job." The words popped right out of my mouth as if I had no control over them.

"Oh, what do you do?"

"Grande, one-pump mocha."

I reached over and took my drink and sandwich from the barista. "Thank you."

Gregg gestured toward an open table. "Do you have time to sit?"

"Yes." I followed him over to where he had pulled out a chair for me. He sat across the table. Maiyun curled up beside my chair and placed her chin on my foot. Now what? I thought. First, I grab a stranger's arm and hold it until his gaping wound stops bleeding, and now I'm asking another stranger for a job? That morphine must have wreaked havoc on my deportment.

I took a bite of my sandwich and managed to miss my mouth. Melted cheese dribbled down my lip. I grabbed the napkin. Great first impression, I thought. I pushed the sandwich aside and decided to wait until after our conversation was over.

"I was wondering," I said, into the napkin. "If—"

"I'm sorry," said Gregg. "I am hard of hearing and I need to read your lips or I don't know what you're saying. Can you remove your napkin?"

Hmm, strike two. I was off to a great start. Maiyun nudged my leg to assure me I was doing just fine. "I'm a massage therapist."

Gregg was silent for a moment, uncomfortably so.

He must think I'm a loony. I couldn't blame him, really.

"You have blood on your sweater," he said.

My face had gone from hot to cold in a matter of seconds. "It's nothing," I said. Rolling up my sleeve. "I cut myself, earlier."

"What is your specialty?" he asked.

"Chinese Tui Na, acupressure, and medical massage."

"How long have you been practicing?"

"On and off for 10 years."

He placed a card in my hand. "Can you come by the clinic tomorrow at 11?"

"Yes."

"Did you need me to arrange a ride for you?" he asked, as he stood from the table.

"No, thank you," I said. "I can drive."

He laughed. "Okay, I'll see you tomorrow then." He gathered his drinks and sandwiches. "Oh, what's your name?"

"Skye."

"See you tomorrow, Skye."

Chapter 4

We cannot stop the force of a tidal wave. Our only chance of survival is to offer it passage without getting caught in its wake.

After driving past the rental property four times, I finally found the tiny driveway that led to the cabin on the water. The address was etched into the wood of the mailbox post, and was impossible for me to read. The neighbor across the street was kind enough to show me the way.

The driveway ended in a circle. I was grateful that I would not have to back out. I parked the truck in front of the small cabin and let Maiyun out while I grabbed my bags. The clouds had moved on and I was able to see with the sun shining brightly overhead. The Father never failed to take care of me and I felt grateful to have His help.

The entrance to the small cabin had a large overhang above the front door and the cedar siding looked freshly stained. The owner said the key was hidden under a fake rock in the garden. Go figure—it was a rock garden with a Zen-like feel. I touched each of the rocks in hopes of finding the fake one.

Maiyun sniffed the one on the far end and sounded a grumbling howl; it was a sound she often made to get my attention. She had found the rock, and under it was the key. "Brilliant," I said. "Thank you, Maiyun." I scratched her ear.

The cottage's front door was cherry wood with an etched oval window at the top. Indoors, the layout and décor were simple. The living room was directly in front of me and was the largest room in the house. To the left was a small kitchen, perfect for one or two people. The bedroom was off to the right. It contained a queen-sized bed, a small closet, and a bathroom with a huge soaking tub. I left my bags on the bed, and then headed toward the sliding glass door off the living room. The floors sloped toward the water of the Hood Canal, probably due to the ground settling beneath the foundation.

I was grateful that the house was not carpeted. I enjoyed the warmth of the hardwood floors. The living room had one small love seat covered in white leather, and a matching chair. There was a square, rosewood end table between them. A sturdy pine dining table separated the living room from the kitchen. It was covered with tinted glass.

I stepped out onto a small cedar deck, just large enough for two lawn chairs, a small barbecue, and a table. The view was magnificent. To the left was Alderbrook

Resort. Directly in front of me was the south coast of Tahuya. The waters of the Hood Canal were as restless as the weather. The presence of white peaks atop its waves indicated that a storm was brewing, although there were no threatening clouds in the sky. That didn't mean much in Washington, though, where the weather changed as quickly as the tide.

Maiyun stood on the deck, ears erect and body poised. She spotted some egrets down on the shore, enjoying the sun. Seagulls cried out in the distance. A soft breeze brushed against my face and hair. It was getting cold.

"Come on, Maiyun, let's go inside."

There was a lot to do. I had to unpack and get ready for tomorrow. I had no idea what to expect, so I wanted to be prepared for anything. I would need my oils, and my music. I planned to forward my resume to Gregg in an e-mail from my iPhone. I was not planning to interview during my vacation, but since the opportunity arose, I found myself giddy with anticipation.

It was only three in the afternoon, but it felt much later than that. Driving always wore me out, especially when I had to travel for long periods of time. My eyes had to constantly scan the road ahead of me, as well as check the mirrors. It took quite a bit of concentration.

I looked forward to taking a hot bath, sipping on a large glass of wine, and listening to a good book. I downloaded Dan Brown's latest novel, The Lost Symbol, onto my iPhone. Listening to it will be a perfect way to unwind before retiring, I thought.

After unpacking, and then marinating the chicken wings I planned to have for dinner, I began sorting through my collection of essential oils. I chose three of my favorites to take with me tomorrow: Calm Spirit, clove, and peppermint. Calm Spirit was a blend that I used to calm the client's mind of clutter. It was a combination of rosewood, cedar, cypress, and frankincense. For a carrier, I chose almond and castor oil. Each bottle had a uniquely shaped bead attached so that I could identify the contents in a dark room. I carefully packed them away in an ornate silk bag along with my CD I intended to play. The silk bag was a gift from my mentor and good friend, Ming Sha. She taught me acupressure and Tui Na, a Chinese form of massage, for two years before returning to Shanghai. The bag was very special to me, and because I had often done impromptu massages during my work week, I was in the habit of keeping my supplies in my bag and close at hand.

The clouds were moving in again, making it difficult to see. I had brought a few full-spectrum light bulbs and began installing them strategically throughout the house: one in the bedroom, one in the living room next to the chair, and one in the kitchen. Without them, I was almost completely blind once the sun set.

I thought back on the past few days and the recent string of events. I had never really heard of Belfair until Dan, the paramedic, told me about Hometown Vets.

I went online and discovered that Belfair was a popular vacation spot. That led me to find this place, and before I knew it, I was here. Because I had to stop at Starbucks to clean myself up after my incident with Doctor Ian, I managed to get an interview for a job. I was fairly sure the Father had something to do with these events. He had a unique way of orchestrating occurrences in my life. Since they always turned out for the best, I really didn't mind. Right now, I was enjoying the ride.

I put the chicken under the broiler, steamed some rice, and sautéed Brussels sprouts with a little coconut oil and green onions. I poured myself a glass of Pinot Grigio, and then sat down to enjoy my meal. I wanted to save the red wine to enjoy while taking my bath.

The setting sun cast a pink hue to the sky, which reflected in the water. The tide must have risen a bit because I could hear it slap against the stone foundation. I wondered how many more years this little cabin would remain standing before it finally gave up the battle and surrendered to the persistent assault of the water.

I looked around at the walls. They were plain, painted white with no pictures. I found that odd. The vaulted ceiling added space to the cabin. Long lamps hung down from the rafters.

After giving thanks to our Father, I picked up a chicken wing and nibbled the meat from the bone. It was tender and slightly salty, just the way I liked it. A little more cayenne pepper would have been perfect, I thought, taking another bite. As usual, I enjoyed my meal, taking time to savor each mouthful.

The evening progressed as I had planned; a hot bath, a glass of Burgundy, and some time with Dan Brown. Sleep came easily afterward. It had been a very long day.

Maiyun's wet nose nudged my hand. My legs were tangled around three pillows and my head was covered by the blanket. I bolted up and tried to focus on the clock. It was too dark to see. I groaned and stumbled out of bed. Pain shot through my big toe as I kicked the foot of the frame. "Ugh!" I fumbled with the light switch, then squinted against the bright light I had installed just the night before.

It was nine in the morning. I had less than two hours to get myself cleaned up and into Belfair by 11. I wasn't sure why this interview was so important to me. It wasn't like me to be so anxious.

I showered, and then fashioned my long, blonde hair into a braid. I banded the end of my braid with a red elastic tie. I removed the upper tie and then flipped the end of my braid through a parting on the top and pulled snugly to form an attractive twist. The end of my braid reached my hips.

Next I attached the charm that Ming Sha had given to me after our first year together. The charm had tiny bells that she claimed would attract the angels. It also had jade charms for bringing abundance into my life. I never left home without it. Whether it worked or not was not the issue; I just wanted to have my friend and mentor close to me, and if it attracted the angels, all the better.

Ming Sha would be so pleased to know that I had returned to body work. She always told me that I had the gift, but I never really believed it, especially since it did nothing to save Derrick or the rest of my family. I shook the thought from my mind. I had to stay focused on positive things.

Maiyun nudged my hand. "All done with breakfast?" I asked. I glanced up at the clock. It was 10:15. I had best get moving.

I loaded everything in the truck, and double-checked that I had not forgotten my oils and CD. They were safely secured in my bag. The engine was running, the cab was heating up, and Maiyun was sitting with her head beside me. I was ready. I took a deep breath and headed up the driveway.

The drive along the south shore was stunning. Fall leaves offered a variety of bright colors, and the water was amazingly calm. There were a few grey clouds in the sky, and the ground was wet. It must have rained last night, but I was too tired to hear it.

I reached Belfair in less than 15 minutes. I decided to grab something to drink and eat so that my stomach didn't make a racket during my interview. Starbucks was familiar and very close to the clinic. I pulled into the parking lot and immediately someone honked. I saw a crazed-looking woman with wild hair glaring at me and I raised my hands.

"What?" My heart pounded double-time. The woman yelled something at me, but I couldn't hear what she said.

I found a safe parking space and made my way to Starbucks. I had about 20 minutes to enjoy my meal. That would be tough, but I could do it.

Standing in line, I decided to stick with tea. I didn't need to have the shakes; I was way too nervous already. At 45, I shouldn't be changing careers like a bored undergraduate. If my father were alive, he would talk me out of this crazy idea, I was sure. For the first time in my life, though, I felt as if I were finally heading in the right direction.

I made quick work of the meal, and then headed toward the bathroom to brush my teeth. I had five minutes to spare. Being slightly early was much better than being late.

I took Maiyun to a private area where she could relieve herself. As a puppy, she learned to eliminate on cue, which proved to be very useful at times like these.

We loaded up into the truck and were on our way. At the stoplight, I glanced at the card Gregg handed me the day before. I was looking for The Wellness Center. The light turned green and I made a left onto State Route 3.

Up ahead was a purple and yellow sign that looked like the top of Gregg's business card. I turned right into the driveway. The back tire caught a curb or something and the truck lurched to the left. I pulled straight into the first parking space in front since there were too many cars at the side of the building. My front bumper hit something. Maiyun groaned in protest when I stopped suddenly. I backed the truck up a bit. "Sorry, Maiyun."

I took a deep breath and hopped out of the cab. The clouds were thick today, which made it more difficult for me to see. I walked to the front to see what I had hit. A small potted tree looked a bit shaken, but not damaged, thank God.

Maiyun panted heavily and paced back in forth with impatience. One would think that she was the one having the interview. I secured her service vest and barely said, "Okay" before she leapt out of the cab. She pressed against my leg and we headed for the front door.

A chime sounded as we entered.

"Dang, Girl," said Gregg. "I thought you were joking when you said you could drive." His hair looked much more silver than I had remembered, and his eyes were deep and brown.

"Why?" I asked.

He stood up and looked out the window. "Well, you killed our brick out front and scared the fruit off our orange tree. God knows what damage you did while getting here."

I felt my face grow red and my confidence fade. "Yes, well I drive much better when the sun is not hidden behind clouds."

"Well, that's comforting." Gregg leaned over the counter. "You do know that this is Washington, right?"

"Gregg, stop it." A woman said as she came down the hall. "She's been here less than five minutes and you're already giving her a hard time?"

She pressed her strong hand into mine. "Hi, I'm Ro. I believe you've already met my charming husband, Gregg."

"I'm Skye, and this is Maiyun."

Ro guided me to a chair. "Have a seat." She was about my height, maybe an inch taller, and had long honey-blonde hair that was pulled back in a braid that ended at her waist. She could have been a dancer, by the way she moved—fluid and graceful. Again, her voice did not match her physique. Both of them appeared so young, but sounded much wiser. It was unusual.

Maiyun laid beside me and placed her chin on my foot. Her warm, soft breath was reassuring. It felt good there, welcoming. The mingled scent of quality aromatherapy oils suffused the air. Product shelves lined the walls, along with some strange-looking lamps that resembled pink crystal. They smelled like salt.

Gregg gathered a few things, and then came to join us in the waiting area.

"So, tell us about yourself," said Ro. Her smile was as bright as her eyes and matched the beautiful energy that surrounded her body. Both she and Gregg radiated with happiness.

I took a deep breath and gathered my thoughts. "I attended The School of Natural Medicine in San Diego for two years. I graduated with 1,100 hours of medical massage training and 630 hours learning herbs and homeopathy. I continued to study under an acupuncturist for two years where I learned Tui Na and acupressure. Between taking care of sick family members and freelance writing, I practiced massage."

Ro pulled her legs into a lotus position on the chair. She was barefoot and wore a pair of stretchy Capris. I loved her carefree disposition. She was a woman who was obviously comfortable in her own skin. "Tell me more about Tui Na."

"It's a Chinese form of massage designed to balance the entire body. It is different from deep tissue and Swedish massage."

Gregg scribbled some notes down. "Are you licensed to practice in this state?"

I nodded. "Yes, I'm nationally certified and have my Washington license with an endorsement to practice large and small animal massage."

"Both?" Ro raised her brow.

I shrugged. "It was a hobby of mine. It only required six months of additional training."

"Can you practice herbs and homeopathy?" asked Gregg, not looking up from his notepad.

Talking about myself was never easy for me. I wanted to know more about them, but I knew I had to endure this first. "I do hold a certificate in both, however, they are not required in this state."

"Fabulous," said Ro. She stood up and took my hand. "You're gonna love this."

I followed her into the back room.

"On this wall, we have over 200 herbs and teas." She

was quiet for a moment. "Well, what do you think?"

"I think if you want me to be able to see any of them, you need to install full-spectrum lights—many of them." There were no windows back here and the lighting was not enough for me to even see shapes.

"How much can you see?" The concern in her voice was familiar. My condition caused many people to second-guess my capabilities.

"Well, in bright sunlight, I see quite well, so long as I am looking directly at something. It would be similar to you peering through a pair of toilet paper rolls. I have no peripheral vision, no depth perception, and absolutely no night vision. I see color, but not like you would expect." I didn't want to go into to that one too much. She might think I'm crazy if I started talking about energy and such. "In low light, I see shapes—kind of like seeing through cloudy water."

"I have the lights on," she said.

"They have to be full-spectrum lights, or my eyes can't process it."

Gregg entered the room. "I'll pick some up tomorrow."

"Am I coming back tomorrow?"

"If you give a good massage, perhaps. If not, I wouldn't bother."

"That's my man," said Ro. "A true master of words." She led me back to the reception area where the sunlight now shone through the windows. The clouds were having a break. "Ah, the sun. Can you see better now?"

I nodded. "Yes, much better, thank you."

Her eyes were an amazing blue, like the deepest depths of the ocean. They were an attractive contrast to her honey-brown hair. "Are you up for giving me a massage?"

"Yes," I patted the bag hanging on my shoulder. "I brought my oils and music."

"Whoa," said Gregg. "A candidate who is prepared?"

Ro patted my shoulder. "Never mind him. He's had too many bad experiences with other candidates."

"How many people work here?" I asked.

"Not enough," said Gregg.

Ro threw something at him. "Don't you have taxes to do?"

Gregg slumped his shoulders. "Great, I have to do real work while you get a massage."

Ro waved her hand. "Have fun, angel." She giggled as he sauntered toward his office.

Chapter 5

When your actions are pure instinct, reality becomes surreal.

Ro handed me a sheet of paper that she grabbed from the reception counter. "I completed this intake form. Will you be able to read it?"

I glanced down at it, and then shook my head. "Not in this light." I reached into my bag and pulled out my iPhone. "I'll record our intake, and then transcribe it later."

"Oh, that'll work." She led me down a short hall and into room with two windows. "This is my room," she said. "You might want to check the table height."

I brushed my hand against the soft blanket that covered the table. It was a bit high for me, but acceptable for one massage. "The table is fine." I continued to walk around the room, familiarizing myself with the furniture and space around the table. My hands and feet would need familiar landmarks when the lights were too dim for me to see any shapes.

Ro set up my CD while I arranged my oils on the small

desk by the door. Soft piano music played against a soothing background of ocean waves. I lit a candle to mark the position of the oils, and to honor my mentor, Ming Sha. She told me to always light a candle in the room when doing body work. It served to carry the woes of the client to God so that the practitioner would not absorb them.

"Do you mind if I remove my shoes?" I asked. "It's hard for me to feel grounded with them on."

"Not at all," she said. "I understand. I work barefoot, myself."

I slid my clogs off and removed my socks. My feet wiggled with appreciation and immediately felt connected to the earth.

I started the record feature of my iPod, and then proceeded to conduct my intake. After asking Ro the standard health questions regarding drugs and medical history, I asked her to stand so that I could check her structure and alignment.

"Can you really feel anomalies with only your touch?" she asked.

"No," I said. "I just do this for show." The sarcasm was uncalled for, but I couldn't help myself.

She turned to look at me, her eyes questioning and her mouth hung open.

I smiled. "Yes, I can feel imbalances in your posture." My hands measured the base of her skull, and then glided down her shoulders and back, ending at her hips.

"Your head has a slight tilt to the left and your hips have a moderate elevation on the right." I was saying that to my iPhone more than to her. "Would you like me to balance your entire body or is there a specific location you want me to focus on?"

"Give me an overhaul, please," she said.

I turned down the corner of the covers and checked the face cradle for the proper position. "Okay, I'll leave and let you get undressed. Lie under the covers, face down. Take your time, I'll knock before entering."

"I'll be ready," she said as I closed the door.

Maiyun waited outside the room. She knew this routine and had learned to stay out of the way. She stood and brushed against my hand.

"Where's the bathroom, Maiyun?"

She led me down the hall to an open door. I found the sink and started washing my hands with hot water. I felt very comfortable here, like I had known this place before. Gregg and Ro were easy to be around and they didn't seem to mind my uncontrollable sarcasm.

For a Monday, the clinic was very quiet. I wondered where the other practitioners were. I found my way back to the treatment room and knocked on the door. "Ro, are you ready?"

"Yeah, come on in."

"It seems very quiet in here today," I commented.

"We're closed," she mumbled through the face cradle. "Sundays and Mondays are our days off."

"Not much of a day off," I said, "if you have to come in to interview."

"I certainly don't mind, and Gregg has some computer work to catch up on."

I positioned a bolster under her ankles and adjusted the blanket. Bodywork always felt right to me—natural. With my hands, I was able to step outside my body and connect with another human universe. What fascinated me the most was how unique each person felt. Their energetic vibrations were their fingerprints, only on an entirely different level than mere physical.

I closed my eyes and touched my right middle finger to the base of her skull. My left hand rested on the top of her sacrum. Her rhythm was slow and rolling like the ocean. I allowed my own rhythm to entrain to hers. This enabled me to sync with her body and discover anomalies.

"You have great command of your energy," said Ro.

"Thank you," I responded. My hands were drawn toward her right hip. When I touched it, I felt a jolt as if I had touched a bare electrical wire.

"Oh," she jumped. "You found it."

I nodded. "Old injury?"

"Five years ago," she said. "I fell from my horse and broke my right hip."

Her right sacroiliac joint protruded higher than her left. "It didn't heal right," I said.

"Yes, the doctors claim that the pins did not hold. They need to re-break the pelvis to set it correctly."

"And what do you believe?" I asked.

"I believe that our bodies can heal if we get out of the

way and allow it to happen."

"I agree. Are you in much pain?" I knew the answer before I asked, but strangely needed her confirmation.

She laughed. "Pain has been a part of my life for so long, I just treat it like my husband's comments, and ignore it." She hesitated before continuing. "It's funny, I can remove other people's pain and discomfort, but I have not yet learned how to remove my own."

Heat began to rise in my hands. "Someone once told me that pain was just an illusion." I placed my hands over her hips.

"Hmm. Sounds like something Shanuk would say."

"Shanuk?"

"Just someone we know," she said. "He's a bit eccentric and…"

"And?" I prompted her to continue.

"It's nothing. He's just different, that's all."

I took a long, deep breath and imagined my body emptying into the earth. An energetic flow poured through me from the heavens as I invited the Father to work through me.

Ro's hip shifted in my hand.

"Oh!" she cried. "Wow, something released."

"Are you okay?" I asked.

"Yes, keep going. Your hands feel good."

I conjured the blue mist from my hands and imagined the pain leaving her body.

Ro's muscles completely relaxed beneath my hands.

The tension was gone. Her tissue yielded under my touch and her breathing kept pace with mine. Our bodies were entrained.

By the time I rolled her over, she was half asleep. I finished with some acupressure and reflexology on her feet.

When the massage was complete I said, "Take your time. I'll wait for you out front."

"Okay," she moaned.

Altogether, I thought the massage went well. After washing my hands with cold water, I waited for Ro out front by the reception area.

Gregg looked up from his computer screen. "Hey, how did it go?"

"Great on my end," I said.

Ro came down the hall. "She's hired."

"That good, eh?" asked Gregg. The perplexed look on his face told me that Ro's comment was a bit of an oddity.

"Good?" she replied. "That's an understatement. I feel no pain and at least 10 years younger. I figure after two more massages by her, I'll feel like 20 again."

Gregg raised his hand. "Sign me up. I'm next."

Ro pushed his hand down. "So," she said. "When can you start?"

Chapter 6

What would happen if greed, anger, jealousy, and other negative emotions did not exist? Would we become gullible, ignorant, and foolish—or just blissfully blind?

I sat on the balcony of the rental cottage enjoying the sunset. Though the sun was behind me, the pink and orange sky reflected brilliantly on the water.

It had been a full yet restful week. I had landed a job and went on some beautiful hikes. Maiyun enjoyed chasing the birds on the shore. She became alarmed, however, when they started chasing her back. I couldn't remember the last time I laughed that hard.

Sam called a few days previously to tell me that he, too, was laid off. He and Karin were planning a road trip to the Oregon coast. He agreed to drop off the rest of my things from the apartment. "Whatever keeps you off the road," he said.

All I had left at my small apartment were a few clothes and some trinkets, all of which fit in my remaining suitcase. Since Derrick died, I kept my possessions to a minimum. It was simpler that way.

Gregg and Ro offered me the studio apartment above The Wellness Center. They insisted that they did not want me driving more than absolutely necessary.

I had agreed to start work and move in at the end of October. That would give me three weeks more of rest.

I took a sip of my wine and savored the bold, spicy hints of cocoa, clove, and black currant. Stagg's Leap Petite Syrah had been my wine of celebration for years. Of course it was better when shared with someone, but Maiyun didn't appreciate wine.

I nibbled a piece of five-year-aged Gouda. Its crystallized texture delighted my palate with a sharp, salty flavor. It was the perfect pairing for my wine.

A fresh breeze brushed my face and I breathed deeply. It was peaceful here. An occasional boat drifted past, and birds played upon the winds that whirled through the canal. I could get used to this.

A somber rendition of Beethoven's Moonlight Sonata contrasted with the idyllic scene, threatening to break my blissful mood when my iPhone buzzed. I reached for it and answered the call.

It was Gregg from The Wellness Center.

"I hate to cut into your vacation time," he said. "But we are in a bit of a bind."

"What kind of bind?" I asked.

"Our other massage therapist was called to work on a cruise ship. She's leaving tomorrow and her schedule is full.

I can reschedule her clients, but I would prefer not to."

I waited for the rest of the story, but nothing followed. I assumed it was his way of asking for help. "Did you need me to fill in?" I prompted.

"Um, if you don't mind."

"Of course not. What time did you need me to come in?"

Gregg cleared his throat. "Your first appointment is at 10."

"Very good," I said. "I'll get there around 9:30."

"Ro and I appreciate it, Skye."

"I know you do. I'll see you tomorrow."

"Have a good evening."

I hung up the phone. The sun had completed its descent and my glass was now empty. A cold breeze sent shivers down my spine. It was time to go inside.

"Well, Maiyun," I said, addressing the limp mass of black and grey fur on the floor. "It looks like we're going to have to postpone our kayak adventure for a bit."

She lifted her head; her grey and white mask gave her a wolf-like appearance. With a long, drawn-out groan, she lowered her head and closed her sleepy brown eyes. She didn't seem too upset. Water was not her favorite place for sport.

I arrived at the office a little after nine. Gregg and Ro had my room well situated and had flooded the entire office with full-spectrum light.

Ro was excited to show me the dispensary where all the herbs and remedies were kept.

I felt like a kid in a candy shop. Along the huge back wall, there were herbs I had only played with back in school. There was even some lobelia, a highly toxic herb with fascinating healing effects. In school, our teacher referred to it as "the mother-in-law herb."

Along the short wall to the left were shelves of tinctures, homeopathic remedies, and herbal formulas. To the right was a prep table and a labeling printer.

Ro led me to another room where Gregg stored his collection of exotic teas. There must have been over 100 different varieties categorized under white, green, red, and herbal. I recognized a few: white silver needle, oolong, and English Breakfast. There were many more, though, that were unknown to me, such as jiaogulan, and pau flowers.

"Gregg is a bit of a tea connoisseur," said Ro.

I nodded then met her gaze with a mock-serious expression. "You think?"

"Come on," she said. "I'll show you where the lunch room is."

I followed her down another long hall and into a room in the far corner of the building. This place was much larger than I thought.

As with most first days at work, I was overwhelmed. I met the other two massage therapists, Kathy and Ann. They were fraternal twins. Steve, the acupuncturist, came in and briefly greeted me before retreating into his room. Khalen, the naturopath, was due to come in later this afternoon.

The clinic was alive with activity and indistinct

conversation. I found my way back to my quiet room and prepared for my first client. Maiyun was enjoying the extra attention from Steve until she noticed that I had left the reception area. She came trotting in behind me.

My treatment room was next to Ro's. The table heater was already turned on. I adjusted the table height, and then continued to arrange my oils on the shelf. I placed my candle next to them.

Gregg stood by the door holding a tall glass tumbler of tea. "I know you enjoy tea, so I made you my famous morning blend. "He pointed to the loose green leaves floating in the water. "It has jiaogulan, High Mountain Oolong, and a hint of peppermint."

I smiled and accepted the tumbler, which was double-wall insulated and crowned with a fine wire mesh below the rim line. The clever design enabled me to drink the tea without having to strain it first. I loved how the tea floated atop the infusion. Its aroma was floral in nature, with a hint of sweetness. I took a small sip. The clean taste of young, green leaves and fermented oolong was playfully strong, yet not at all bitter. It left a pleasant sweetness on my tongue. "Oh," I said. "This is fantastic."

Gregg's smile was radiant. "Whole tea likes to have the freedom to swim," he explained. "I wash it first to get rid of the bitterness."

"Wash it?"

"Yeah, I steep it for about a minute, and then drain the liquid. It's kind of like having a second-press espresso—all the flavor and none of the bitter caffeine."

I raised my cup. "Good to know. Thank you." I typically drank black tea English style with honey and cream, but this tea was truly delightful.

My first appointment arrived. The voice sounded vaguely familiar. I made my way toward the lobby to meet him. The blood rushed from my face as I realized who the man was, and my heart pounded as Gregg turned to introduce me.

"Ian, this is Skye, our new therapist. She'll be working on you today."

Ian smiled as if he knew we would meet again soon. His wavy blond hair and green eyes were alluring. He stood at least six foot one and was in excellent shape. His skin was tanner than it should be for this area. He had to be an outdoorsman or something athletic. I took a deep breath and extended my hand in greeting.

"We meet again," I said.

"Indeed, we do, Miss Taylor." His eloquent smile conveyed his amusement.

Gregg handed me his file. "You two know each other?"

"He tended to my dog," I quickly said, hoping the good doctor would take the hint and keep his mouth closed about the bite incident.

"And she tended to my arm after I was bit," he said.

So much for hints. "Well, are you ready?"

"I'll tell you about it later," he whispered back to Gregg.

I turned to meet his gaze then motioned him into the room. "I wish you wouldn't," I said, closing the door. Maiyun followed the doctor to the chair where she was sure to get some good attention. She was not disappointed.

"May I ask why?"

"Because the entire incident was just a bit odd and I don't want my new friends to think I'm a lunatic before they get to know me."

He laughed, displaying a set of brilliant white teeth. This town obviously attracted people of unusual beauty. The light surrounding Ian was just as bright as the light that surrounded Gregg and Ro. Kathy, Ann, and Steven didn't have the same brilliance to their energy, but they were still beautiful in their own way.

"How about after they get to know you?" he asked.

I picked up my clipboard, ignoring his jest. "I see on your self-assessment form that your lower back is hurting you?"

His green eyes sparkled. His charm was irritating. I glanced at his mouth to regain my composure. It didn't help. Even the subtle curl to his lips was entrancing.

"I picked a dog up onto the exam table, he wriggled, and I heroically tried to save him from falling onto the hard floor."

I held back the smile that tugged at my mouth and avoided looking up at him. "I see." After scribbling some notes on my chart, I placed it down on the desk and asked him to stand. He towered above me, staring down with the same scrutiny I cast upon him. I motioned for him to turn.

"Hmm, it looks as if you have strained your right QL. It's pulling your hip up and your left trap is complaining of overwork." I made a few more notes on my chart. "Take your shoes off and lay face up on the table."

His questioning expression was playful and annoying. "Do you intend to massage me with my clothes on?"

My blood betrayed me by rushing to my cheeks. I quickly reached for the light dimmer and turned down the lights. "I am going to release your hip, and then massage you."

I did a series of Tui Na manipulations, and then asked him to stand. "I want you to walk up and down the hall a couple of times to reset your hip."

He hopped off the table, appearing much younger than his intake form suggested. There was no way this man was 52 years old. He looked and behaved more like 30, maybe even 20.

I watched as he strode up and down the hallway. As anticipated, his right hip dropped and his gate became much more fluid. "How does your lower back feel?"

"Better," he said. "That nagging pinch is gone."

I motioned him back to the room, then left him to undress. When I returned, he was leaning off the table to pet Maiyun. I looked at her and shook my head. As if reading my thoughts, she lowered her ears and laid down in the far corner of the room. It was unlike her to forget her place and fraternize with my clients.

"You have quite a gift," he said.

I didn't like talking during a session; it distracted my concentration. I replied with a terse "Thanks." I then used an acupressure point that my mentor showed me to put clients at rest. Oftentimes, they became so relaxed that they snored. Having it done to me several times, I knew the move made one feel blissfully drunk without the horrible side effects. Within minutes of applying the technique to Ian, his body relaxed and his breathing slowed. I finished my work in silence, disturbing him only enough to roll him over.

Knowing he had to return to work and be coherent, I stimulated the appropriate reflex points on his feet before ending his session.

"Wow," he said, before I left the room. "I feel great. My big brother is going to love you tomorrow."

I swallowed hard. "Big brother?"

"Aye. Aidan. I told him all about you." His charming Irish accent seeped through.

"Perfect." I smiled back at him and left him to dress. The session was not as disturbing as I had expected. Once he was on the table, he was no longer a dashing veterinarian with mesmerizing eyes. He was simply Ian, with an aching back. Perhaps his older brother would be just as easy tomorrow.

I retreated to the back room to finish my charting. I heard Ian talk with Gregg at the front counter, but could not make out their conversation, only some laughter. Maiyun nudged me, encouraging me toward the reception area. "Then go," I told her. "You don't need me to come with you."

She made a low howl.

"Shh," I scolded. "This is a wellness clinic, not home."

She lifted her head and made a louder howl. Her golden eyes sparkled with mischief.

I glared. "Fine!" I stood then looked down at her. "You pick this moment to act more like your breed?"

She shoved the back of my leg with impatience.

"Okay, I'm going." I knew what she was up to. It wasn't going to happen. Derrick was my life and now he's gone. There will not be another to replace him, ever.

Ian's eyes glistened like a young baby's after waking from a deep sleep. His boyish half-grin made me wonder why he was not already married. Perhaps he liked to play the field. If that were the case, I wasn't too eager to give him the ball.

"How is your back?" I asked, already knowing the answer.

"Good as can be expected," he said. Not the answer I had anticipated.

My brow furrowed. "Is that good or bad?"

He and Gregg both laughed as if I was the blunt of some inside joke.

Ian waved as he left. "I'll see you next week, Skye."

I pursed my lips and turned to Gregg. "What, exactly, did he mean by that?"

"Oh," he said, looking over at his computer screen. "Ian made another appointment to see you next week."

"Not that, his other comment about feeling good as can be expected?"

Gregg shrugged, feigning innocence. "I guess he

expected to feel good?"

I narrowed my eyes. "Uh huh."

I left to clean up my room and ready the table for my next client. When that was done, I took Maiyun out for a break. When we came back inside, she made a beeline for the first office on the right. I called her back, but she ignored me.

"Why is there a dog in my office?" asked a deep, angry voice.

I peeked in and grabbed Maiyun by her collar. "Sorry, she's with me."

The man turned around. He looked eerily familiar. What caught my attention were his amazing hazel eyes. I thought I saw flecks of gold in them, despite his anger. He was definitely taller than Ian by at least four inches. My guess was that he was Native American. His hair was dark and pulled back into a thick five-inch braid. He wore a tan silk shirt with the first two buttons open, a pair of black Dockers, and expensive-looking dress shoes. I knew I had seen him before, but where?

He extended his large hand toward me. "I'm Khalen."

I accepted his hand and nearly winced at his strong grip. Not wanting to seem like a weakling, I matched his grip with my own feeble strength. "I'm Skye, the new therapist."

His full lips curled into a smile as if enjoying my façade.

"Maiyun is my service dog. I'm sorry about the intrusion. It won't happen again." I shook her collar. "Right?"

Maiyun sniffed the man's pant leg. He quickly brushed the wet mark as though he could remove it. My eyes grew wide. What had gotten into Maiyun?

Khalen looked at me with an odd expression. Perhaps he did not approve of my knickers and bare feet?

"Do you not have shoes?" he asked, almost amused. His accent sounded faintly British.

"I take them off when I'm working," I explained. It wasn't the entire truth. The real truth was that I didn't like shoes. I was barefoot most of the time, unless shoes were absolutely necessary.

"Hmm," was all he said. He brushed past me and headed for the front desk where Gregg was working. "Do you have Sarah Richlie's chart?"

Gregg handed him a manila chart that was two inches thick. "I see you've met our new therapist, Skye."

Khalen opened the chart and nodded. "I did." He then retreated back to his office.

Gregg smiled. "You must have made an impression."

"A bad one," I grumbled. "I don't think he approves of my dog or my bare feet."

His smirk told me that Khalen's reaction was the least of my worries. "Is that all?"

My face contorted with confusion. "All that I noticed."

Ro came down the hall and poked her head in Khalen's office. "Good day to you, happiness. Did you meet—".

"I met her," he said tersely.

She approached Gregg with a wry smile. "He must approve, eh?"

I shook my head. "You all have a warped idea of approval." I led Maiyun back to my room and scolded her for her insolence.

"What is wrong with you?"

She licked my hand. Her innocent face made it hard to stay mad. I cupped her muzzle in my hands and looked into her deep brown eyes. "You need to stay in my room," I told her. "Leave Khalen alone."

She placed her paw in my hand and cocked her head to one side. Her tongue hung out of her mouth sideways.

"Yeah, you have that whole cute thing down, all right. It won't work with him, you know."

Another client walked into the lobby. I looked at Maiyun. "You stay," I said in a firm voice. She hadn't been this difficult since she was six months old.

Chapter 7

If I could just escape from myself, I know I could be truly great.

The week ended and Gregg and Ro made me promise to move into the studio apartment earlier than expected. Since my work had begun prematurely, there really was no need to continue renting the cottage. Sam and Karin offered to help me move, but there was not much to take over—just a few bags. I expected them at the cottage at any time.

I checked around each room one more time to ensure I hadn't forgotten anything and that the place was left cleaner than how I found it—which was difficult, because it was very clean to start with. I replaced the full-spectrum bulbs with the original lights and made sure that all the doors were locked.

Maiyun came to me and laid down, hoping for some attention. I knelt down and stroked her exposed belly. Her behavior improved somewhat as the week progressed, but she was still excessively infatuated with Dr. Khalen.

Unfortunately for her, the feeling was not mutual nor was her attention reciprocated.

He was not a happy man. It seemed he always wore a frown until one of his patients came to visit. His face suddenly lit up and he seemed like a normal man—just not around me.

I frowned at that thought, wondering what I had done to merit such treatment. While other people in this town seemed to be drawn to me, he was repelled. I had always found it easy to make friends and kept a small circle of them close to me. I loved people, but also appreciated my alone time.

Derrick had been the social one. He was the one who taught me to like myself and be confident with my true self. As a kid, that was difficult. I often felt as if I didn't belong in this world where everything was temporary and disposable. I was more of a long-term kind of gal. I still carried and used the purple pen Derrick gave to me on our anniversary 10 years ago. He was my first and only true love, and the only man I ever slept with. We met as freshmen in high school and got married shortly after graduation.

I laid my head down on Maiyun's large chest and breathed in her musky scent. It always provided comfort to me.

I heard Sam's Outback pull into the driveway. I stood up and wiped the tear that trickled down my face. I hadn't even noticed I was crying. I opened the front door and smiled at Sam, who wore a bright orange Carhart t-shirt, lime-green shorts, and hiking boots. Karin walked up behind him wearing a grey sweater and blue jeans. She was obviously the conservative one.

I smiled at her and gestured toward Sam. "You let him leave the house like that?" I asked.

She laughed. "As if I could stop him."

Sam glared. "You two just don't appreciate the expression of color," he said.

I smiled. "Is that what you call it?"

He brushed past me and went straight toward Maiyun. They wrestled like two bear cubs on the floor. Karin was polite enough to give me a gentle hug first.

"It's great to see you, Skye. You look much better than the last time I saw you."

My leg had healed much faster than my doctor anticipated. Of course he attributed that to his skillful work. I did not mention the mysterious minister who had visited me in the hospital.

Karin and I glanced down at the two on the floor. Maiyun had her tongue hanging out of her mouth and Sam held her paw between his teeth, pretending to bite it as he growled.

Karin and I stepped over them.

"This place is cute," she said, looking around the living room and kitchen.

"Yes," I said. "It was a very comfortable stay. "It's available for three more weeks, if you two are interested."

She glanced back at Sam with a smile.

He rolled his eyes. "Okay, we'll stay for a week."

Karin jumped up and down and clapped her hands like a young girl getting her first puppy. "Yea!"

I led the way to my new place. It was a 600 square foot apartment next door to the 24-hour gym. My apartment was next to the yoga studio, where hopefully it would be quiet.

I had a decent-sized room and closet against the right wall, a tiny reading area against the left wall, and a kitchenette just left of the entrance way. It was perfect.

"It's a little small," said Sam.

"I think it's cute," added Karin.

"It's free and it's close to work," I said. "I love it."

Sam raised his thick, bushy brow, giving him a rough Neanderthal look. "Free?"

"Yeah," I explained. "Gregg and Ro don't want me driving any more than necessary."

Sam laughed. "You must have made quite an impression. What did you do, run into their building or something?"

I glared. "I ran over a brick and bumped into their orange tree."

Karin giggled, and then quickly covered her mouth.

"Did you kill it?" asked Sam. "I didn't see one outside anywhere."

"No, I didn't kill it. Gregg moved it indoors because it was getting too cold for it outside."

"An orange tree in Washington. This I have to see," said Sam.

I gave them a brief tour of The Wellness Center, and then showed them the tree. There was a tiny scuff on the edge of the pot but it didn't look too bad.

"Hey," I said, "are you two hungry?" It was almost five o'clock and my stomach was growling like a grumpy old bear waking from a long hibernation.

Sam shrugged then looked to Karin who nodded enthusiastically.

"I'm starved," she said.

Sam looked her plump, short body up and down. "Trust me, Honey, ya ain't starvin'."

She slapped him on the shoulder. Her auburn curls bouncing against her neck. "Where did you have in mind?"

It was always fun being with these two. "There's a new Mexican restaurant in Allyn I wanted to try."

"Ooh," said Sam. "Margaritas." His Spanish accent on the word did not do it justice.

I offered to drive, but Sam insisted that I leave my keys in my bag where they belong.

It was a short jaunt to the next town south of Belfair. The restaurant resided on the second floor of a mini mall, and had a wall of windows that opened to a brilliant view of North Bay. Mt. Rainier reflected the sunset with a light pink and orange hue.

"Wow, I could get used to this," said Karin as they were led to a table next to the window.

"Don't get too used to it," said Sam. "A town this small would kill me for sure."

"A small town might do you some good," said Karin. "Make you respectable."

He scoffed. "You wouldn't want me respectable, honey." He pinched her under the table and she let out a muffled shriek.

I had left Maiyun at home and was starting to miss her.

A waiter named Tavo took our order, and then quickly returned with our drinks. As soon as he was gone, Sam mentioned that Tavo winked at me when he lowered my Tequila Sunset onto the table in front of me. It had been several years since men had taken a notice in me. I was slightly overweight, wore no makeup, and was really not that attractive at 45 years old. By the sound of his voice, Tavo couldn't have been more than 25.

"Hey," said Karin. "I think he likes you."

I fumbled with the napkin on the table. "Yes, well, he's half my age."

"You don't look your age," said Sam. "Never did."

I could feel a sudden rush of blood warm my cheeks. Thank God the place was too dark for anyone to see.

"Now you've gone and made her blush," said Karin.

So much for dim light. I stood from the table. "I'll be back." As I made my way to the ladies room, I could hear Sam and Karin giggle. It was difficult to see with the lights so dim. Perhaps I should have brought Maiyun, or at least my cane. Sam must have noticed my struggle because he was by my side in less than a minute.

"It's over here," he said, leading me back toward the front

of the restaurant. "Did you need me to wait for you?"

"No, I can find my way back, thank you."

"So independent," he said, shaking his head.

"You forgot stubborn," I shot back at him.

Minutes later, I exited the well-lit bathroom and struggled to see anything in the dark dining room. I could see the windows and started heading in that general direction. I was doing fairly well until I ran into something incredibly hard.

"Are you all right," said a familiar voice. "Skye?" I wanted to die right there. It was the deep, husky voice of Dr. Khalen Dunning. His firm grip pulled me up by my upper arm.

"I'm so sorry, Dr. Khalen. I didn't see you."

"I hate to be the one to bring this to your attention," he said, "But you are blind. Where's your dog?" Irritation laced his words, but there was also concern, which managed to choke my response.

"Um, she's at home," I stammered.

Sam came to my rescue once again. "I'll take her from here, sir. Sorry for the mishap."

Khalen let go of my arm without another word. I could feel his eyes boring into me like red-hot pokers, or perhaps he was admiring my escort's fine apparel. It was hard to tell.

Sam led me back to the table, mumbling. "Yes, Sam, in the future I would appreciate your help. Please stay and wait for me to come out." His derogatory tone was not missed.

"Jeez, Skye. Why is it so hard for you to ask for help?"

I rubbed my arm where Khalen had gripped me. It felt bruised.

Karin nodded toward the other room. "You know him?"

"He works at The Wellness Center. He's our naturopath." I furrowed my brows, disappointed in myself for not having the foresight to bring Maiyun or my cane. What was I thinking?

"He's cute," said Karin.

Sam nudged her in the arm. "You think everything is cute," he chimed.

"Is he married?" she asked.

Sam's eyes grew wide in the candlelight. "Are you asking for yourself?"

"No." She shoved him hard. "I'm asking for Skye. It's about time she gets hooked up with a good-looking man."

I looked down at the table and carefully unfolded my napkin. I knew my face was red again. "I'm not interested in finding a man."

"Oh," said Karin. "So you're finally giving in to the dark side and scoping out the women?" Her tone matched my own familiar sarcasm, confirming my notion that you become like those you hang around.

"No," I shot back, "I'm perfectly happy being alone."

Karin sighed. "That's too bad. He looks like a real catch, if he's single."

"I don't know if he's single or married," I said. "The

man absolutely abhors me, so I do my best to avoid him."

Sam huffed. "The way he was staring down at you did not exactly scream abhorrence."

"Well, yes," I explained. "I'm sure his emotions toward me were colored by anger, and perhaps frustration just now. Believe me, his distaste for me will return on Tuesday."

Sam flicked his napkin. "Whatever, Skye."

Tavo returned with our meals. He placed mine down first and warned me about the plate being hot. The tangy aroma wafting up from the lamb made my mouth water. I said a silent prayer, and then familiarized myself with where the meat was on my plate. It had been awhile since I had eaten dinner out. I had forgotten how dark it was in most dining areas.

"Have you got it?" Sam asked.

I obviously needed more practice at this. "Yes, thank you," I said a bit too tersely.

He slid the candle closer to my plate. It didn't help much, but I could at least identify different shapes of sorts. "Thank you." This time, my tone was more grateful.

"You're welcome."

To keep them out of my love life—or lack thereof—I drove the conversation toward their trip to Oregon. Karin took the bait and excitedly told me about all the wonderful places they wanted to see.

We were just about ready to leave when Khalen stopped at our table. He leaned over and whispered to Sam. "Make sure you lead her out to the car. We need her at work on

Tuesday." His scent was intoxicating. It smelled earthy and spicy at the same time.

I took a deep breath and bit my lower lip, fighting the urge to fire back a retort. He stood with four other people, two men and two women. Their energy was just as bright as Khalen's. It was rare to see so many people who radiated their energy so far from their bodies, yet there seemed to be a plethora of them in this small town.

Khalen touched my arm. "I'll see you on Tuesday," he said, his voice deep and disturbingly silky.

My throat closed. "Tuesday," I finally managed to squeak out. He released my arm, leaving a searing patch of heat in his hand's place. I resented the discomfort he instilled in me.

After he left, Sam and Karin stared at me in silence. Sam cleared his throat then took the last sip of his margarita.

Chapter 8

Fear is nothing more than a mystery yearning for solution—a gift that can only come from peace.

I spent the rest of the weekend with Sam and Karin kayaking along Case Inlet. We said our farewells on Monday, since they were planning to leave for Oregon Saturday. They promised to swing by on their way back to Seattle in a few weeks.

My apartment was beginning to feel more like home as I spread my few belongings about the place. Tuesday had come so quickly. I ate a bowl of oatmeal for breakfast and headed down to the center for work. Maiyun wondered off toward the woods; she would join me back at the center when she was done. We had a routine down now and it felt comfortable.

Gregg and Ro were going over the day's schedule. They glanced up as I passed the lobby.

"Good morning," called Ro.

"Morning," I called back, and then continued to my room to prepare it. When I returned to the lobby, Maiyun

stood outside, waiting to come in. I opened the door for
her.

I walked into the office and wandered over to glance
at the day's schedule. As I leaned over the counter, my hip
ached as if a knife were being stabbed into my flesh. I placed
my hand over it, but the pain intensified. It had been aching
a bit the entire weekend, but I paid it no mind. I figured I
had pulled a muscle or something. This, however, was not
a pulled muscle.

"Are you all right?" asked Ro.

The pain traveled down my leg, causing it to buckle.
"My hip aches," I said. "It started aching this weekend, but
not this badly."

Ro palpated my hip. "It's hot and firm."

She led me over to a chair, but the pain was too intense
for me to sit.

"Let's lay you down," she said. "I'll take you into the
exam room. Khalen will be here soon, he can have a look to
see what's wrong."

The thought of having him look at my hip was encouragement enough to feign the dismissal of pain. "No, I'm
okay. Just give me a moment to work it out. I'll be okay."

"You don't look okay, Skye. Your brow is damp and your
color is pale."

I hobbled toward my room. "Just give me a moment.
I'll be fine."

She watched me for a moment, and then returned to the
reception area, mumbling something incoherent.

I closed my door and finessed my way onto the table. The pain was intense now, almost debilitating. I placed my hand over the heated bump rising over my right hip and concentrated on removing the pain. It worked some, but not entirely. My leg began to spasm. I bit my lower lip, trying not to cry out.

I could hear Ro and Gregg discuss something in the lobby, but their words were indecipherable.

The front door chimed as it opened. It was Khalen, no doubt.

I heard them all converse, and then a sudden knock on my door made me jump.

"I'll be out in a moment," I called, not wanting anyone to enter.

Khalen opened the door with Gregg behind him.

I kept my hand over my hip.

"Let me see it," said Khalen, lifting my hand.

"I'm okay," I cried out. "Please, just leave. I'll be fine."

Khalen lowered my pants and I gasped; not so much from the embarrassment as it was from the searing pain that ripped through my flesh.

His jaw clenched. "Bring her to my exam room," he instructed. "We need to remove it, immediately."

My heart beat so loud, it was the only thing my ears detected. Whatever they were planning to do, it did not sound pleasant. Gregg effortlessly carried me to the exam room. Khalen was not too far behind.

"Do I have a say in this?" I asked.

Both Gregg and Khalen answered simultaneously. "No."

"Is it a capsule?" Gregg asked.

"I'm not sure," said Khalen. "We don't have much time."

I wanted to know what they were talking about, but fear held my tongue. I laid on my side as Khalen scanned me from head to toe with his electrifying eyes. The gold specks glowed beneath the lights.

Gregg didn't seem to notice, so I ignored the oddity as I had done for many years. It wasn't unusual for me to see what wasn't real.

"It is a capsule. Thank God she has only one." He slid the top of my pants down to expose my hip.

My face grew red and I wanted to shrink under the table. I tried to sit.

"Lie down, Skye," he said. His voice was deep and soft, making it impossible to ignore.

"Has it exploded?" asked Gregg.

Khalen shook his head. "No, her body is rejecting it."

I took a deep breath, wanting this to be over with soon. Maiyun peered into the room and started to whine. She must have sensed my discomfort and fear.

"It's okay, girl," I whispered. The trembling in my voice gave away my fear.

Khalen placed his hand on my shoulder. "Skye, this won't hurt. Just be very still." Again, his voice was soft and low, like an angel whispering down from the heavens.

Gregg donned a pair of gloves and assisted the doctor as if he had done this a hundred times.

"I'm going to numb you a bit," said Khalen, just before he pricked a needle into my hip.

My breath caught in my throat. Warmth spread under my skin and I felt strangely vulnerable. My hip would not move, even if I willed it to. It felt warm and heavy as a sack of sand.

"Scalpel," said Khalen.

I felt heat where he sliced and a trickle of blood. Gregg dabbed the area.

"It's deep," said Khalen. "Pray it's not protected."

I didn't want to know what that meant. I just prayed.

"There," said Gregg. "To the left."

"I see it," Khalen grumbled. "Damn."

Both men were silent. My heartbeat was all I could hear. Whatever they saw, it couldn't be good.

"It's protected," said Gregg.

"What does that mean?" I asked, my voice weak and low.

"If we remove it," Khalen explained. "It releases cyanide."

"What if we remove the tissue around it?" said Gregg.

"We'll have to work quickly," said Khalen.

I now knew what the holiday turkey felt as its flesh was torn from its bones. The pain was beyond anything I had ever experienced. I wanted so badly to place my hand over the area and make the pain go away, but Khalen instructed me to stay very still. Instead, I imagined my hand there and envisioned the blue mist rising from my body. Pain is just an illusion, I told myself. It's just an illusion, nothing more.

"Khalen, the serum," Gregg warned.

"I know, I see it." He pulled out the broken capsule, along with a chunk of my tissue. "Suction it, quickly," he instructed.

"I can't get it all," said Gregg. "It's being absorbed."

Khalen rushed out of the room. He returned with a bowl.

"What is that?" asked Gregg.

I felt something cold press into my flesh. It burned.

"Plantain, bentonite clay, and cyanide homeopathic. It will draw out the poison and neutralize it." He placed a bandage around my wound and secured it with tape.

Sweat moistened my forehead and I felt a strange calm come over me. I wanted to sleep.

"Get her up," said Khalen. "Don't let her sleep."

I felt them wrench me up by my shoulders. My body was very relaxed, almost as though I were drunk.

"Skye, stand up," Khalen demanded.

My legs were limp and non-responsive.

"Get some ice-cold water," Khalen told Gregg. "Quickly!"

"I don't like cold," I mumbled. "I want to sleep."

"Don't sleep," he whispered. "Stay with me." He slapped my face, but I barely felt it. My body slipped down onto the cold surface of the floor.

Maiyun scratched me with her paw, and then howled as if trying to get my attention. Her cold nose touched my hand.

Gregg returned with a bowl of ice water and a cloth. Khalen wet the cloth and then rubbed the cold liquid over my face and head. I shivered in response.

I tried to move his hand away, but he continued to wet me down. My muscles felt tight and threatened to spasm. They ached. My bones felt as if they were being crushed. The sleepy sensation soon gave way to the immense pain that caged my body. I screamed in agony. My body writhed in pain.

Khalen continued to wet my head, face, and neck.

"What's happening?" asked Gregg.

"The poison is trying to take hold." He placed some drops under my tongue, and then held my mouth closed. "You can beat this," he told me. "You're strong enough, Skye. Come on."

His voice grew distant. I felt separated from my body, and peace surrounded me completely. I was free.

Chapter 9

Love is a power all in itself. It offers unbelievable strength and debilitating weakness in the span of a heartbeat.

Derrick appeared before me. His soft, brown eyes looked down at me, his sweet breath caressing my cheek. We stood outside by a waterfall, in a meadow of pink and purple flowers. The sun warmed my skin. This must be heaven, I thought.

I wrapped my arms around him. "God, I miss you," I whispered. "It feels so good to have you back in my arms."

"You cannot stay," he said. "You must go back."

My stomach felt hollow, my heart slowed. "No," I cried. "I cannot leave you."

"You must," he whispered. His warm lips brushed the top of my head, and then gently pried my arms away from him.

"Don't leave," I pleaded.

"I never have," he said. "I am always with you."

I held his hand to my face and kissed his soft skin. A tear rolled down my cheek. "I love you."

I opened my eyes. The meadow was gone, along with the waterfall and warm sun. I was in my bed. The hand I now held belonged to Khalen. I released it immediately and took a deep breath. Tears continued to stream down my cheek.

"Welcome back," he said, smiling. I had never seen that expression on him before, and it was disturbing. He looked happy and dashing all at the same time. I swallowed hard, praying he hadn't heard my words.

He placed a few more drops of liquid under my tongue. "The worst is over," he said.

I tried to sit up, but a sudden rush of dizziness kept me still. "How long have I been out?"

"Three days and seven hours," he said.

"That long?" It seemed like only minutes to me. I tried to move again. A stabbing pain bit at my hip where the capsule had been removed.

"Stay still," he instructed with obvious impatience. "Give yourself a chance to recover."

"I've had three days and seven hours to recover. Now I need to get up." Again I tried to sit, but his strong hands held my shoulders down. "Are you always this stubborn?"

I knew that I couldn't fight against him right now and I snapped back, "I can be worse." I wanted to get some answers. "Why was a capsule inside me?"

"They wanted to track you," he said.

"Who are they?"

His brow wrinkled as if what he had to say caused pain.

"You should get some rest." He stood up from my bed.

I grabbed his arm. "Don't go," I said, shocking myself at the same time. It was unlike me to act this way.

He glared down at me and I released my grip. "I'm sorry," I said. "I'm not sure why I did that." I shook my head, embarrassed. "Of course you can go. I'll be fine."

"Are you trying to convince me or yourself?"

The draw I had toward this man was unnerving, and definitely unwarranted. "I need some answers," I said, my tone low and controlled.

He sat down beside me and dried my tears that had dampened his hand. "When you were unconscious," he said. "You were talking to someone. Who was it?"

I closed my eyes. "Derrick, my husband."

He lowered his head and his eyes darkened. "You're married."

I shook my head. "No, he died nine years ago from cancer."

He looked thoughtful and his eyes brightened again. The gold flecks in them began to glow.

"What are you looking for now?" I asked.

He looked surprised and speculative. "Why do you ask that?"

"When you were looking for the capsule inside me, your eyes glowed like that. So I'm wondering what you hope to find this time."

His dark brow arched as if he were doubting what I saw. "For someone who is supposed to be blind, you sure do observe a lot."

"Also," I added, "this is going to sound crazy, but I figured I have nothing else to lose here, so I'm just going to say it."

"I'm listening," he said.

"You, Gregg, and Ro have amazing energy surrounding you. I have not seen that type of energy since my husband died. This town seems to be flooded with high-energy people." I blurted this out, knowing how crazy I must sound.

He cocked his head and smiled. "High-energy?"

He was mocking me, I was sure. "You vibrate at a very high frequency," I explained. "White light surrounds you all and radiates far from your bodies."

"Are you talking about our auras?"

I shook my head. "I don't know what that is. I just know what I see, and what you have around you is different from most humans."

He laughed. "And are you like most humans?"

I swallowed hard. "Yes," I lied. I had never been like most humans, even as a young child. I often saw things that were not real, and felt my instincts were sharper than normal. It often made me paranoid. After drawing unwanted attention to myself, I learned to ignore my feelings and visions, but not entirely.

Crossing his arms, he began to study me. I could feel him probing into my soul. "Hmm," he said. "You never questioned why you look so much younger than you are? You talk about energy and vibration, yet you know nothing about auras. You claim my eyes glow, yet you cannot tell me what color shirt I'm wearing right now. And you can heal with your touch. Yet you feel as if you are the same as everyone else?"

I kept my surprise and fear veiled behind a calm façade, unwilling to satisfy him with any confirmation. "You have a great imagination," I said, but the catch in my voice betrayed me.

"Yes," he said. "I've been accused of that a time or two."

The silence that followed was unnerving.

"What are we?" I finally said, admitting what he knew to be true. I was different, and so was he.

"We are Spirians," he explained. "Not quite human, and not fully spirit. We are in between dimensions, you might say."

Welcome to the Twilight Zone, I thought. I could almost hear the music playing in the background. "You said that they would use the capsule to get to me. Who are they?"

"The Shadows."

My brow arched. "Who are the Shadows?"

"Spirians who choose to live their lives in the dark. They use their gifts for personal gain and often hurt others in the process."

"Their energy is cold," I said, "and dark." I thought about the female paramedic I had met in the hospital. She had that kind of energy.

"Yes," he confirmed. "What you sense around me and

the others of our kind is the universal light of God, the creator of all life. We are called the Protected."

My curiosity was aroused. "Can a Protected one become a Shadow?"

"Yes," he said, "and a Shadow," he swallowed hard, "can choose to become Protected."

I shook my head. "Why would anyone choose to be a Shadow?"

He wrung his hands together as if trying to remove some hidden germ. "It's easy to become like those you hang around," he explained. "When you are surrounded by negativity and ugliness, it becomes the norm and the light that accompanies positive thoughts and actions is shadowed. The difference between what is right and what is wrong becomes less defined."

There was more to his story than he was willing to share. It intrigued me, but I was not quite ready to venture there. "So why do the Shadows want to track me?"

"They are interested in your gifts, no doubt."

Again, I thought about the strange paramedic in the hospital, and how she looked at me as if trying to figure me out. "I met someone at the hospital four months ago. She was a paramedic. She asked me to…" I shook my head.

"To what?" he prompted.

I looked into his unusual eyes, which were more gold than green. He didn't think I was crazy. That was a first. "I took away the pain in my dog's hip. She witnessed it and asked me to work on her wrist. She claimed she had injured it, but there was nothing wrong with her, nor did she have any pain. She lied to me. Was she a Shadow?"

His gentle smile faded. "Most likely, yes."

"Good versus evil," I said. "But how did the capsule get inside me?"

"Typically through a shot. I'm sure they gave you pain meds in the hospital."

I frowned. "That was through an IV drip. I don't remember having a shot in my hip." I frowned. "Then again, I don't remember much of anything after the morphine kicked in."

"Well, you must have sparked an interest in that paramedic. She could have injected you when you were asleep."

"Are there many of them?" I asked. "The Shadows?"

He nodded, hesitantly. "Yes. Right now, the balance between good and evil is weighted in their favor. There are more of them than of us."

I considered this. Kids did seem more unruly these days, and the prisons were packed more than ever. Drug use was at an all-time high, and the majority of humans were on some kind of antidepressant. This whole thing made sense. I just hadn't seen it until then.

"Am I in danger?"

"They are curious about you. If they wanted you dead, you would be so. The capsule is something they use to track a Spirian of interest. If they prove to be useful, the Shadows will claim them. If they prove to be worthless, or a threat, the capsule explodes and the Spirian dies from poison."

He said it all very matter-of-factly, as if this were a well-known tactic that had been used for many years.

My eyes widened. "So I'm being tracked?"

He smiled, but it was guarded. "Not any more, but they know you are here."

"Then I should leave." I started to move, but he held me down.

"No, you shouldn't."

The warmth of his touch overwhelmed and frightened me. I was a frog in heating water, waiting to fall victim to the boiling point of his alluring charm. I moved my hand and, again, tried to sit. "I'm feeling better now, can I move?"

With hesitance and a tired sigh, he helped me.

"Things are about to get interesting around here," he said. "Be careful who you treat. Keep your instincts sharp."

"Why?"

"I don't want you to become one of them."

My eyes widened. "I will not become a Shadow."

"Good," he said. "That's a promising start."

I noticed that Maiyun was not around. "Where's my dog?"

"She's at the shop," he said. "She kept trying to lie on top of you."

I frowned. That was unlike her to behave that way. She must have been really worried. "I want to see her."

"I'll get her," he said, standing up. When he left, the place seemed oddly empty.

Judging by the dim light outside, it must have been early

evening. I turned on my reading lamp and swung my legs out of bed. Pain ripped down my thigh and through my hip area. I chose to ignore it as I padded my way to the kitchen to make some tea. My stomach grumbled. The shortbread cookies in the cupboard looked inviting, so I grabbed the open package.

I heard the front door open and Maiyun's nails against the hardwood floor. I bent down to greet her. She licked my face and pushed against me with fierce enthusiasm. I fell back onto my aching hip and released a sharp cry. She must have sensed my pain, because she laid down right away with her ears flat and down.

"It's okay, Maiyun." I reached my hand out to her.

She scooted toward me and placed her head on my lap.

Khalen looked at the cookies on the counter and shook his head. He then put them back into the cupboard, and pulled down some brown rice. "I'll make you some real food to eat," he said, as he pushed his sleeves up. His white turtle-neck sweater provided an attractive contrast to his dark skin. The blue jeans were also a shocking change from his usual high-priced slacks—although the jeans were perfectly pressed with sharp creases down the front and back of the legs.

I shook my head wondering what kind of person presses blue jeans.

"Did you work at all today?" I asked, rubbing Maiyun's belly.

He pulled some chicken out of the freezer, along with frozen beans. "No."

"Yesterday?" I asked.

"No." He turned to look at me. "I haven't left your side."

I suddenly felt very uncomfortable. His face was impossible to read. I pet Maiyun in silence as I watched him prepare the food. He was obviously skilled in the kitchen and knew his way around my kitchen far too well.

"Why are you so concerned for my welfare?" I finally asked. "Last week, you made me feel like the plague."

"Last week, I questioned who you were, or wondered what you were pretending to be," he explained.

I pursed my lips, trying to comprehend why he would think such things.

"There are many like you who try to infiltrate our kind. They pretend to be one of us, and then too easily turn our people into one of them—like a virus." His knuckles turned white as he gripped the knife tighter. There was a story there, I was certain. "Gregg and Ro have too much trust in people. They believe everyone is good until proven otherwise."

I watched him cut the frozen tenderloins into chunks and toss them into the pan with heated coconut oil. He turned the rice down to simmer. Its nutty aroma permeated the air.

"And you believe that everyone is bad?"

He glanced at me over his shoulder. "I've run into quite a few Shadows."

An image popped into my head. The woman with red hair and green eyes. The one from my dreams. She was beautiful, elegant, and very tall. The image of her faded when he turned to face me. Then it dawned on me. The man in my dream was Khalen. I was Khalen. My stomach felt sick. I knew he looked familiar the day that I met him, but I could not put the pieces together until now. This man was much more refined than the one I saw in my dreams. It couldn't be him. Or could it?

"What was her name? The redheaded woman with the green eyes?" I asked, throwing all caution aside.

He shook his head. "You seem to have many gifts," he said. "Be very careful how you choose to use them." His voice was almost a growl.

I took that as a warning and dropped the subject for now. He, too, had many gifts that he had not yet revealed to me. He pulled his energy in and kept me out on purpose.

I stood up and walked toward my stash of wine. "Are you a wine drinker?" I asked.

He glanced at me and arched his brow. "That depends upon the wine."

I pursed my lips and tried to guess what type of wine this man would drink. He was definitely a red-wine soul. A full-bodied one with some attitude and a strong finish. I pulled out the 1998 Robert Mondavi Cabernet Sauvignon.

I opened the bottle and allowed it to breath for a few minutes before pouring a little bit into two large-bowled Riedel glasses. I picked up one of them and swirled its contents around, then breathed in the fiery aroma. This year of Mondavi's Cab never disappointed me. I took a small sip and held it on my tongue to enjoy all the subtleties this juice had to offer.

Derrick had introduced me to wine. He never took his first sip before giving me a very passionate kiss. Even in fancy restaurants, he would clink my glass, lean over, and linger a warm and inviting kiss on my eager lips. I closed my eyes, trying to imagine his tender lips on mine right now. My heart ached with his absence. Before tears could fill my eyes, I swallowed and looked away.

The wine was just as bit as good as I had remembered. Having regained my composure, I handed Khalen a glass.

He looked at me with a questioning glance, then swirled the deep burgundy liquid in his glass. I watched as he closed his eyes, and breathed in the aroma I knew he would find pleasing. He curled his lips into a smile, and then took a slow sip. He took his time swallowing. A man after my own heart.

I watched patiently, anticipating his reaction.

"A woman who knows her wine. I'm impressed." He looked at my shabby grey sweats and bare feet. "Judging by the way you dress, I would never have thought you would know anything about wine."

Okay, he was no longer after my heart. My eyes narrowed. "Perhaps good judgment is not one of your gifts?"

He laughed. "Touché."

"You still have not answered my question," I reminded him.

His body stiffened.

He must have thought I was going to ask about the red-headed woman. I ventured to prove him wrong. "Why are you taking care of me?"

"Would you prefer someone else?"

He kept his energy close and unreadable. I found it both intriguing and frustrating.

"I never said that."

He added the rice and green beans to the chicken, then added some cayenne pepper, sea salt, and tamari sauce. The smell made my stomach roar. "It smells good," I said, trying to lighten the mood.

He carried the frying pan over to the table and set it on top of a trivet. He then retrieved two bowls from the cupboard and set out some silverware.

I placed two napkins on the table, along with the bottle of wine.

"You really shouldn't drink," he said. "It dulls your gifts."

I laughed. "Yeah, it's been a real problem."

He downed the rest of his wine in one swoop, and then poured more for both of us. There was definitely a story to discover here. I just wasn't sure if it wanted to be discovered, or if I would like what I found.

Chapter 10

When one realm becomes imbalanced, another realm becomes concerned. The food chain must start at the bottom. When realms collide, however, it is difficult to know who is at the top and who is at the bottom of the food chain.

We enjoyed our dinner in silence, and then retired to the reading area. We finished our glass of wine with a little small talk. He continued to protect himself from me, and I was impressed at how persistent he could be with that shield.

His somber mood was getting to me. I stood up and clenched my teeth, biting back against the pain in my hip. "I need to take a shower," I said.

"I'll do dishes." He stood and headed for the kitchen. "After that, I'll change your dressings."

The blood drained from my face. He had said that so casually, yet to me it felt like a violation. I knew he was a doctor and had probably seen many backsides before, but that was different. He was talking about my backside. "I'll take care of it," I said, almost too hastily.

He smiled, as if enjoying my obvious discomfort. "It

really shouldn't get wet." He went to the kitchen, tore off a piece of plastic wrap, and folded it in half. He then dug through the black bag he'd brought with him and pulled out some hefty-looking tape. "Come here," he said.

Whatever blood was left in my head abandoned my face all together. "What?"

He pulled me toward him and turned me around. "I don't want you to get it wet," he explained. He then lowered my sweats much lower than necessary. I pulled them back up a bit.

"Skye," he grumbled. "I have seen your hip, it's okay."

I allowed him to tape the plastic wrap, and then made haste toward the bathroom.

From inside that sanctuary, I washed my hair and shaved my legs, grateful to be feeling human again. The hot water did a great job of clearing my thoughts. After drying myself and using copious amounts of lavender lotion on my skin, I realized that I had not brought clean clothes in with me—and I did not intend to wear my stinky sweats again.

With a large bath towel wrapped around me, I opened the door and peeked outside. Khalen was still cleaning the kitchen. I quietly slipped into the bedroom and looked for some clean sweats. I found a pair of purple workout pants and an old green t-shirt.

The pain in my hip throbbed. I placed my hand over the area and envisioned the blue mist rising from my wound. Heat coursed through my body and out through my hand. My breathing increased and the pain faded, leaving an intense itch in its place. The heat was almost too much. I sat on the floor for a moment to cool down.

Maiyun found me, and then howled to gain Khalen's attention.

He entered the room and knelt beside me. "Bloody hell, you are way too hot." He felt my forehead and laid me down. "How hot was that shower?" he asked.

"Too hot," I mumbled.

He drenched a towel in cold water and placed it under my shirt. I bolted up in shock and tried to remove the towel.

"Leave it," he demanded. "It'll cool you down."

The room finally stopped spinning, and I felt the color return to my face. "Thank you," I said, removing the cold towel from my belly. The last of my clean shirts was now soaking wet.

"Didn't anyone tell you that hot water and wine don't mix?"

I groaned and held my wet shirt out away from my body.

He left, and then soon returned with one of his shirts in hand. It was a grey, long-sleeved turtleneck ski shirt made of very soft cotton. "Here, put this on."

I waited for him to leave, and then donned the oversized shirt. The arms draped past my hands, and the hem fell almost to my knees. It smelled like him: cedar and clove.

He returned shortly after.

"Thank you," I said. "That was my last clean shirt." I

glanced over at the wet shirt on the floor.

He picked it up and placed it into the basket. "You don't have much of a wardrobe," he commented. "I'll take these to the center tomorrow and wash them for you."

I closed my eyes. "Please don't," I asked. "You've done enough. I'm able to take care of myself now." It was difficult to allow someone to care for me and it made me very uncomfortable.

"Yes, well, I'll be the judge of that. Let me change your dressing."

At least the pain was gone, I thought. I laid down on the bed and lowered my pants just enough to gain him access.

His annoying laugh did not escape my notice. "You were much easier to care for when you were unconscious."

"I'm sorry to disappoint you."

He tore the bandage from my rump.

I held my scream in, not wanting to give him any satisfaction.

"It's healed," he said. "No wonder you were so hot and drained."

"I just took the pain away," I said.

"Well, you did much more than that," he added. "The wound is closed and looking great." He covered my hip. "I guess you don't need me anymore."

My heart skipped at the thought of him leaving. I was just getting used to his company.

"You're welcome to stay the night, if you want," I said, my voice low and unsure.

He smiled. "I'm sure you miss your privacy," he said. "You'll sleep much better if I'm gone."

"Oh, okay," I said, trying to hide the disappointment in my voice.

He packed his few belongings and waited for me to crawl into bed. "I'll see you tomorrow," he said.

His energy was expanded again, no longer guarded. He was happy to leave, I thought. Of course he was. He no longer had to shield himself from me.

"Tomorrow," I mirrored.

He turned to leave.

"Khalen," I called.

"Yes."

"Thank you for everything."

He nodded, and then left.

It was rude of me to pry into his personal life, and ask about a woman who obviously distressed him. What difference did it make anyway? The anger inside me was self-inflicted, and I promised myself to stay out of his business, not read him anymore.

For the first time in my life, I felt as if I had found people who truly understood me. I was not so vulnerable, nor was I the only one surrounded by weirdness that could not be explained. I closed my eyes and tried to push the redheaded woman I saw in Khalen's past from my mind.

I switched my thoughts to Derrick and the way he looked in the meadow. Over the past nine years, I had forgotten the details of his face. He seemed different in the meadow, taller and much more muscular than I had remembered him. I laughed at the absurdity of my dream. It seemed so real. "Why can't I let you go?" I said quietly.

I turned over in bed, hoping the new position would offer some peace of mind and perhaps some sleep. It did neither. A cold, dark nose rose over the edge of the bed. Out came a warm, wet tongue. I reached for Maiyun's head and pet the top of it. "Hi Maiyun. You can't sleep either?"

I considered listening to one of my audio books. I was not in the mood for Dan Brown, and the other books in my collection were sappy love stories. I got out of bed and padded over to the window. It was dark outside and quiet in the parking lot. The gym next door seemed like a good alternative, but my energy level just wasn't there. I walked to my dresser and pulled out my sketchbook and pencils.

I turned on my light and started drawing a pair of eyes. They looked like Derrick's, almond-shaped and set wide apart. I added some eyebrows and his straight nose with a triangular end. Next I drew his lips. They had a curl to them that I always found attractive. His square chin and jaw line came next, which tied in nicely with his ears. I sketched a wild disarray of hair, and started filling in the shadows.

An hour later, I finished my sketch of the most perfect man ever. His charismatic eyes stared back at me. My brow furrowed. I grabbed the sketch and added a short braid to his head. Then, I widened his jaw a bit, and darkened the shadow under his nose. His lips became slightly fuller, and his chin more square. I darkened his eyebrows, and added distinctive flecks to his eyes.

"Khalen Dunning," I whispered. I slapped the sketch-book closed and tossed it back into my drawer. I let out a sharp laugh and shook my head. "Always drawn to the impossible," I said. "Imagine that."

Maiyun cocked her head. I placed my hands on either side of her face and kissed her soft muzzle. "Let's make some cocoa, girl."

Chapter 11

The grey-eyed one who is blind but sees will heal the temple of our souls and bare the life of our future.

I came down to the center wearing my purple workout pants and Khalen's grey shirt. My plan was to change into a work shirt. There wasn't much I could do about the pants. I would get overheated working, but I would just have to deal with it until I could wash my clothes.

Ro came around the corner then stopped dead in her tracks. "Skye, what are you doing here?"

"I came to work," I said.

Everyone stopped what they were doing and stared in my direction. I looked behind me feeling as if there were some evil monster standing there.

"How are you feeling?" asked Gregg.

"Great," I responded. "Why are you all staring at me?"

Ro came over and gave me a big hug. "Thank God you're all right." Then, she stepped back. "Does Khalen know you're here?"

"No, should he?"

Gregg chimed in. "He will not be pleased."

My eyes narrowed. "Well, he has his own life to tend to. I'm sure mine is no concern to him."

Gregg and Ro exchanged glances as if they knew something that I didn't.

"It might be kind of a slow day for you," said Gregg. "I didn't expect you in all week."

"I'll catch the walk-ins," I said.

Kathy and Ann just stared at me as I walked past them toward the storage room to get a clean work shirt. They always kept to themselves, and didn't really talk to me much, so their aloofness was not a huge surprise.

"Welcome back, Skye," Steve called out from his room.

"Thank you," I responded.

Khalen was not in yet. His office was still dark and his Escalade was not out front. I opened the door to the storage room and saw my clothes folded and neatly stacked on the counter next to the laundry machines. He must have done them last night before going home, I thought.

I gathered my clothes and headed back to my apartment to change into something more reasonable. I took my time heading back to the center, anticipating a slow day.

Two women and a man stood in the lobby asking to book an appointment with me. Gregg looked very uneasy, and the energy in the room felt cold and heavy.

"She's booked today," he said. "And all into next week. We have two other therapists if—"

"We want to see Skye," the man demanded.

I walked past the three people, and headed toward the back room to check the schedule. There were many openings today, and several for next week. The man's eyes followed me and locked in when he caught my focus on him.

"We'll take her next available appointment," one of the women said.

"Do you all want to come in on the same day?" asked Gregg.

"It doesn't matter," said the man, still staring in my direction.

Gregg booked an appointment for each of them.

"You will call if there is a cancellation?" the man asked.

"Of course," said Gregg. "See you all in two weeks."

The three people left. I peeked around the corner to make sure they were gone, and then walked toward the front counter.

"What was that all about?" I asked. "I'm not booked."

"Do you know them?" asked Gregg.

I shook my head. "No, why?"

His lips grew firm. "They certainly seem to know you."

Khalen walked in carrying a Nordstrom bag and two cups of coffee. He must have noticed Gregg's bleak expression, and then cast a warning glance in my direction. "You should be resting."

"I'm fine," I countered.

He was about to come toward me, but Gregg cut him off. "Can I talk to you for a moment?"

Khalen cast a warning glance in my direction, and then

followed Gregg into the office and closed the door, but my senses were on the alert and I could clearly hear Gregg's voice.

"Talon and his mates came in to the office today to see Skye," he explained.

Khalen was silent, and then said something too soft for me to hear. They must have known I was listening. I heard them speak but could no longer make out the conversation. I barely heard Khalen say, "I'll talk to her," before the door to his office opened.

Gregg walked past me with a look of concern.

"Skye," Khalen called to me. "We need to talk."

I looked back at Gregg, and then entered Khalen's office. He closed the door behind me, and then handed me a cup of coffee. "One-pump mocha with whole milk and a splash of cinnamon powder."

I took the coffee from his hand, clearly confused. "Thanks." How did he know my coffee drink? I stepped around his desk and sat in one of the chairs.

He sat down across from me and folded his hands. He looked down to gather his thoughts. When his eyes met mine, there was more than just concern flashing in them. "Skye, you really shouldn't be here. You need to rest."

"I want to work," I said. "I feel fine."

"Yes, well, it seems you have drawn attention to yourself."

An image of some crazy person wearing a huge tent sign and loud clothing flashed through my mind. It was unlike me to draw attention to myself. I took a sip of coffee, feeling the need to hide my embarrassment. I did not like being the cause of concern, but somehow I attracted it into my life. Another one of my fabulous gifts, I presumed.

"Gregg said that the three people who wanted to see you were persistent, as if they knew about your gift."

My brow creased. "I barely know about my gift," I retorted. "How could they possibly know? That man looked at me is if I were his next meal."

"The people you've worked on," he said. "Did anyone seem—different?"

I laughed. "This whole town seems different. Somehow it attracts beautiful people with unusual gifts. Ian, Aidan, Ro, you—"

"Did you use your gift?" he interrupted.

"No. I removed their pain, that's all," I said.

His expression was filled with speculation and doubt. "Like you removed your pain?"

My heart skipped and I suddenly felt very warm. I knew my face was glowing red. "My intention was not to heal," I explained. "I just wanted to stop their pain."

"Hmm." He studied me with those golden green eyes. He stood up and walked out of the office, motioning me to follow him. He stopped in front of Gregg's desk. "Does she have anything this morning?"

Gregg shook his head, and then looked at me.

"Good," said Khalen. "Block our schedule out for the next two hours." He walked into my treatment room and greeted Maiyun by scratching her under her chin. He then turned his piercing eyes on me. "I want you to work on me as if I am a stranger," he said. "Can you do that?"

I nodded. "You practically are a stranger."

In truth, this was going to be difficult. I always read my clients as I worked on them because it enabled me to remove any emotional blocks they might have. I had promised myself not to do that to Khalen. I would have to keep my energy in check.

I took a deep breath, and tried to ground myself—a difficult task while he was in the room. "I need you to stand up," I said, my voice just barely above a whisper.

He must have sensed my discomfort. He smiled warmly and softened his eyes. "Remember, I'm just a stranger," he reminded me.

"Yes, you are." I touched him and immediately noted that his guard was down. I stayed focused on what my hands felt and not on the dark images that hovered peripherally in my mind. His structure leaned to the left, indicating a heaviness he felt toward a female in his life. It could be anything, I reminded myself, but I was not very convincing. My instincts were much stronger than my logic.

I made some notes on my chart regarding his burdened structure and muscle tension then set the chart down on my table. "Okay," I said. "Get undressed and lie face down on the table." I dimmed the lights on my way out.

"I'll only be a moment," he said.

I closed the door and left to wash my hands. They shook

as I held them under the warm water. I closed the door to the bathroom and turned off the light. I had to get control of my emotions. My mind was all over the place and my bare feet barely felt the floor beneath me. I took some long, deep breaths and allowed God's love to pour through me, purging the black tar that held me bound. I was feeling lighter now, and ready to work. With one more breath, I raised my arms over my head and centered myself. "You don't know him," I told myself. "He's just another person, nothing more."

As I approached the door, my calmness gave way to anxiety. I forced myself to breathe deep and concentrate on the task before me.

After placing a bolster under his ankles, I measured his legs and found the left one two inches shorter than the right. This difference was not unusual if his body had suffered a trauma. I moved to his side and placed my right index finger at the base of his skull and my left palm over his sacrum. His vibration was strong, fast and steady, like the hum of a large engine. I allowed my vibration to entrain to his, and then continued to calm that frequency down to induce a relaxed state. We were connected now. After feeling the subtle shift under my hands, I rechecked his leg length and found them even. His body was ready to receive treatment.

I placed my hands on his lower back and took a deep calming breath. The images that flooded my mind were disturbing. I did my best to block them, but could not. I couldn't swallow, my throat was constricted and tense.

Breathe, I told myself. I started on the right side of his back where there was little tension. His left side would take some work and quite a bit of concentration.

That was an understatement. He had injuries on his left side. My hands felt scars that ran deep into his tissue. His lower three ribs had been broken a long time ago. His spine wanted to curl as if the muscles were pulling it over. His tissue was taught and dense, unyielding to my touch. To invoke change, I would have to enter that place he kept so guarded. I was unwilling to do so. I stuck with working the surface of his tissue, instead, praying he wouldn't notice.

"You pulled out," he said. "Why?"

"It's rude to enter that space," I said. "You are not guarded and I don't feel right entering a place that brings you discomfort."

"You have to," he said. "If I didn't want you to, I would have prevented it."

With a deep breath, I placed my hands on his back and entered that sacred space he left open for me. Images flashed in my mind and pain racked my body so deeply I almost hunched over. The source of this pain was the redheaded woman I saw the other day and in my dreams. She had attacked him with violence and anger. My stomach wrenched and my hands were shaking.

I focused my thoughts on removing this pain, for both our sakes. Father, I silently prayed, I need your help. I opened myself to Him, the source, and waited for His peace to surround me. The blue mist pooled around my hands, and then drifted upward. My body felt hollow and filled with light. My feet were anchored to the earth like the roots of an ancient cedar tree. The images cleared from my mind, and were replaced with peace that could never be described with mere words.

When the vibration in Khalen's body slowed, I removed my hands. They were burning hot. Perspiration beaded on my forehead.

Khalen rolled over, and then sat up. I couldn't move. Never in my years had a session been so intense. He took my hands in his.

"Release it," he whispered. "Let it flow out of your hands and into the earth."

I did as he asked, feeling the heat move out through my fingertips. When I stopped shaking, I hesitantly pulled my hands from his and brightened the lights so I could see his face. "What just happened?" I asked.

"I had to see what you are capable of," he said. "I had to open you up to something that most people keep hidden."

I shook my head, trying to purge the memory of the images in my mind. "Who… Why?" I covered my face.

"It doesn't matter," he said. "We have a much larger issue here."

It was hard to see a much larger issue when my own world was swirling around like a muddled whirlpool of strange gifts and inexplicably beautiful people trying to kill one another.

Khalen was much too calm about all this. It was

irritating and confusing. I wanted to slap him and bring him back to my level so that he could feel my frustration and confusion.

Maiyun pressed against me, offering comfort. I scratched her head and ears, and then looked into Khalen's eyes, which were more green than gold right now. They were the same eyes that stared back at me in the mirror of my dreams.

"I dreamt of you," I said. "Months before I even met you. I was you, and there was another man who looked like you. Then there was a redheaded woman. She stabbed me here," I pointed at the scar on his back. "And then she died. I, too, felt almost dead."

"I know," he said. "I have dreamt of you as well." The sound of his voice was eerie, like a familiar tune from another lifetime.

"Are the people in your dreams trying to kill me?"

"Not exactly."

I sat down on my stool and shook my head. "I don't understand all this. I don't want to be an issue for you or anyone else. I want to go back to being plain, anonymous me."

"Then you need to learn to pull back. You cannot heal everyone of everything. Sometimes, people need to experience something to gain something greater."

I was confused and shook my head. "Explain."

"You can heal, yet you are still blind. Why?"

"I didn't know I could heal," I said. "I thought I just took away the pain."

"Then how do you explain what happened to Ian at the vet hospital? Or to Ro after your last session with her. How do you explain your hip?"

I couldn't. I remembered about Ian, but did not know about any healing I had done with Ro. I was just trying to remove her pain. I thought back in the hospital when the Reverend came to visit me. He, too, removed the pain, but I also healed much faster than the doctors had expected.

"I thought Ian was a fluke," I said quietly. "I..." My stomach was turning and my head felt ready to explode.

Khalen sat quietly, studying me. I could feel his gold-laced emerald eyes bore into me, but I had nothing to hide, so I didn't care. The blanket had slid down to his waist, exposing his smooth chest and well-muscled stomach. My nausea turned to flutters, as if a billion tiny bubbles were fighting to escape my gut.

"I'll leave," I said, "so you can get dressed."

"Not yet. Tell me what happened in the hospital."

My eyes widened, betraying my shock. Did he read my mind? I suddenly felt very vulnerable. If he knew about the hospital, he could also feel how his presence affected me. Heat rose in my cheeks, making me even warmer than I was.

I cleared my throat. "A man came to visit me," I began. "He said his name was Reverend Mark." I shook my head, trying to ignore how silly this was all going to sound. "He told me that pain was just an illusion. Then—"

"Pain is just an illusion," he repeated, his eyes in distant thought. "Hmm, tell me more about this man."

I squinted and shook my head, certain he was playing with me. I retrieved the image I had stored of the old man, and marveled at the level of detail I was able to recall. "He had short grey hair and amazing blue eyes with silver specks." I looked into Khalen's eyes. "Very similar to yours, but different colors, of course."

He smiled. "Go on."

"Anyway, his eyes were like an ocean, and he moved so fluidly, like a 20-year- old, but I was certain he was well over 50." I frowned. "I'm not sure why."

"Tell me about his smile."

"Oh, it was stunning. He had the most perfect set of white teeth I had ever seen on another human being. They were much too perfect to be real."

Khalen laughed. "Shanuk," he muttered.

My jaw dropped open and my vision grew dim. Shanuk was the same name that Ro had mentioned when I told her that pain was just an illusion. "Who is Shanuk?"

He shook his head. "That's not important right now. Tell me what he did during his time with you in the hospital."

I frowned. "He placed his hand on my leg. It felt pleasantly warm and oddly electrifying. After a few moments, a blue mist rose upward and my pain went away. After that, he was gone."

"Gone?" Khalen's questioning expression suggested more interest than I felt the Reverend merited.

I concentrated for a moment. "I don't remember him

leaving. I must have fallen back asleep."

"Did anyone else see him?"

I shook my head. "My nurse said that there was no one on the floor that fit his description." A sharp laugh escaped my lips. "I thought it was the morphine messing with my imagination."

"Did you have these gifts before that man touched you?"

I shook my head, "Not healing," I said sadly. "When my family was sick, I prayed for the Father to give me the gift to heal, but I could not save them. If I had that gift, they would still be alive."

"You're not telling me everything, Skye."

Jeez, this man was annoying. "You seem to know everything about me, why don't you give me your explanation of all this?" My tone was much sharper than I had intended. I looked away from his piercing eyes.

"Like you," he said. "I see images, flashes of things that don't always make sense. Is that a new gift for you?"

"No," I said. "I have been able to do that since I lost my vision 12 years ago. I thought it was a product of my other senses kicking in. I never looked at it as 'a gift.' Khalen," I said calmly, shunting the subject into a new direction. "If me being here is causing a riff, I'll gladly pack my things and leave."

"And then what?"

"I won't be your problem anymore, that's what."

"It's too late for that." The tone in his voice was too

quiet for the intensity of his words. It left me confused. "They will come looking for you, and they will find you."

A shiver shot up my spine. "Who are they?"

"Shadows." There was a long pause. "They are very dangerous," he added.

I narrowed my eyes and shook my head. "What do they want with me?"

"You're a healer," he said. "Very useful."

Maiyun nudged my hand, offering some comfort. Life was so simple two weeks ago. I was just starting to enjoy the calm, not knowing the storm was just around the corner. "Can I turn it off?" I quietly asked.

He hopped off the table and grabbed his pants. I closed my eyes and looked away. "Um, did you want me to leave?"

"No," he said, fumbling with his pockets. He sat back onto the table, covered his lap, and then opened the blade of the knife he had just retrieved. "I want to see if you can turn it off." He then slid the blade over his index finger, drawing a thin line of blood.

My eyes widened and I swallowed hard against the lump lodged in my throat. I grabbed a small towel from my table and held it under his hand. I didn't want blood spilling all over my carpet and bed. That would not be a huge vote of confidence for my clients, I was sure. The scent of his blood caused my hands to shake—not because I was queasy, mind you, but because of a need, a craving that wouldn't be denied.

"Place your hand over it," he said. His voice was demanding.

I did as he directed. I did not conjure the blue mist, nor did I attempt to relieve his pain. I just held his finger.

"Remove just the pain," he instructed.

I opened myself to the universal flow of God and envisioned the blue mist rising from my hand. The familiar vibration of energy coursed through my fingers as if a thousand violin strings had been plucked at the same time. I could almost hear the clear tone of A sharp ringing in my ears.

The heat of his warm, flowing blood turned to a sticky coolness against my touch. When I no longer felt the high-pitched, buzzing vibration in my hand, I released his finger.

"Hmm," he said, examining his self-inflicted cut. "It seems your pain control has more behind it than you intend it to." His wound was healed. He wiped his finger with a disinfectant wipe, and then handed me a clean wipe for my hand.

"You need to learn to control this gift, Skye."

"Why?"

If there was one thing in this world that really plucked my chord, it was someone telling me what I had to do. I'm not sure how that irritation started, or when, I just knew that my rebellious shield went up when I was ordered around. I felt my jaw clench to the point where the muscles in the back of my neck ached for release.

"When those three people come in two weeks from now, I need you to be able to control their pain, but not heal them. If you do neither, it will only alert them. Right now, you cannot remove pain without invoking a healing effect. If they see that all you do is remove pain, their interest in you will not be as great. You will not be the one they are looking for."

"You and Gregg know who they are," I said, fighting the restriction in my throat. "I heard him call the man Talon."

Khalen looked off into the distance. "Talon and his two mates, Mira and Lonnie, belong to the local Shadow clan. They are scouts sent to find those with gifts who have not yet been claimed."

"Claimed?"

"Taken by a mate," he said, rather flatly.

"How very barbaric."

He laughed. "More than you know," he added.

I took a much-needed sip of my coffee. For what should have been a simple feat, it wasn't. My hands were shaking so fiercely, the coffee ended up dripping down my chin. I grabbed the towel from Khalen's lap and dabbed my face, my shirt, and a spot that landed on my pants. "Perfect," I mumbled.

I clenched the towel, now dappled with coffee and with Khalen's blood. Still, the soft cotton felt comforting in my trembling hands. All of this was too much for me. I had to keep my feet grounded more in reality and not so much in the quantum zone.

"What do they want with me, other than the fact that I am not 'claimed'?" I asked.

"There is a legend that very few people know about, but which exists nonetheless. No one knows how the legend was started or where it originated."

"Let's hear it," I said. What he was about to tell me certainly couldn't be any more bizarre than what I had already heard—or so I thought.

He smiled, as if enjoying my predicament. "My father told it to me once, and made me remember it. He said I would know when it would become important." Khalen shook his head and laughed. "I was just and kid then, and never put much thought toward it—until I met you." His face was serious again. "The legend says that the grey-eyed one who is blind but sees will heal the temple of our souls and bear the life of our future."

I laughed, seeing the absurdity of his interest in me now. "And you believe that I'm that grey-eyed woman?"

He laughed too, and shook his head. "Apparently, I'm not the only one."

My laughter stopped when my stomach sank to the depths of my bowels. "You think that the three people who came in today believe that I'm the legend?"

"Yes, I do."

I threw up my hands. "Oh, for Pete's sake." I stood from my stool, eager to be moving. "I assure you, Khalen. I'm as ordinary as the rain in Washington."

He laughed. "Define ordinary."

"As in, not out of the norm. There is nothing special about me."

He held up his finger. "Of course there isn't. Everyone can heal a cut in less than one minute. No big deal."

My head was pounding. "Are we done?" I needed to go for a walk and clear my thoughts.

He studied me with those piercing eyes of his, and then hopped off the table. "For now."

I grabbed my bag from under the table and left the room. Maiyun followed me. I went straight out the front door without saying one word to Gregg. It was rude, of course, but my attitude was less than positive right now and I really just needed to be alone. I decided to walk to Starbucks for a cup of tea and something to eat. I was sure that Khalen would fill him in on the details.

As Maiyun and I crossed the street, my body grew rigid and my attention was drawn to a black Audi across the street waiting at the red light. I could not see who was inside, but I could feel their eyes upon me.

Great, I thought. Now I'm even more paranoid.

Chapter 12

When we challenged our Father to show us the truth, we opened our hearts to the destructive lies of illusion.

I sat in the corner of the coffee shop, where it was dark and quiet. The hot tea steamed in my cold hands, warming them. I nibbled on my almond scone as Maiyun munched on the biscuit the barista offered her.

People meandered into the shop; some stood impatiently in line, while others pursued the extensive collection of unique coffee presses and tea infusers. Mugs of every shape, color, and material cluttered the see-through shelves that allowed for a potential consumer's access from both sides.

Abstract art decorated the walls, though the café lighting was insufficient for me to see much detail. The walls were dark as was the furniture. This hardly allowed for light to reflect, even when the days were sunny.

I purposely chose the darkest corner to sit in, mainly because I just wanted to think without distraction. Also, I didn't want to attract attention, which often happened when Maiyun was by my side. She could effortlessly attract the most wary bystander.

So many things flowed through my head. For years I had prayed for something different, something exciting. Now I just wanted to say, "Whoa, Holy Father, stop the train." None of this was rational; I felt as if I had fallen headlong into a science fiction horror flick with no script to follow. What was I going to do? People were after me for a gift I couldn't control. What would happen once they found me?

I took a sip of my Zen tea and another bite of my scone. Khalen would, no doubt, be miffed to hear that I took off, nor would he like not knowing where I had gone. I was sure to get an earful upon my return.

Maiyun perked up as someone walked through the front door. Her tail wagged and her ears pricked forward. Khalen walked around the corner and quietly took a seat across from me. It was not so much his face that gave him away as it was his movement and scent. Maiyun rested her head on his polished shoes as he gently rubbed her ear.

"You found me," I finally said, wanting to break the silence.

"Pack your things," he said. "I'm taking you someplace where you will be safe."

Again, he was telling me what to do, as if he owned me. "I'm happy here," I said. "A safe is where you store precious items, such as diamonds and gold. It is not a place for me."

He reached for my hand. His firm grip was a more honest display of the anger he felt, as opposed to his seemingly calm composure. "Skye, I will not argue with you here and now. You are coming with me, whether you are willing or not. You can cause a scene, or walk on your own accord, the choice is yours."

I tried to pull my hand away but it was impossible against his unyielding strength. He pulled me up to a standing position and led me out of the store. I barely had enough time to grab my bag. I left my tea and half-eaten scone on the table.

"Not much of a choice if you ask me," I replied sarcastically.

Maiyun remained dutifully at my side, but did not seem the least bit protective. She trusted Khalen—perhaps too much for my comfort. I knew that arguing with him at this point was futile, so I allowed him to take me home in his SUV. I was surprised he allowed Maiyun in the back as opposed to tying her to the bumper and making her trot alongside us.

The short ride back was silent. He instructed me to pack my things while he took care of his schedule in the office. "I'll be back for you in 15 minutes." The look in his eyes was a warning for me to do as he asked.

A small part of me wondered what would happen if anyone ever went against his commands. Running away would be silly. Where would I go? I decided to make his life simple for now, too curious to see where he intended on taking me.

I packed my few belongings in my largest bag, and then waited for him out front. Maiyun did not look at all concerned, so I made the decision to enjoy the ride and trust in fate. There was always a part of me that craved adventure and the excitement of the unknown. It often overshadowed the haze of fear that kept most people from doing something new. But this was somehow different. It also involved emotions I was not ready to feel.

Khalen tossed my heavy bag in the back of his Escalade as if it weighed no more than 10 pounds. "I sure hope that bottle of wine survived," I commented.

Khalen smiled, and then shook his head. "There was no bottle of wine in there."

"We'll see," I said, as I opened the door for Maiyun.

Khalen opened my door for me, and then helped me into the tall seat. Noticing that I did not need further assistance, he made his way to the driver's seat. He started the engine, and stared at me. Without another word, he groaned and got out of the car to inspect the bag. There really was a bottle of wine inside, but I had nestled it in my clothes to keep it safe. He straightened my belongings, and then carefully tucked my bag between two containers.

"The wine is safe," he said, climbing back into the driver's seat.

I looked out the window, suppressing an urge to smile. I wasn't sure if he checked the bag to make sure the wine hadn't spilled or to ensure that it wouldn't stain his precious SUV. The mysterious Khalen had limitations after all, I thought. There were times I felt he could read my mind, but he couldn't. He mentioned that he picked up images, like I did as I worked on people. I wondered what else he was capable of doing.

We turned south onto Highway 3 and were heading away from Belfair before he spoke again. "I'm curious," he said. "What you would have done if a Shadow had picked you up instead of me?"

I glanced over at him with confidence. "I would have stood my ground and said, 'in the name of Jesus, I demand that you get behind me Satan and leave me alone.'"

He rolled his eyes. "I'm being very serious, Skye."

"I felt them earlier," I said.

His muscles tensed and his grip became more firm on the steering wheel.

"As I was crossing the street toward the coffee shop. I looked directly at them. They were in a black Audi, waiting at the red light across the street."

"It would have taken them nothing to pick you up."

"That wasn't their intent," I said. "They were merely curious, that's all."

"I could well imagine why," he said then pounded the wheel for emphasis.

I ignored his sudden outburst. He was a typical angry soul looking for a willing victim. I was neither willing nor a victim.

"It was strange, really," I muttered, mostly to myself. "It was almost as if they had tossed a pebble at me to see if I would look."

"Did you see their faces?"

I laughed. "No, I'm blind, remember?"

"Well, you certainly don't act it," he grumbled. There were times when he reminded me of a grumpy bear waking from a long winter slumber. All he needed was a full beard and bed-head hair to complete the simile.

I ignored his obvious derogation. How he believed blind people should act would have been amusing, I was sure, but his anger had already peaked and I had no interest in rousing him further.

"So where are you taking me," I said, changing the subject.

"To my home."

The lump in my throat constricted a verbal response. I chose to stay quiet until it dispersed. I pictured a large mansion with white carpet and expensive paintings on the walls. I then pictured Maiyun having one of her insecure moments and chewing a hole in his white leather sofas that probably cost more than my truck.

"And where is home?" I asked, still a bit shaken.

All he said was "an island," never taking his eyes off the road.

We passed through Allyn and continued toward the small town of Grapeview. There were several islands on the peninsula.

"Are you always this calm?" he asked.

If he could feel what my stomach was doing, he would not ask that question. "No, not always."

"How about when you felt the Shadows?"

He was like a pit bull with a juicy bone in his teeth. He wasn't going to let it go. Despite my efforts to change the subject, he brought it right back again. "Like I said, their intention was curiosity, nothing more."

"And what if you were reading a false intention?"

"Then I would be in their car right now instead of yours."

It occurred to me that Khalen didn't completely reveal his own concerns. He had feelings for me, that was evident, but they were guarded and tethered by something I couldn't touch or see. I was peanut butter to someone who was deathly allergic to peanuts, or at least that's how I felt. He could enjoy the aroma and the presence, but not the taste.

We turned left onto Pickering Road toward Harstine Island. I had heard about this place, but didn't know too much about it. "If the Shadows can find me in Belfair, what makes you think they won't find me on this island?" I asked.

Khalen looked at me with those stunning green eyes with the golden flecks. He was clearly perturbed about something other than me leaving to get coffee. His knuckles were white and his jaw looked as if it were chiseled out of marble. "They will have no problem finding you, but they won't be able to get to you."

I laughed. "So, am I to be your prisoner, then?"

The tight muscles in his jaw rippled. "No."

"Khalen, this whole thing would be easier for me to

accept if you would just explain where I'm going and what I can expect when I get there."

He continued onto the Harstine Island bridge.

"It's difficult to explain," he said, but it was not the truth. He pulled his energy in, trying to keep me out. He was oddly uncomfortable.

"I don't believe you," I said. "What I do believe is that this is far more difficult for you than it is for me. You know that bringing me here is the right thing to do, but you fight within yourself and want to distance yourself from me emotionally, but not physically. What I don't understand is why?"

He looked genuinely intrigued. "You don't need to know why."

I laughed. "Of course not." I decided to let the subject go for now. It was clear he was not going to discuss this further—today.

We turned right onto Harstine Island and headed south. The narrow, two-lane road twisted through thick walls of evergreens laden with moss and lush ferns. The sun was beginning its descent, making it even more challenging for me to see under the trees' thick canopy.

"If it makes things easier for you," I said. "I'm not looking for a lover or a serious relationship. I'm happy just being your friend."

His frown indicated displeasure where I was expecting relief. "That's good to know," he grumbled. "Thank you for the clarification."

THE PROTECTED

Jeez, there was no pleasing this man. I shook my head and laughed. "Albeit a very moody friend."

I felt his glare in return.

He turned left onto a dirt road that was only wide enough for one vehicle. It wound and twisted for half a mile before he turned toward a cluster of tent-like structures. Several pit fires burned, warming small groups of people standing beside them. It reminded me of an upscale homeless camp.

He pulled up to a large, circular structure that resembled a cross between a tent and a stick-built home. I felt the weight of many eyes staring in our direction and was overcome with the urge to stay right where I was, safe and warm behind the tinted windows of the SUV. Maiyun spotted a few large dogs playfully running with some children in the distance. She whined and paced back and forth.

Khalen opened the back door. She waited for my command, and then bolted straight for the other dogs who did not look so willing to let her play.

"She'll be all right," said Khalen, noticing my concern. He opened my door then guided me out of the car. Gravel ground under my feet. It was difficult to see in the encroaching darkness. If there was a sky overhead, the trees prevented me from seeing it.

"Where are your shoes?"

I shrugged. "I didn't pack them."

"You clearly decided not to wear them, either," he exclaimed.

He grabbed my bag, and then led me toward the big

circular tent structure that sat upon a raised platform. We walked up three steep stairs onto a 12 foot by 12 foot landing. He opened a heavy cedar door with an ornate, cut-glass window in it—not something one would expect to see on a tent-like structure.

Inside there was room for a small gathering. In the center was a circular fireplace, constructed of grey flagstone, Where embers glowed warmly. The floor was made of dark wood that had been polished to an impressive satin smoothness. The rich, reddish-brown colors and intricate patterns indicated their origin was not of this continent. My guess was that the wood was Brazilian or perhaps South American.

To the left was a small, open kitchen. The cabinets were made of cherry and the counters were black granite. The place smelled like Khalen: earthy cedar, with a hint of clove.

A tan, leather couch was on the right next to a small end table that was once an impressive tree stump. On the far side of the room was a king-sized bed with a dark, royal purple covering and ample pillows. My stomach sank as I realized there was only one bed.

He laughed. "I'll take the couch." He carried my bag over to the bed and opened his arms. "Welcome to my home."

It was not at all what I had expected. Somehow, a GQ man who creased his blue jeans did not fit well with the tent he called home. Given the rest of the day's events, however, it fit perfectly with all the other stuff that didn't make sense.

I looked around at the lamps he had scattered throughout the place. They did not match the décor, but each of them had full-spectrum bulbs so I could see. "Were you expecting me?"

"I called Ian and asked him to set up some lights."

My heart skipped a few beats. "Ian O'Dougherty?"

"Yes, Ian and his brother Aidan live here, along with Gregg and Ro at times."

"At times?"

He opened a cedar door beneath the raised fireplace and took out a few logs. After strategically placing them over the embers, he closed the door and brushed his hands off over the crackling embers. "Gregg and Ro have several cabins they like to frequent."

"I see." I really didn't, but for now, his explanation would suffice. There were no windows in the place, except the ornate one in the door. "I should check on Maiyun."

"She's fine," he said. "Let her be a dog for Christ's sake." The harshness in his tone was alarming.

"As opposed to what?" I questioned.

"A lap dog."

The air was becoming stuffy as well as the company. I needed to step out. I made my way toward the door but before I could reach it, his hand was around my arm.

"Hey, I'm sorry." He turned me to face him. "I didn't mean it tha—"

"It's okay," I interrupted. I knew that pulling my arm from his tight grip was futile, so I didn't even try. "I don't expect you to understand." My tone surprised me. There was a hardness to it that was not intended. His grip fell away from me.

I opened the door to find my dog covered in mud and something that smelled like rotting oysters. "Oh, Maiyun." Her sheepish grin confirmed the fun she obviously had with the other dogs. I closed the door, unwilling to invite her inside. Perhaps Khalen was right. She needed to be a dog occasionally and not my constant companion. That realization stabbed at me like a dull, rusty blade.

"I'll have the kids clean her up for you," said Khalen.

"It's too cold for a bath."

His sideways glance and twisted frown was another confirmation of my smothering love for the dog.

"I'm sure she'll survive the ordeal," he said.

"Fine," I agreed. "Perhaps it will teach her a lesson."

He laughed as he closed the door.

When he returned, he had a sheepskin rug and a few bamboo mats. He carefully placed them next to my bed. When he opened the door, he instructed my pitifully wet dog to lie only on the rug and nowhere else. With her ears laid flat to the sides of her head, she meandered through the door and immediately laid upon the rug he had prepared for her. She glanced up at me as if to reveal her most sincere apology.

I patted her head, assuring her that she was forgiven. She smelled of eucalyptus and something reminiscent of myrrh. It wasn't the most pleasing scent, but it was better than rotting oysters.

I stood from the bed. "Would you mind if I thanked the kids who bathed her for me?"

"Later," was all he said. He was preparing something in the kitchen. It smelled Italian. It seemed strange that he had not introduced me to the people outside. Common etiquette called for some familiarity among communities. I felt more like a new toy that was not meant to be shared or even revealed, in fear of it being stolen or destroyed.

He had opened a bottle of Barbera wine earlier and allowed it to breathe before serving us each a glass. His fine stemware made my simple Riedels look like Walmart specials. The crystal felt so delicate in my hand, I wondered how Khalen was able to hold the fragile stem without snapping it in his brawny hands. As I glanced through the glass at the beautiful color of the wine, I noticed the subtle rainbow tint in the glass. It was beautiful and very thin.

The wine was the epitome of complete balance between tart and sweet with just enough spice to dry the tongue. Its aroma lingered, suggesting sweet fruit. It had been a long time since I had luxuriated in such a treat. I savored each sip, allowing the flavors to seduce my taste buds into an appreciative frenzy.

"You know," I said, trying to break his solemn mood. "If you wanted to ask me out to dinner, all you had to do was ask." I raised my glass to him in hopes of sparking a smile.

He raised his glass in response, but no smile. "If I asked you out to dinner, it would have been under more promising conditions."

What he meant by that was yet another mystery to solve. I was not in the mood for more puzzles this evening. I simply let it go.

Khalen was a man of complexity that I could not unravel quickly with impatient efforts. Part of me was afraid of what I might find behind that tangled web of mystery, while another part of me was intrigued. He was very much like this fine glass of wine I enjoyed— something to be savored, and not swallowed with a careless whirl.

Chapter 13

We are born into this world but are not of this world. When the physical blinds the spirit, we cannot see. When the spirit blinds the physical, truth is revealed.

I woke up alone. Maiyun and Khalen were gone. I reached for my iPhone and glanced at the time. It was ten in the morning. I never slept in that late. I didn't even remember going to bed last night. I looked over at my empty wine glass and remembered having only two glasses of wine, not enough to become oblivious.

My clothes were tossed on the floor. I must have removed them last night during my sleep. That was not uncommon for me. I never could stand wearing clothes in bed. I pulled a clean white cotton long-sleeved shirt and a pair of khaki capris from my bag and quickly donned them before placing my dirty clothes next to Maiyun's bed.

Eager to go outside, I ran a brush through my hair and left it loose. It fell to the top of my thighs in thick waves. I would have to trim it again soon. I then brushed my teeth and tossed everything back in my bag. I did not intend to leave my stuff around as if I belonged here. I was hoping it would only be temporary.

I padded my way to the front door and opened it. The fresh air that greeted me was beyond inviting. I breathed the crisp, cold air deep into my lungs and stepped outside. The cold damp wood felt good to my feet as I made my way down the three steep steps. The gravel was sharp, but I didn't care. I walked toward a group of ladies chatting and laughing near an open fire. The sweet smoke smelled of cedar and alder.

Their conversation ceased as I approached. "Hi," I said shyly. "I'm Skye."

The oldest woman with shoulder-length grey hair and black eyes was the first to answer. "Welcome, dear. We've heard so much about you." Her British accent was slightly thicker than Khalen's. She walked over and wrapped her frail arms around my waist. She only stood about five feet tall. "I'm Eve." She looked to be about 80 years old, but moved as if she were only 50. She dressed casually in blue jeans and a floral sweatshirt with pink cherry blooms. The color matched the beautiful blush on her rose-petal cheeks.

A younger woman about 40 years old approached me next. Her short auburn hair, cut in a bob, glimmered like copper against the flames. "I'm Ember, and these are my sisters, Kate, Rose, and Jade," she said, gesturing toward the rest of the group.

All of them shared the same flaming hair, but their eyes were different. None of them glistened with the gold flecks that Khalen's had, but all of them had variations of hazel hues. Ember's looked more green than gold. Ember's sisters raised their hands in greeting. They all looked between 30 and 40 years old, with Jade being the youngest. The light was not good enough to make out the details of their faces, but they all carried themselves well, and had the same inner glow that Khalen displayed.

I looked around for Khalen and Maiyun. They were not in sight.

"Khalen took her hunting," Eve explained, as if reading my thoughts. "They left early this morning before sunrise."

It was unusual for Maiyun to leave my side. She never had in the past. I frowned, slightly disturbed by Khalen's influence over her. I glanced up and barely detected sunlight through the trees. It seemed strange to be under such thick cover but not be surrounded by endless moss and moisture.

"It's a shroud," said Ember. "Khalen had it installed to prevent our location from being detected from satellite. It allows the moisture to leave and the sun to shine through, but nothing can be seen from above."

There were several people gathered around the area that must have spanned 20 or more acres. It was difficult to tell since I couldn't see past the first few fires, but I could hear activity far away.

"It's actually 50 acres," said Ember.

Could she read my thoughts as well? I wondered.

She smiled, and confirmed my suspicion. "Yes, I can."

Eve glared at her. "Rude," was all she said before reaching for my hand. "Come, Skye, I will introduce you to the elders." Eve was clearly the leader of that group. Ember's shame was evident when she lowered her eyes and folded her hands as if to apologize.

"Forgive her," said Eve. "This gift is new to her and she is so curious about you."

Her hand was soft in mine, and warm. It carried a similar electric buzz that Reverend Mark's had.

"What is this place?" I asked.

"It is a sanctuary."

"Who are all these people?" There must have been at least 20 families here.

"The clan," she said. "They are family."

There were people of varying race. I found it hard to believe they were family by the true sense of the word. "I don't suppose they are all related by blood."

She smiled. "Well, technically, we are all related by blood. Mostly, though, we are of like mind."

"Spirians," I said, trying to grasp her meaning.

She nodded. "Yes, we are all Spirians. They come here to live and contribute to the clan's way of life. Some only come for training, while others decide to stay. Either way, everyone is expected to contribute."

"Who owns this land?"

She looked at me and smiled. "It belongs to the Squaxin tribe. The chief granted it to Khalen to house his clan."

"His clan?"

"Yes, he started it many years ago."

She said it with such pride in her voice, it made me curious how she was related to him, if at all.

"I'm his mother," she offered.

This whole mind-reading thing would take some time to get used to, I thought. As we made our way across the vast camp, the fallen leaves crunched beneath my bare feet.

"Where are your shoes?" asked Eve.

"I don't like wearing them," I said. "I prefer to go barefoot."

She gestured with amusement. "I'm sure Khalen loves that," she smiled.

I shrugged. "If so, it would be the only thing he does love about me."

"He's a complicated man," said Eve. "But one who knows what he likes." She gave me a look as if I would know what she meant.

I didn't, but chose not to question her.

She led me to a group of old men in deep discussion by a crackling fire. Despite our interruption, the warmth in their dark eyes was inviting and full of a love that was indescribable. I couldn't keep from returning their smile.

Eve bowed her head and touched the oldest man's arm. He had short grey hair and obsidian eyes. "Husband," she said with utmost respect. "This is Skye." She then turned to me. "Skye, this is Case, my husband, and elder of this clan."

Case took my hand and patted the back of it. "Welcome, my dear."

Khalen did not resemble Case or Eve in any way. Both of them were pale-skinned, of European ancestry. Khalen was more Native American in appearance.

The other two men nodded and their smile deepened. The youngest man had short black hair, and seemed to be about 50 years old. His amber eyes glowed against the firelight. He reached out his hand. "Hi, Skye, I'm Caleb."

The other man with brown hair and brown eyes offered his hand next. "And I'm Drew." He and the youngest man must have been brothers. They had the same bright smile and similar mannerisms.

"Come," said Case. "Let's walk." He offered his arm as if knowing I had a vision impairment. "You must have many questions?" he said in a delightful British tone.

I laughed, partly because I felt inadequate in his presence, and because his statement was true. "Just a few," I said. The crack in my voice betrayed my frazzled nerves.

He laughed. "Relax, my dear. I'm not going to eat you." He led me over to a log that loomed above a hidden lake I never would have known was there.

"This is Khalen's thinking log. I thought it would be appropriate to talk with you here." He gestured to the well-worn cedar log, smooth from years of use. Someone had taken the time to remove the bark and flatten the top with a plane. I wondered what had cured it and kept it from rotting.

Two blue egrets waded in the lake searching for something to eat. They looked unperturbed by our presence. From the lake's reflection, I could see the blue sky above slowly giving way to a thin scattering of grayish-white clouds.

Case sat quietly beside me for a moment, as if weighing his words carefully. "Khalen tells me you're blind, and can heal with touch."

So much for subtleties. "According to the doctors, I'm completely blind, but I am able to see, I assure you. I can see what you look like, providing there is enough sunlight." I glanced up at the interrupted sunlight looming above us. "The only time I cannot see is when the sun goes down, or the lighting is inadequate."

He nodded. "Yes, I am aware of your condition," he said. "Retinitis Pigmentosa. Tell me about your healing abilities."

I frowned. "They are new to me. It seems to concern Khalen, so he brought me here." I waved my hands to emphasize the vast surroundings. "Problem is, I don't know where here is or why he brought me." Or why he cares, I added in thought.

The old man laughed again. "Yes, that is quite another story, indeed." Like Khalen, he had a flair for vagueness. His expression indicated an uncanny knowing. "The part about why he cares," he clarified.

Apparently, Eve and Ember were not the only one with the ability to read thoughts.

"The entire clan is connected in thought," he explained. "Only a few of us can connect to those who are not in the family."

"Like me."

"I would not jump to that conclusion," he said. "Khalen brought you here so that you could learn how to control your gift. From what I understand, you have drawn the attention of the Shadows and will be tested in two weeks time."

That was the short of it. Case certainly did not waste words or time. His comment about not jumping to the conclusion that I was not part of the family was in the back of my mind, just like all the other questions plaguing my thoughts. To maintain what little sanity I had left, I decided to let them go for now and focus on the issue at hand. "Can you help me?"

He nodded. "I will certainly try, but not today. We will begin tomorrow when your mind is fresh."

We sat in silence for a moment before the questions in my mind nagged at me like tyrant children wanting some kind of treat. "Why is this happening?" I finally said.

He glanced down at me, his dark eyes glowing like rainbow obsidian. I didn't notice how tall he was until now. He probably equaled Khalen in height.

"The world is in transition," he explained. "For several years, we will be caught between the physical and spiritual realms until the two complete their union."

"Which means what?"

"As we draw closer to the spirit, our pineal gland opens and becomes active. We develop the gifts of the angels. Some of us have more gifts than others, but each of us has at least one gift." He smiled down at me. "Of course, these gifts can be used to help or destroy. With good, there is always an equal evil; that is the law of homeostasis, the balance of all life."

"Yes, I've heard about the Shadows," I said.

"When the ego becomes the ruler of one's soul, it is easy to lose sight of good."

I looked down, suddenly realizing why Khalen was so concerned about me. "Khalen believes that I could be used by the Shadows, doesn't he?"

Case's eyes turned dark and deep. "He fears you will be consumed by them."

"Consumed?" I tried to swallow, but the lump in my throat stopped me.

"They devour every bit of light in your soul until you no longer care about anything or anyone. You will know no guilt, fear, or regret."

My words were also caught behind that constricting fear. I shook my head, trying to convince myself that this was just another nightmare, nothing more. I would wake up soon.

"That won't happen," I finally choked out. "It won't." I started to stand, wanting to leave this place.

Case wrapped his large hand around my forearm and gently but firmly guided me back down. He had the same strength as Khalen. There were times when I thought he could crush me, but restrained himself. That thought brought another smile to the old man's face.

"Then you must be prepared," he said. He looked down at my feet, curling around the leaves and debris. "Do you not have shoes?"

"I do," I said. "I just don't like wearing them."

"Hmm," he said, clearly not approving.

A gentle breeze kicked up and brushed against my face. My hair brushed against the old man's arm. He didn't seem to notice.

"Eve said that she was Khalen's mother. I'm assuming that you are his father, but—"

"We look nothing alike," he finished for me. "Yet I am his father," he said, staring out in the distance.

Eve said that the clan was family. Since Case was the elder, it would make sense for him to be the father of the family, including Khalen.

A rustling in the bushes drew our attention. Ian, the familiar doctor from Hometown Vets, came rushing forth looking right at me. "You are needed at camp," he said hurriedly.

I looked at Case, assuming Ian was talking to him. Case took my arm. "Let's go."

Ian led the way and Case all but carried me. I guess I walked too slow. I had never seen urgency in Ian's eyes. He always seemed so relaxed the last two times I saw him.

Maiyun laid in a pool of blood, her legs were twisted and she was unconscious. I dropped to my knees, my heart ached deep in my hollow chest. It was hard to breathe.

"You can heal her," said Ian.

Visions of my dying husband flooded my mind. I prayed

for the ability to heal him and could not. He faded beneath my touch like fog against the morning sun. I couldn't save him. What if I couldn't save her?

Maiyun's breathing was slow and uneven. I closed my eyes and prayed. "Father, I need you. Please work through me," I whispered. I laid my trembling hands on Maiyun's sticky fur, concentrating first on her heart and organs. I conjured the blue mist and imagined the pain rising from her body. My hands grew hot and my forehead perspired. The images around me faded, as if the sun had set very quickly. I could see nothing.

Maiyun's breathing grew stronger and more rhythmic. My own grew weaker, more labored. I moved my hands to each of her broken limbs, envisioning their perfect form. Deep inside, I could feel her bones mend and her tissue grow firm. My thoughts grew weary and it seemed as if I were no longer present in a camp full of people. I was elsewhere.

The familiar meadow with the waterfall and fragrant purple flowers surrounded me. Derrick stared down at me, touching my face. His features morphed into Khalen's. He and Derrick were the same. Was I dead? I couldn't speak, and my inner vision saw surreal colors that were not of this world.

The images faded in and out like waves crashing upon the shore then retreating again for another approach.

The redheaded woman invaded in my thoughts. I felt the cold, sharp blade of her knife pierce my back. I arched in pain, and then felt nothing. Everything disappeared.

Chapter 14

The duality of good and evil is as perpetual as the tide. In duality, there is balance—you cannot have one without the other.

What happened next challenged my fading grasp of reality. My head spun; my ears heard conversations that were too far away to make sense of them. I felt foreboding and empty of purpose or care. I felt movement without moving, for I had no body. Light surrounded me with colors that didn't exist on Earth. Where was I?

Bitterness lingered in my mouth, yet I had no tongue. Whatever I thought about presented itself to me in vivid detail—detail I hadn't seen for many years, but had not forgotten. I thought of Derrick, and he was there, in front of me, smiling and curling those lips the way I had remembered. I could hear his voice, his laughter. I thought about the children we wanted to have but couldn't. Two young ones entered my thoughts, but they had no face, no gender.

My imagination was rampant, uncontrolled. I wondered if this was what it was like to be high on drugs. I was frightened, yet calm at the same time. Perhaps I was in limbo, a place where people go before they are sent to heaven or hell.

I felt heat on my face. Firelight danced all around me, and I could hear music playing in the background. There were ceremonial drums and an Indian flute. Occasional chanting accompanied the liquid rhythm. I felt a cold mist fall upon my chest and abdomen. My eyes fluttered open, but I could see nothing but the light of the fire. Dark shapes moved around me, talking quietly. My head throbbed and my heart matched its cadence.

I urged myself to sit up, but something heavy pressed against my chest. "Stay down." The voice was deep, demanding, and familiar.

"Khalen," I whispered.

"I'm here," he said. "Stay still." His arm was bandaged and cold.

"You're hurt?"

"No," he said. "I'm fine. Maiyun saved my life."

"What happened?"

"We surprised a bear and she attacked."

Again, I tried to sit up but was firmly restrained. "Where is she?"

Khalen patted my leg. Maiyun pressed her head against me and groaned. "She hasn't left your side," he said.

"Is she all right?"

"Good as new," he said. "Are you surprised?"

I shook my head. "I feel horrible, like I overindulged in

bad drugs and wine." I pressed my cold fingers against my temples.

"Yes, well, what you did surprised us all," he said.

I wrapped my hands around Khalen's arm. My inner vision revealed broken bones and torn flesh. Without even trying, the blue mist rose from my hands.

Khalen pulled away. "Not now," he said. "You are still too weak."

Not enjoying being told what to do and when to do it, I projected my thoughts back to his arm and continued the healing. My heart pounded in my chest as if trying to get out. My breathing slowed, and my temperature rose. Another hand rested on my feet and I felt as if roots sprung out of my heels and pressed through the earth. My strength slowly returned.

"She can project," another voice said. I recognized it as Case's. "Her gifts come too fast. I need to teach her to ground herself."

Khalen removed the bandages from his arm. It was completely healed.

Case stepped closer and looked into my eyes. "We begin training tonight," he said sternly. "Get up and get something to eat."

I felt a wave of energy unlike anything I had ever felt. A bolt of lightning would have been more subtle. My head felt clear, and my body strong. I brushed off a sprinkling of herbs that were scattered on my stomach, and rose from a makeshift bed of furs and bamboo mats. The heaviness of many eyes rested upon me as I rose and followed Khalen and Case toward my temporary home. Maiyun pressed against my side, guiding me safely toward the towering circular structure.

I followed the men inside, then closed the door. It was warm; the fire was crackling loudly, almost hurting my ears. I covered them and closed my eyes.

"You're hypersensitive," said Case. "It'll pass." He guided me to the couch.

Khalen handed me a cup of hot tea.

"Did we run out of wine?" I asked.

"No wine," said Case, "not until your training is complete."

I frowned and sipped the hot tea Khalen handed me. I looked around, wondering what such an elaborate tent was called.

"It's a Yurt," said Khalen. "This one is fashioned after the ones used by the tribes in Siberia."

"It's rude to read people's minds," I said, taking another sip of tea. I glanced over at Case, who was smiling at Khalen.

Case was cooking something, and flipping some food in a pan. My vision was not completely restored and I was having some problems even with the abundant supply of full-spectrum light.

"Keep drinking the tea," said Case. "It will help restore balance to your senses."

It tasted good, but slightly bitter. I thought it was some

kind of black tea. "What is it?"

"Evening primrose, jiaogulan, and oolong for flavor," said Khalen. "It's father's favorite blend." He sat down beside me, studying my face. I could smell the sweetness of his breath and it made me feel uncomfortable, especially when he smiled.

"I make you uncomfortable?" he said smugly.

I turned my head, disgusted with his constant display of rudeness. Perhaps Case could teach me how to block that gift in others.

Case flipped a sandwich onto a plate, and then proudly carried it over to me. "Lamb and mushroom on sprouted wheat bread."

It smelled better than it sounded. "Thank you." My stomach was game whether the meal sounded good or not. I felt as if I hadn't eaten in days. My first bite was unexpected. Flavors of tart yogurt, tangy cheese, and spicy cayenne pepper flooded my taste buds with a delightful orchestra of flavor. The lamb was tender and played well against the mushroom relish. Good was an understatement.

"Oh," I said, after swallowing my first bite. "This is amazing."

Case smiled with pleasure. "I'm glad you like it." He bowed his head. "Eat quickly. We have work to do."

Reluctantly I did as he asked. Food this good should be savored, not devoured with mindless intent. He seemed impatient, though, and I, too, was eager to get this over with so I could return to my normal life—or so I thought.

I had spent most of my life looking for adventure, the bizarre, and the unbelievable. Now it stared me in the face and I refused to acknowledge its existence. I felt as if this was all some distant fantasy that I had conjured, just like the blue mist that miraculously healed wounds. When Derrick died, I thought my life was over. I gave up on the notion that I was even remotely special in any way, shape, or form. At my age, what could I possibly hope to change?

I swallowed the last of my sandwich, and sipped the last of my tea. Both Khalen and Case stared at me as if I were an interesting creature from another planet. I almost wished my eyesight had not returned. Their probing eyes were like scalpels in the hands of skillful surgeons.

"You're staring," I reminded them.

"We're strategizing," Khalen corrected.

"Strategizing," I repeated. I felt as if I were about to become their meal, but unlike a normal human being, I was not afraid. Here I was, in the midst of a camp full of gifted people, in front of the two leaders who could restrain me with one finger and control me with a simple look. Their eyes were hypnotic—Case, with his dark pupils that glimmered with subtle colors, and Khalen's that flickered with gold.

"She's a wild bolt of lightning with no ground," said Case. "Dangerous and unpredictable."

I hadn't heard a compliment like that since my early 20s, I thought, amused.

"She's easy to read," Khalen added, as if I were not even in the room.

I pursed my lips and added a few thoughts of my own, just to remind them both that I was sitting here, in their presence.

"Nice, kitty," said Case, smiling. "Stand up," he instructed. He then demonstrated the basic Qi Gong practice known as The Eight Pieces of Brocade. I mimicked Case's movements effortlessly.

"You've done this before," he said.

"My husband, Derrick, was a Kempo Master. He used to do these moves every morning." My memory of him was vivid.

Khalen looked distant. He clearly didn't like me thinking about Derrick.

"Why did you not join him?" asked Case.

Khalen looked at me as if measuring my response. I did not intend to lie. "I liked watching him move," I said. "It was peaceful and meditative."

Khalen moved with the same grace, only he had power to his movement, and authority. He was secretly demanding my attention. When I looked at his face, he was smiling, obviously pleased at his ability to attract me.

"Focus," said Case, "or must I separate you two?"

My face immediately turned red and my attempt to perform Qi Gong resembled wet clay collapsing on a turn table.

Case pushed his palm toward me. I fell to the floor as the wind was knocked out of my lungs.

"You are a bright, shiny lure in a sea of barracudas,

my dear. You best learn to ground yourself before you are snatched up as someone's very alluring meal."

It took me a moment to restore air to my lungs. When I did, they felt as if they had been crushed by a fast-moving truck, yet he was nowhere near me. "How?" I stammered out.

"Energy is a powerful thing," he said. He then directed his palm toward Khalen. Nothing happened.

Khalen continued to move through the Qi Gong positions with amazing concentration.

"You need to learn to protect yourself and turn off that flashy lure that screams, 'look at me,'" said Case.

I frowned. He made it sound as if I were purposely trying to gain attention.

Again, he pressed his palm toward me, knocking me back a few paces. "Focus!" he demanded. His eyes were dark now and I was truly alarmed. "Don't allow that ego to surface, keep it in check."

My ego really didn't like that statement. Anger began to rise in my chest in defense. Again, his energy knocked me back. I fell against the soft cushions of the couch. He lifted me back up again from several feet away. I suddenly felt very vulnerable. Khalen did not look concerned, which was oddly comforting.

Maiyun looked at me, and then at Case with apprehension. She didn't dare growl, knowing she would not stand a chance against him. She came toward me and offered an assuring nudge of her head.

"Out," Case demanded. He pointed toward Maiyun's bed. She quickly complied with his demand. She rarely listened to anyone but me. Fear began to constrict my chest.

"Throw it to the ground," he said, aiming his palm toward me. The sting of his energy felt like a horde of angry bees attacking me all at once. A muted scream escaped my lips. Again I fell to the ground. The sting continued.

"Direct it down," he said.

Just like I had conjured the blue mist, I envisioned an iron wall between me and my attacker. His energy stopped at this wall and traveled deep into the earth.

"Ah, very good," he said.

My heart felt heavy but strong. I stood up, this time on my own accord. The stings that invaded my body still lingered, making me itch.

"That wall," he said, "will save your life. Use it each time you use your gifts or encounter an unfriendly soul."

"A Shadow," I confirmed.

"Not all dangerous souls are Shadows," he said. "There are those without gifts that will also try to snuff out your light. We call them the Influenced—those who are not yet enlightened."

"And why do you call yourselves the Protected?" I asked, still a bit out of breath and recovering from the painful stings.

"So long as we are filled with God's light, we can distinguish right from wrong, good from evil, and creation from destruction."

"If I am Protected, then how can the Shadow's threaten me?"

"The same way that darkness makes you blind, my dear. It takes nothing to snuff out a light, but much effort is required to keep it lit."

"Never stop caring," Khalen added. "Once you do, your flame will be snuffed out and darkness will prevail."

The image of the redheaded woman engulfed my mind. When Khalen sensed it, he pulled the image back like a child not willing to share a toy. For the rest of the evening, he was distant and unreadable.

Case wasn't much help in that area, either. He was so focused on helping me with controlling my gifts that he was becoming quite a bore. After healing his self-inflicted wounds repeatedly, I was getting irritated. "I cannot remove the pain without healing the wound," I claimed.

Khalen remained distant and almost sulky in the kitchen. He was cooking something on the stove. "Find a way," he grumbled.

I was growing tired and it was clear that neither of them would allow me to sleep until I had found a way to remove the pain without healing the wound.

"I need a break," I said. "Please, just a few minutes of peace."

Khalen returned with three mugs of hot cocoa topped with cayenne pepper and cream sherry. It was a welcome indulgence.

"Thank you," I said, with genuine gratitude.

ROWENA PORTCH

He did not respond. I tried probing Case's mind for some answers, but he, too, sensed my silent inquiries and shut me out. So it was possible to close your thoughts to others. Khalen had demonstrated that before. I just wished I knew how he did it.

I sipped my cocoa slowly, knowing that the grueling training would begin again once my last sip was taken. I thought, for a moment, about the paramedic in the hospital who claimed to have an injured wrist. I knew she was lying, and therefore I was able to work without healing. There simply was nothing to heal. My intention had been to comfort her wrist, nothing more.

I put my cocoa down. "I want to try something," I said.

Having read my intention, Case cut his hand with a knife.

Instead of removing the pain, I decided to touch him with compassion. My hand wrapped gently around his wound and I filled it with thoughts of love, nothing more. His blood flowed beneath my hand. The warmth mingled with the warmth of my touch, but continued to flow.

"The pain is gone," he said, a big smile on his face.

I removed my hand. The wound remained, still bleeding and red. The injury drew me in, begging for my help. It was like a sickness—a drunk looking for one more drink.

"Leave it," said Khalen.

I stood and washed my hands of Case's blood. The smell was intoxicating. I had to stop the bleeding.

The need finally outweighed the victory, and from across the room I felt his wound close.

Chapter 15

We are each a mere cell in the body of life that is plagued with disease. Why are we surprised when the fever of our host rises to eliminate its offenders?

"Your intentions are powerful," said Case, "but wild and out of control."

"I am drawn to heal in a very compelling way," I explained. "It's like an addiction for me; I cannot fight it. The more I heal, the stronger the need becomes." My hands ached with burning heat, but they wanted more, craving the pain. Yet my entire body felt spent.

"She's had enough for tonight," said Khalen.

Case stood to leave with great concern etched in his face. "Get some rest," he called back over his shoulder. "You will need it come morning."

Khalen walked his father to the door, they exchanged some words, then hugged each other good night. Khalen bowed as his father took his leave. He then filled two plastic bags with ice and sealed them shut before joining me on the couch. He placed a bag in each of my red hands, which were now shaking.

"Is Case really your father?" I asked.

The guarded expression on his face told me there was more power to that question than he wanted to reveal.

"For all intents and purposes, yes."

"But not your biological father."

He shook his head and lowered his eyes. "No, I met him when I was nine years old." He examined my hands, more to pause the conversation than to check the cooling progress.

"Where did you meet?"

He took a deep breath, clearly exasperated by my persistence. "Brighton Mental Institute." He glanced up to measure my reaction. "I had serious anger issues. He was my doctor." That last part was stated rather sharply.

I carried the ice bags over to the sink, and then allowed cold water to rush over my hands. "Where are your parents?"

"My mother is dead," he said with bitterness. "I left shortly afterward."

I walked back to the couch. There was a lot he was leaving out, I could feel it. Not wanting to discourage him, I played him along. "And you checked into Brighton, on your own?"

"Case took me home and became my father," he said abruptly. His evasion would have been less obvious if he had stood and walked away.

He never did answer the question. The gap in his story

was much like the images that littered my mind. It was like looking at a complicated puzzle with several missing pieces.

"What about your real father? Is he not concerned?"

Khalen stood and retrieved a log from the hold beneath the fire pit. He poked at the embers a bit, and then carefully added the log. "No, he is not concerned." His brows drew together in thought. His hands tightened into fists, and his jaw clenched.

"And what about your anger issues?" Judging by his body language, I sensed I was treading on dangerous ground. Still, I had to ask.

His lips grew firm. "If you had Case for a father, would you throw temper tantrums?"

Memories of the energy stings played fresh in my memory. "Uh, no," I laughed.

Khalen relaxed at bit. "Case understood me," he explained, "and helped redirect my anger into something more useful. I never felt accepted by my family, but Case knew me. He could read my thoughts and switch off the pain that ripped through me from the inside out."

"Pain?"

"From the nightmares. Premonitions of what was to come."

"Premonitions?"

He wrung his hands together, clearly uncomfortable with the conversation. "More like possible outcomes."

"Hmm." I nodded. In the silence, I wanted to ask him

about the redheaded woman, but refrained. He looked tired. "You should get some rest," I said.

"And you shouldn't?"

I felt energized, and my mind was thinking a million things at once. I had some journaling to do and needed some quiet time. "I'll sleep soon," I assured him.

I made my way to the bed and waited for him to settle onto the couch. I stood and placed another log on the dwindling fire, and then crawled back up onto the bed. Maiyun looked up at me and nuzzled my hand for attention.

"Hey, Girl. What a day, huh?" She licked my face. "I'm scared," I whispered to her. "I don't feel strong enough for all this." She licked me again, offering her own kind of encouragement. I reached over and gave her a hug. Her scent was always comforting to me, even when she smelled of bear and woods.

She curled up on her bed and settled down. I slid down from my own bed and snuggled with her until her breathing slowed into a deep slumber. Something under the bed reflected the firelight. I reached under and felt a spiral notebook. I pulled it toward me. A box of pencils rested on top.

I glanced toward Khalen. He was dead asleep.

Sitting next to Maiyun, I opened the notebook and saw pictures sketched with amazing skill. They resembled black and white photos, soft, yet full of detail and precision. Most of them were pictures of nature, trees, animals, and water. Some were dark and abstract, depicting pain and anger.

There was one of a woman with daggers in her hand and death in her eyes. Her shoulder-length hair was in disarray, and her teeth were bared like an angry wolf. She had the body of a Barbie doll gone army. Her shapely form was well muscled and lean. She resembled the woman in my dreams. A chill ran up my spine.

The next few pictures were women without a face. All of them had long braids. Two of them were barefoot but still faceless. I flipped the page and my stomach turned. The last picture was of me hugging Maiyun. My eyes sparkled, and my cheeks were wide in a smile. He had detailed my bare feet and added a toe ring. There was a band on my left ring finger and a silver necklace dangling over Maiyun's back. I had not worn jewelry since Derrick died. I closed the book and returned it under the frame as I had found it.

Khalen slept soundly on the couch. His deep, rhythmic breaths were almost mesmerizing. I picked up my journal and began documenting the day's encounters. Even in writing, the day seemed like an out-of-control fantasy. For years I had prayed for the gift to heal. Today literally confirmed the adage to be careful what you pray for.

Sleep finally came over me, along with the dreams that demanded my participation. Darkness clouded my vision, but the forms that came toward me were clear: three men and two women. Their eyes glowed with an eerie redness, demonic and sinister. I backed up, my feet heavy like bricks of iron. The faster I tried to move, the heavier my feet became. The five Shadows grew closer.

My feet betrayed me, holding me firm. I was now face to face with them. The men were incredibly handsome, the women beautiful. Their friendly smiles bared perfect sets of sharp teeth, like those of wolves. Their eyes locked me in their gaze. I couldn't move. One of the men reached for me.

"No!" Khalen screamed.

I bolted up, out of bed, my heart pounding. I crossed the room. His blanket was wet and his pillow had been tossed across the floor. "Khalen." I shook his shoulders.

His hand reached up and grabbed me. "Run!" he screamed. "Run!"

"Khalen," I called louder. "Wake up."

His eyes fluttered open. My arm ached under his intense grip.

"Khalen, you're hurting me. Let go." I placed my hands over his, encouraging his release.

He reached over and pulled me close to him. I felt like a fragile child in his arms. He crushed me to his chest. His earthy scent was intoxicating. His breath, uncomfortably inviting. With hesitance, I returned the hug as a mutual friend. His grip did not cease. I now felt awkward and clumsy. Unable to break away from his hold, I continued to wrap my arms around him, offering the comfort he apparently needed. He cradled my head in his hand and gripped my hair with gentle affection.

"Khalen," I whispered. "What's wrong?"

He slowly released his hold on me. "Go back to bed,"

he said quietly. He stood from the couch and walked out the front door.

Maiyun cocked her head and whined softly.

I shrugged. "I don't know," I said. "He's crazy." For two hours I waited for him to return. He never did.

Chapter 16

Our greatest triumphs await at the end of our fiercest battles, as does the calm follow the storm.

This morning, I would have to find a place to bathe. Khalen had a convenient composting toilet in the yurt, but there was no place to shower.

I rummaged through the kitchen and found enough food to make a camper's breakfast. It was my father's favorite. While it was cooking, I opened the front door to let Maiyun out for some fresh air. She didn't venture too far before coming right back. Perhaps yesterday's ordeal imprinted a fear of separation on her psyche. I couldn't imagine being attacked by a bear.

I found a container of ground coffee and a French press in the cupboard. A rich cup of joe sounded perfect this morning. I heated up some water and prepared my thick ceramic mug with honey. The mug felt good in my hand proportion-wise, and the white satin glaze provided a sound grip. There was no milk in the refrigerator, so I would have to endure my coffee black. It wasn't ideal, but better than nothing.

Khalen opened the door carrying a basket of eggs and a jar of milk. He looked a sharp sight better than he did last night after his nightmare. His dark hair was smoothed back into a neat braid at the nape of his neck. He smelled fresh and his clothes were neatly pressed. Why anyone would press a pair of blue jeans eluded me, but there they were, perfectly pressed from the pockets to his cuffs. His long-sleeved, button-up shirt looked as if he had just picked it up from the cleaners. I wanted to touch it to see if it was made from some special type of material. There wasn't a single wrinkle in sight. Of course, even if there were, I wouldn't see it, but still, I was sure there were none. The light beige of the shirt played well against his dark skin. The man had good taste in clothes.

I smiled and took the milk from his hand. "Perfect timing," I said. The milk was warm. "Is this fresh?"

"Of course," he said. "We have several goats."

I poured milk into my mug, and then poured the boiling water into the waiting coffee grounds in the press. "Would you like some breakfast?"

"What are we having?" he asked, taking a seat at the kitchen bar.

I smiled. "My father's favorite—camper's breakfast."

He glanced toward the frying pan as I poured him a cup of black coffee.

"Bacon, corn tortillas, onions, eggs, and cheese," I said. "I couldn't find any bread for toast, or fresh fruit."

"Look in the egg basket," he said. "My mum made us

some fresh bread this morning." He stood and opened the pantry and pulled out a jar of peaches. "Will these do?"

I smiled. "Ah, lovely. Thank you."

The bread was encrusted with various seeds and was dark brown in color. When I sliced into it, nutmeg, cardamom, and allspice aroused my appetite. "This smells good."

I served breakfast, and then went around the bar to sit next to him.

"Do you see your parents often?" he asked.

I swallowed hard and shook my head. "They died shortly before my husband passed."

"Do you have any family?"

Again, I shook my head.

He must have sensed my discomfort. His questions ceased.

"You left, last night," I said.

He acknowledged my statement with a curt glance, but said nothing.

"Where did you go?"

He looked at me, swallowed his food, and then sipped his coffee. "For a walk," he finally said. The anger was back in his voice.

"Hmm." I continued to eat. Apparently, what happened last night was a touchy subject for him. He was about as moody as any hormone-imbalanced female I had ever known. I didn't want to push him over the edge.

"Nice clothes," I commented. "Do you have a separate yurt dedicated to your wardrobe?" It was sarcastic, I know, but I failed to see where he could possibly keep the amount of clothing he had here in this tent. There were no closets that I knew of.

He stood and walked toward the wall between the kitchen and the front door. He grabbed a small handle that was camouflaged against the wood grain and slid the panel open. It collapsed on itself like an accordion drape. He then proceeded to open the other walls in a similar fashion. The cleverly hidden closets contained more clothing than Walmart in December.

I raised my coffee mug. "Impressive."

He nodded, closed all the accordion doors, and then joined me back at the breakfast bar.

"How did you sleep last night?" he asked.

"Sporadically."

"Any dreams?"

"I always have dreams."

He turned to face me better. "About?"

Now it was my turn to feel discomfort. How would I explain that attractive demons chased me in the night, threatening to eat me? I was sure that Freud would have a field day analyzing that one. "Well, they're different every night."

"How about last night?" he asked, with an expression that dared me to stretch the truth. He probably already knew what happened, so why bother asking?

"I believe you already know the answer."

"Perhaps." He took a long sip of his coffee.

"Do you like the eggs?"

He nodded and took another bite.

"My father used to make them for us every Sunday morning, along with fluffy biscuits and sliced apples."

"You're changing the subject," he reminded me. "What did you dream about last night?"

The man was persistent.

"Demons," I said. "The same dream I have had since those three people came into the office to book an appointment with me. There are five of them, three men and two women, all very attractive. Their eyes are hypnotic, and their teeth are sharp like wolves'. The tall man with lighter hair reached for me, and then you screamed and woke me up."

He frowned. "Do you know this alley?"

"I never mentioned an alley."

"Do you know it?" His voice was louder, more demanding.

"No." I stood and carried my plate to the sink. "Are you always this moody?

He glared. "Only around you," he said.

To my surprise, his words stung. They shouldn't. This situation was temporary at best and I would soon be on my way. "We can change that, you know."

He looked at me, still frowning.

"I could stay with someone else until it is safe for me to return home."

He stood and carried his plate to the sink. "You want to go home?"

"Everyone is more comfortable at home, Khalen. I don't belong here."

He seemed hurt by my words and that confused me even more. In one moment, he claimed I make him moody. In the next moment, he acted as if my leaving was not a viable option.

"Would you be more comfortable in another's tent?" he asked.

"No," I said, shaking my head. "I would be more comfortable at home."

"I meant until your training is complete." He spoke through his teeth now, and his words had an edge to them.

"This is not about me, Khalen, and you know it. I'm not sure what is going on with you, but it feels like I'm in the eye of a hurricane. So long as I stay there, all is calm. Heaven help me if I bump into the edge."

"Ugh," he slammed the granite table with his hand. His face was contorted with pain as if he wanted to say something, but couldn't. "I'll find another place for you to stay," he said.

I did the dishes as he gathered a few things and left. My heart felt constricted and heavy. Every pump of blood seemed like an effort. Relationships were a dicey thing. I wanted to be his friend, but he kept pushing me away.

It reminded me of a horse I had long ago. His name was Keko. I used to place apples in his water tank to keep him entertained. Try as he might to grab the apples, his eager efforts merely pushed them out of his grasp. Finally, after hours of frustration, he learned to finesse the apples toward the edge of the bucket, and then gently wedge them between his teeth.

Perhaps Khalen would learn some finesse once I was gone? I didn't really want to leave, but I didn't want to be the source of his frustration, either. My attraction to him was obscure. It was like I had known him for many centuries, not just days or weeks. I knew him, though we had never really shared affection. He was a part of me that would never leave. I doubted he felt the same way.

I packed my things and laid them on the bed. It was time to find a place to bathe. Towel in hand, and a clean change of clothes under my arm, I headed toward the water.

"Where are you going?" called Khalen.

"The water," I said, turning to face him. "I need to bathe." Maiyun pressed against my side.

He pursed his lips. "And you were thinking about using the lake?"

"Do you have a better suggestion?"

"Come," he said, taking my hand. "I'll show you to the showers."

My hand felt comfortable in his, yet strangely wrong. There was a sense of belonging in his grip, but also a possessiveness that didn't quite fit. My hand felt small and weak against his warm hold, yet protected. It was not hard to imagine how Ann Darrow felt as King Kong carried her up the Empire State Building.

He led me to a wooden building. "Would you like me

to wait for you?"

I shook my head. "No, I can find my way back, thank you."

"My father and I will be waiting for you at the yurt," he said, still holding onto my hand.

Again I thanked him, but there was much more sincerity in my voice this time. Mostly, I was grateful for the kindness he displayed. It was a refreshing change from his recent fluctuations of anger, pain, and disappointment.

He slowly released my hand, nodded, and then retreated back toward the yurt. Maiyun followed me into the shower room. It was spacious, with ample room for my clothes and towel. There were no doors, just shower heads spread along the back wall.

I took my time, enjoying the heat surrounding my body. I shampooed my hair and was tempted to bathe Maiyun as well, but knew it was pointless. She would, no doubt, find something else to get into during our stay. Her bath would have to wait until we returned home.

Brushing my hair while it was wet was frustrating at best, so I decided to allow it to dry naturally. The long walk back to the yurt would help some, especially because the sun was out. It was still cold, though—not freezing, but close to it. I flipped the hood of my old grey sweat shirt over my head and gave up the notion of trying to dry my hair in this environment. The men would just have to endure my damp head for the morning.

Maiyun expertly lead me around obstacles that could

potentially trip me or twist my ankles. We arrived at the
yurt to find the two men laughing outside. Khalen was
quite attractive behind a genuine smile. His eyes were
more green today than gold. I followed the men up the
steps and into the yurt.

I removed my hooded sweatshirt and stood by the fire to
shake out my hair. I was wearing the grey turtleneck Khalen
lent me in the apartment, and he looked pleased to see me
wearing it again. "I will give it back," I said, smiling.

"Keep it," he said. "It looks good on you."

I liked it because it covered the top of my white capris,
which were much too small for my comfort. I preferred my
clothes to be loose and comfortable. I had limited selection,
though, and knew I would have to do some washing very
soon.

No healing was done that morning, only pain relief. The
urge to heal was not as strong today, but the smell of blood
still tempted me to close the wound. It was becoming easier now, and required only a suggestion on my part. It was
scary, really, how easy it was to project my intentions and
seeing them manifest so quickly.

I was becoming connected with Case, and was able to
communicate more freely with him, both in thought and
with words. He was a kind and gentle man, but one who
demanded the utmost respect.

We made good progress this morning, and I was
ready for a break. I quickly brushed my hair, and then we
stepped outside to mingle with the ladies out by the fire.

Jade greeted me with a smile.

"Hi Skye," she said. "Remember me?"

"Jade, right?"

Her smiled beamed. "That's right. You're good." She glanced over at Khalen, who was talking with Case, Ian, and Aidan.

"He likes you," she said. "The entire clan is talking about it."

I looked at her with doubt. "Khalen?"

"Of course, who else would I be talking about?"

"Ian, Aidan?" I was joking, of course, although Ian was not shy about his advances, as insincere as they were.

She giggled. "They are the clan's playboys. They chase all the women." There was a sudden sadness in her eyes as she glanced back at Ian. "Khalen, on the other hand, is very particular. Women were taboo to him until you came along."

"Taboo? Why?"

Khalen and Case shot Jade a look, and she grew pale. "Never mind. I shouldn't have said anything." She stepped away.

"Jade, wait." I started to go after her but was cut off by Ian and Aidan.

"Hi, Skye," said Ian. He was the more boisterous of the two. Aidan was older by two years, and much more sophisticated. They were both unbelievably tall and looked very much alike. Aidan was slightly taller and more muscular in his arms.

"Ian, Aidan." I nodded toward Jade. "What was that all about?" I asked.

"Nothing," Aidan said. "She's a gossip queen."

"Hey," said Ian. "Are you up for an adventure?"

My brows furrowed. "Uh, what kind of adventure?"

"Dunna matter," said Aidan. "Are you up for one or not?" His Irish accent was slightly stronger than his younger brother's.

"Sure," I said. Compared to this week, what could be worse?

Aidan grabbed my arm and led me toward a large jeep with mud slung along the sides.

"What are you boys up to?" said Khalen, removing Aidan's grip from my arm.

Ian stepped around the truck. "We're just showing her the sights," he said. "We'll have her back in time for her next training session."

"It's not safe," Khalen seethed. His eyes were darker now.

"Relax," said Aidan. "She needs a break."

They locked eyes for a moment, obviously having a silent conversation.

Maiyun whined and paced anxiously. "Stay with Khalen," I told her. "I'll be back soon."

I looked at Khalen. "I want to go."

He growled in response, like some lead wolf warding off the pack from a fresh kill. "Nothing dangerous," he warned.

"Pst," Aidan laughed. "What's dangerous? We're showing her the sights."

Khalen glowered at him. "You know what I mean."

Ian guided me into the jeep. "Relax, Khalen. We'll take good care of her."

"That's what worries me," he said.

I shook my head. Three middle-aged men acting like high-school boys over the new girl in class—pathetic.

"Billy," Aidan called out to a teenager chatting with a group of girls. "We need a driver."

The boy eagerly ran over and hopped into the driver's seat. His black, curly hair draped over the headrest. He was a good-looking kid with obvious mixed heritage. He looked part Nigerian and part Finnish with a bit of Sicilian mixed in.

"Keep it slow," Khalen instructed the teen.

"Yes sir," the boy replied.

Khalen looked at me as if warning me to stay safe. I shook my head in response. He was possessive, yet held me at bay. He cared for me, but couldn't be around me for long. Honestly, I felt like a ping pong ball in a solo match.

Billy drove slowly away from the camp, just as Khalen instructed. Like his father, Khalen demanded respect. That was evident, except when it came to Ian and Aidan. They didn't seem to be as intimidated by Khalen.

"Billy," Aidan said, punching his shoulder. "This is Skye. Skye, Billy."

I nodded.

"Yeah, no kidding," Billy replied. "The entire clan knows about you." He looked at me from the rearview mirror.

"Perfect," I mumbled.

Ian placed his warm hand on my leg. "All good things," he said, glaring back at the young teen.

When we reached the main road, Billy cut loose and skidded away from the dirt driveway. "Whoo hoo!" he yelled, pressing down on the accelerator. The engine roared to life, and then shut down.

"Damn it, Khalen," Billy muttered under his breath. "I was just having a bit of fun, that's all." He got out, slammed the door and opened the hood.

Ian and Aidan laughed.

Billy hopped back into the jeep and restarted the engine.

"Distributor cap?" asked Ian.

Billy looked back in the mirror. "No, the fuel line."

Aidan shook his head. "Dang, it's worse than we thought, brother."

"Uh huh."

"Anyone care to fill me in?" I said, feeling a bit left out.

"We are not at liberty to say," said Aidan.

I threw up my hands in frustration. "Of course not."

Chapter 17

To define what is real is to negate the power of intention, imagination, and desire for all that is yet to come.

Billy drove more carefully during the rest of the trip. In less than an hour, we reached the top of a cliff. Billy stopped the jeep in a heavily wooded spot. I assumed they were going to show me the town from this high vantage. My fear of heights reared its ugly head to remind me that I was merely human and that falling could cause injury if not death.

"Come on," said Ian, opening his door. "You're gonna love this." He opened the tailgate and grabbed two long bags.

We were parked on top of a hill that resembled a bald head of a really big man. Sparse sprigs of dandelion squeezed their way through the cracks in the smooth stone surface beneath my feet. There were few trees around, and no signs of animal life, including humans. Beyond the cliff, I could see the Case Inlet sparkling beneath the pristine sky. A gentle, salty breeze blew steadily off the coast.

I went around to the back to see what they were doing.

Aidan pulled out a pale blue suit and stepped into it. Ian's suit was white.

I frowned. "What are those things?"

"Not things," said Aidan. "Squirrel suits."

Ian laughed. "Ha, flyin' squirrel suits," he corrected. "We had to modify them for this area. They are quite unique, I assure you." He gave his brother a knowing wink.

My mouth opened and my eyes grew wide. "You aren't seriously considering flying off this short cliff?"

"No," said Ian. "We are flyin' off it."

Aidan tossed me a harness. "Here, put this on."

It landed on my outstretched arm like a snare before it was set. I turned it around in my hands. It resembled a clump of rubber bands that were horribly tangled.

Billy came to my rescue. "I'll help you." He untangled the mess. "Step your feet in here." He held open two holes then slid the harness up my legs. "Where's your shoes?"

"I don't like wearing them."

He laughed. "Cool." He guided my arms through another hole, and then began buckling the straps. Most of them needed adjusting. The last person to use this harness must have been twice my size. Compared to Ian and Aidan, though, I felt tiny. "There," said Billy. "Snug as a shrink-wrapped tenderloin."

I frowned. "Nice analogy."

He grinned with pride. "Who's she riding with?"

"Me," said Aidan. "My suit is larger, and I'm a much stronger bird than baby brother over there."

"Ha," Ian laughed. "You wish."

Billy brought me over to Aidan and began securing me to the front of his chest. My stomach sank to the center of my gut, twisting and grinding in protest. My instinct screamed that this was a bad idea and that I should return to camp with Billy.

"You're not scared, are ye, lassie?" asked Aidan.

"Shouldn't I be?"

"Na, we've done this a hundred times, maybe more. The trick is waitin' for the perfect conditions, ye see. If the wind currents aren't just right, we fall to the ground and—splat."

Ian cleared his throat. "We've only done this three other times with another person. The other two times didn't end well, but, we're getting better each time, eh big brother?"

Aidan laughed, causing my body to shake with him.

"Mmm, ye smell good," he said, taking a long whiff of my hair.

"Careful, brother," said Ian. "She belongs to Khalen."

"I what?"

"Ye belong to Khalen," Ian repeated.

"I most certainly do not," I protested. "We are barely friends, and I'm not even sure he wants to be that."

Both Aidan and Ian laughed hard.

Even Billy chuckled a bit. "I'll see you at camp," he said, heading back to the jeep.

"What?" I inquired.

"Well," said Aidan, "apparently you're blind in more ways than one."

"Meaning?"

"Everyone but you knows that Khalen has claimed you."

"I'm not a chunk of land, you know. No one can just claim another being without the other's consent."

We started walking toward the cliff. My heart was pounding hard and loud. It was a challenge to keep breathing. I tried to dig my heels in but my legs were strapped in. I kicked and wriggled against the rubber straps, but they held firm. Aidan didn't even seem to notice.

"So according to you, you're available for other suitors?" he asked.

"Yes, no—I mean, I'm not looking." Oh Lord, I had no depth perception, but the cars below looked like matchbox toys.

Aidan laughed. "Neither is Khalen." He leaned forward, allowing us both to fall. My breathing ceased, my heart raced as if to complete its allotted number of beats in that very moment. My feet felt heavy. I was sure it was because my stomach had sunk there.

"Ahhhhhh!" I screamed, wiggling against the tight constraints. We were falling fast. Soon I would resemble pizza meeting the floor.

Aidan's suit fluttered in the breeze, yielding to the current that drew us ever closer to the ground. Slowly, he spread his arms and the wind caught beneath the fabric that connected his arms to his legs. Our descent slowed dramatically and we began to glide.

"Whew," Ian called. "What a rush."

"You can open your eyes now," said Aidan. "We aren't going to die."

I hadn't realized I had closed them. I gasped as Aidan made a sharp left turn.

"Below us is Treasure Island," he said. "Beyond that is the Key Peninsula." He caught an air current over the water and it pulled us upward.

Again, my stomach fell somewhere between my thighs and my feet.

"If we catch the right air currents, we can fly for miles," he said.

"How do you find them?" I asked, feeling naive.

"You feel the wind," he said. "Become part of it." This was obviously his and Ian's element up here. They both flew as if each of them were born with wings.

"Look to your left," he said.

I did. There was an eagle flying side by side with Ian. When Ian turned left, so did the eagle.

"That's incredible," I said. The fear that had gripped me minutes ago had given precedence to awe and wonderment. I raised my face to feel more of the wind. I was tempted to spread my wings as well, but decided to just stay still, instead.

"Go ahead," said Aidan. "Spread 'em."

I did, and it felt amazing. The wind supported me as if it were water. I felt its strength, yet it was soft and yielding.

"Take her over McMicken Island, and then circle back,"

Aidan instructed his brother.

"Okay," he called back.

They headed toward a small island surrounded by boats.

"It's a state park," Aidan explained. "The entire island is owned by Washington State. It is a very popular camp site for boaters." He adjusted his arms and legs and they banked right. "You can breathe now, we're headin' back."

"That's too bad," I said. "I was starting to enjoy myself."

"Ah, a girl after me own heart," said Aidan. "I may just claim ye for myself."

I knew he was joking, so I didn't bother rebutting his remark. This recent attention I was suddenly getting felt oddly out of place. I didn't consider myself an attractive woman, nor one with assets that typically lured men. I was simple, independent, and not in the market for companionship. These traits were hardly those that drew a man's attention. I wouldn't complain, however. This attention made me feel young again, and somewhat alluring. I was having fun.

We flew low over Harstine Island. "Okay," said Aidan. "Lean back and lift your legs. Let me do all the work."

He pulled a string to open the parachute. It gripped the air and yanked us to a slow descent. The straps around my legs bit into my flesh.

Holding my breath, I did as he asked as we approached a clearing near a lake. I pressed back against his chest and drew my legs up to keep them from getting tangled up with his. He curled his arms around me then pressed his legs forward. We hit the ground with a gentle thud.

Ian landed behind us. "Whew!" he yelled. "I love to fly."

"I could get used to this," I said.

"So, ye liked it then, eh?" Aidan released the buckles binding us together.

My face felt cold and refreshed, my mind clear. "Yes, very much."

He removed his suit, and then helped me out of my harness. He was taking a bit too long for my comfort. I did not look up at him because I didn't want to see those green eyes staring down at me. I had enough problems with Khalen.

Aidan chuckled as if feeling my discomfort. "You're a real gem, Skye. If Khalen doesn't want ye, I'm definitely next in line."

"Behind me," said Ian.

"Do I get a say in this?" I asked.

Both of them answered simultaneously. "No."

I noticed that neither of them gathered the harnesses and suits. When I looked behind us, the gear was gone. "Where are the suits and harnesses?"

Ian and Aidan laughed. "Don't worry 'bout them," said Ian.

My eyes grew wide. "Don't worry about them? You said that they were custom made, and were one of a kind." I turned and started to head back.

"Skye," Ian called. "There are no suits and harnesses."

I stopped. Both of them looked at me with utmost seriousness. "Explain," I said.

Aidan opened his arms as if gesturing toward the entire forest. "It was all an illusion," he said. "We never left the island."

My hands sat perched on my hips. "An illusion."

"Aye," he laughed. "An illusion."

I huffed. "We never drove up to the cliffs or jumped off, or flew with an eagle?"

Both of them shook their heads. If they were lying, they certainly weren't showing it.

"Technically no," said Ian. "But imaginatively, we all enjoyed a great adventure."

"But the cliff was so real. The wind blew my hair." I lifted the tangled mess as if to prove my point.

Aidan put his hand on my shoulder. "Skye, lass, there are no cliffs in this area that are suitable for jumpin', especially in a squirrel suit."

Ian placed his hand on my other shoulder. "It's one of our gifts," he said. "Did you enjoy it?"

I nodded, and then shook my head with confusion. "It seemed so real."

"Aye, it did," said Aidan.

As we approached camp, Khalen and Maiyun waited at the outskirts of camp. "Watch this," Aidan said as he wrapped his arm around my shoulders.

Khalen noticeably stiffened. "I'll take her from here," he said, removing Aidan's arm from around me. He held my hand and nearly crushed it. Maiyun flanked my other side making me feel like a prisoner being escorted back to my cell.

"I'm not running away," I commented. "You can ease your grip."

"Are ye still thinking you're available now, lassie, eh?" Aidan called out.

I looked back over my shoulder. He was smiling.

Khalen's grip was still firm, but not quite crushing. Maiyun continued pressing against me. I didn't even get a chance to say hello to her. I scratched her head as we walked, offering a silent apology. Men could be so rude.

As we neared the yurt, I felt a familiar sting at my back. I blocked it and sent it immediately to the ground. The next thing I knew, I fell to my knees and was unable to stand. Khalen released my hand.

"You're late," Case said, standing at the top of the stairs. "We have work to do."

Try as I might, I could not stand. Khalen left me and joined his father in the yurt. He took Maiyun with him, despite her resistance.

Something told me this training session would not be as easy as the one this morning. The longer I sat there, the more painful the stings became. My best effort to block them failed me. Now I was scared.

Chapter 18

*D*o we truly know anything, or do we simply manifest our perception of the truth?

Panic gripped me. The eyes of Eve and three other women peered over at me, pleading me to stand, but I couldn't. The pain increased and I cried out. The ache reminded me of when Derrick died. It crippled me for weeks until I learned to ignore it. That's what I had to do now—ignore it.

"Pain is just an illusion," I told myself. "Nothing more." I shifted my intention to getting up and into the yurt. My legs felt weak, but I wouldn't allow them to quit on me now. I was half way up, they were shaking. I focused on sending Case's energy to the ground. My shield grew thick and dense, like the wall I had built around my heart after Derrick died. I hadn't realized it was there until now. From my cocoon, I was safe—protected. I walked up the stairs with confidence, but not too much to open myself to Case's next blow. It was sure to come swiftly if I let my guard down with any hint of cockiness.

His obsidian eyes met mine as I walked through the

door. The sting in my chest was present, but no longer debilitating.

"You took much longer than I anticipated," Case said. He and Khalen were sitting on the couch.

Maiyun laid in her bed, but her tail was wagging. The men must have warned her to stay there.

The old man's disappointment returned me to childhood, when I brought home my first D. My father broke my heart with his expression. I wasn't used to disappointing him and after that day, I vowed never to cause it again.

This situation was slightly different, but it felt the same. I lowered my head, offering this great man the respect he deserved. "I'm sorry." My words were sincere.

"Ian and Aidan know better than to have taken you away."

I shook my head. "It wasn't their fault, Case. I wanted to go."

"At their suggestion," he added.

"It was still my decision. I could have said no, but I didn't. The mistake is mine and mine alone." I lowered my eyes, waiting for his response.

"Refreshing."

I looked at him. His eyes had softened. Khalen was pleased, but he tried very hard not to show it.

"I expect you to be prompt next time," said Case.

"Yes, sir," I replied. It felt odd addressing another adult so formally, but this man made me feel young and vulnerable in his presence. It was no wonder he was the leader of this clan.

An urgent knock rattled the door. Khalen stood to answer it. A young man with short, sandy hair spoke through labored breaths.

"Khalen, it's Pete. He's back." The boy shook his head. "Not good."

Case stood with a look of concern on his face. "Come with," he told me. "You might be able to help."

We followed the young boy to a small yurt at the far end of camp. Inside was a teenage boy. His black hair was tangled and damp, his half-naked body curled in a ball. He was shaking and glistening with sweat.

Khalen knelt down to examine him. "Ah, Pete. What have you done?" He rolled the boy over and looked at both eyes. He then examined his gums. "He's overdosed again."

"Jimmy," he said to the younger boy. "Ask Eve for hot, wet towels and a bowl of bentonite and kelp. Make sure they are hot."

"Okay," he called back, racing out of the yurt.

"Lobelia," I said. "It'll help."

"I don't have any here," Khalen said.

"I do." I looked at Maiyun. "Find my bag," I told her.

Maiyun ran back toward Khalen's yurt.

"The door," he said. "It's closed."

I knelt down beside the boy and placed my hands on his chest and abdomen. "She can open it," I said, closing my eyes.

I conjured the blue mist and prayed for the boy's health. My insides ached then I remembered to send the pain to the ground. It worked. My hands grew warm but not hot. The boy's breathing grew stronger, but he was still unconscious and shaking. I felt a strong connection to the source, our Father. The vibration I felt in my hands was slow and deep, like sound waves traveling through water. I waited for them to fade. The boy's shaking calmed, and he was no longer curled in pain.

Maiyun returned with my bag in her mouth. She waited for my command to release it. "Good girl." I loosened the small, ornate bag's red drawstrings and pulled out a dram of lobelia homeopathic remedy. I banged it against my hand several times, and then filled the dropper with the remedy. I placed five drops on the boy's gums. "This will help," I whispered to him, keeping his lips closed.

By the time Jimmy returned with the hot towels, his brother had stopped shaking. Khalen rubbed his body with the clay and kelp, and then wrapped him in the steaming hot towels. "This will draw out the toxins," he said.

Case dragged a cot close to the fire, then helped Khalen lift Pete onto the cot so he could be closer to the heat.

Jimmy offered a blanket. Khalen smiled then took the blanket to wrap around the teen. "Your brother will be fine, Jimmy."

Tears glistened in the young boy's eyes. "Mom won't be happy," he said.

Case stood. "I'll talk to her."

I placed another few drops of the remedy in Pete's mouth.

"Good thinking," said Khalen. "We make a great team." His bright smile was welcoming and appreciative.

I had seen drug overdoses before, but never this severe. "Does he do this a lot?" I asked.

Khalen shook his head. "His dad passed away a few years ago. He had a hard time dealing with it. He cleaned up for a while, and then disappeared three weeks ago."

Jimmy tossed something against the wall. "It's those stupid kids on Timothy Drive," he said. "They got to him real bad."

Khalen sat the boy on his lap. "We make our own choices in life, Jimmy. No one makes us do anything."

Ember crashed through the door with Case close behind. "Pete!" She rushed over and placed her hand on his forehead. She still had her gardening gloves on. With haste, she yanked them off and tossed them to the floor. Wisps of copper hair floated around her face as she knelt down closer to her son to check his breathing.

Khalen set Jimmy down then put his hand on Ember's shoulder. "He'll be okay, Ember. Calm down."

"He was with the Rogers again, I know it." She looked back at Case. "Something has to be done about them," she said.

"There will always be people like the Rogers," he said.

"Then we'll get rid of all of them, one at a time," she seethed.

"And when all is done," said Case, "what makes us any better than them?"

She glared at him. "I'll do it myself, if I have to."

"Come," said Case, looking in my direction, "we have training to do."

The look on Ember's delicate face was one of hate and revenge. It seemed strange to see it in this camp, as if it didn't belong.

I gathered my bag and followed Case and Khalen out the door. It had turned dark, so Khalen took my hand to guide me. Maiyun flanked my other side. She seemed comfortable allowing him to take her place, but she did not want to relinquish her job completely.

Small fires crackled loudly as groups of people gathered around them. Young children giggled and squealed as their marshmallows burst into flames. There were no televisions here, or sound systems that caused your bones to vibrate with heavy bass. The strong sense of community was solid here and comforting. I loved the quiet that filled the day and the peace that blanketed the night.

We entered the yurt. Khalen went straight to the kitchen while Case and I retreated to the couch. I set my bag on the coffee table. The fire was still smoldering. It was warm enough without adding another log. The smell of cedar mingled with the burning fir logs.

"Apparently," said Case. "You are unable to cure illnesses, yet you can heal wounds." He rubbed his tanned, clean-shaven chin. "Interesting."

"It doesn't make sense," I said. "If I can heal flesh, why can't I affect individual cells?"

"You do," he explained, "so long as the cells are healthy."

I shook my head and frowned. "But when flesh is cut, the cells are compromised."

"But not reprogrammed," he corrected. "Unhealthy cells have strayed from their primary DNA; they are no longer structured to perform their original function. Hence, they are diseased."

"That explains why she cannot heal her vision," Khalen said from the kitchen.

"Exactly," Case confirmed. "Injuries typically occur by accident, but illness is a product of our life choices." His eyes widened as if realizing something profound. He stood and started pacing. "If we could reverse the effects of our choices, there would be no consequence. Without consequence, there would be no accountability. Chaos would reign."

I thought about my family and all the pain they went through. What life choices had they made to earn them the suffering they endured? I could not imagine anything they could have done to bring cancer upon themselves.

"And what if disease ends in death?" I asked.

"Everything ends in death," said Case.

I wrung my hands together until they ached. "I don't understand disease." I truly didn't. If all things with God were possible, then why couldn't their illnesses be healed? My family were good people who certainly did not deserve the torture that marked the last months of their lives.

Khalen chopped the ends off carrots and tossed them to Maiyun. "If we are given the ability to heal sickness as well as injuries, we would never die. Without death, there can be no rebirth."

"Balance could not be restored," added Case.

I chimed in. "So, if some evil entity wanted to rid the planet of individuals, all they would need to do is introduce some horrid disease?"

Case looked at me with surprise. "What makes you think they haven't already?"

"AIDS, for one," said Khalen, holding up the knife as if it were an extension of his finger.

My eyes grew wide. "AIDS?"

Case nodded. "Man-made."

I shook my head, having a hard time believing that other humans could do such a thing. "Why?"

"To rid the planet of undesirables," said Khalen, popping a carrot chunk into his mouth.

My stomach felt sick, my heart heavy. So many people suffering at the hands of other humans. It all seemed so unreal, yet horribly plausible at the same time. "There are times," I said, "that I really don't feel as if I'm a part of this race."

"All humans are not evil, Skye," Case explained. "There are those who follow their hearts and do their best to help others. Part of being human is accepting the law of duality, but not giving into it haphazardly."

"I don't understand," I said.

Case sat next to me on the couch. "When I hurt you out there, you had two choices. You could get angry at me for causing you pain, or you could accept your condition as a consequence of your own actions. You chose to learn rather than react, but it was your choice. You could have blamed Ian and Aidan for taking you away, but you chose to accept your own decision."

My discomfort at hearing his praise surprised me. My parents often praised me for right choices; why would this man be different?

"My mother often told me that we are responsible for our own actions. No one makes us do anything we don't want to do, she always said." I laughed. "At the time, I never understood how she could say that, but it stuck with me."

"She sounds very wise," he said.

"She was," I replied sadly. "She passed away several years ago."

"Hmm," he said. "She's home."

I nodded. In many ways, I wished that I could join her, my dad, my sister, and my beloved husband, but deep down, I knew that there were many things I had yet to complete before our Father called me home. Four months ago, I would have been ready. How could so much have changed between then and now?

"I still don't understand why humans have to hurt one another."

"For the same reason that most doctors address the symptoms but ignore the cause of disease," said Khalen.

"On the surface, the patient feels healed, but it's only an illusion."

"Exactly," said Case. "Now back to your training, young lady."

As Khalen finished making dinner, Case presented situations that I could potentially encounter, should the Shadows come for me. The discussion disturbed Khalen. His chopping grew louder, and his face was contorted as if he were trying his best to contain the storm that stirred his emotions.

"Remember," said Case. "God gives everyone the gift of discernment. Listen to your instincts; they never lie or cloud the truth."

Dinner was fabulous: tuna salad blended with yogurt, finely chopped carrots, celery, pickles, onions, and garlic, served over fresh baby spinach and accompanied by Eve's bread and goat butter. After enjoying all this, I was ready for sleep. It had been a long day. So much had happened.

Unfortunately, Case, was not finished for the day. He had me exercising my ability to project. To demonstrate, he manipulated the stream of water Khalen used to rinse the dishes. A hefty spray of water drenched the front of his shirt and splattered his face.

I couldn't stifle my laugh as Khalen turned with a look of shock on his face. He pulled his drenched shirt away from his stomach, and then proceeded to remove the dripping garment. With a huff, he tossed it toward his father. "Very clever, old man."

Case stopped the cloth in midair. He waved his hand, guided the cloth down, and then folded it neatly. It was completely dry. He was laughing the entire time, clearly enjoying Khalen's predicament. "You let your guard down, dear boy."

Khalen glared. "I believe this is Skye's training, and not my own." He dried the water from his bronzed skin. His well-muscled arms and chest held me mesmerized.

There was no hair evident on his chest, and arms, which helped confirm he was of American Indian descent. His thick black hair and chiseled jaw line also conformed to my suspicion. His hazel eyes, however, were a mystery. They changed color drastically, depending on his mood. Right now, they were dark gold, betraying his underlying anger at having been caught off guard.

Case glanced over at him. "Every moment is an opportunity to hone your skills, son. Always be prepared."

Khalen nodded with a slight bow as if conceding to his father's wisdom. When his gaze fell on me, I quickly looked away, embarrassed to be caught staring at his impressive physique. When I glanced up again, I noticed the corners of his full lips had a slight curl to them.

Case stood up from the couch. "Well, enough fun for tonight," he said. "Shanuk calls for me."

"Shanuk?" I inquired.

"My grandfather," Khalen answered. "He is very sick."

Case's expression reflected the pain he tried so hard to hide. He came over and gave me a warm, sincere hug.

"Sleep well, my dear."

He hugged Khalen next, and then took his leave.

Case looked to be about 80 years old, which would make his father at least 100. The man who had visited me in the hospital was nowhere near that age.

"How old is your father," I asked, as Khalen walked toward the fire to stoke it.

He glanced up. "How old do you think he is?" A slight smile curled his lips, drawing me in like a hummingbird to nectar. This man is dangerous, I told myself.

"Eightyish," I said, picking up the fuzzy blanket on the bed and rubbing it softly in my hands.

He laughed. "That's my age," he said.

My eyes grew wide and my breath caught in my throat. "You are not."

"Eighty-three, to be exact."

He had the body of a 30-year-old. "How is that possible?"

"Have you looked in the mirror, lately, Skye?"

I did, just that morning, but didn't really notice anything special. "Why?"

"You're 45, but you look as young as most 20-year-olds."

People always commented how young I appeared, especially Sam. I thought they were merely being kind.

He placed another log on the fire, and then came to sit with me on the bed. His sudden closeness made my heart race.

"The more we exercise our pineal gland, the stronger our gifts become, and the younger we appear. It's like reverting to our teenage state, but without all the emotional drama."

"So, we don't age?"

"Oh, we do, but very slowly." He glanced over at my bag packed and resting on the bed. His smile was replaced with disappointment. "Gregg and Ro said you could stay at their cabin for as long as you like." He reached over and grabbed my bag. "Come, I'll walk you over."

I was hoping he would ask me to stay. Instead, he was eager to help me leave. "I don't have to go right now," I said.

He turned to look at me, his eyes now green with gold flecks. "It's best if you do."

In an odd way, I understood. Our attraction to one another was difficult to comprehend, and could easily get out of control. Although our worlds were the same, they were miles apart, or so it seemed.

I gathered Maiyun's bedding and followed him out the door. Maiyun hesitantly followed, looking confused.

We walked in silence across the camp, his hand holding mine protectively. "Case," he said, breaking the silence. "Is 152 years old."

"And Shanuk?"

Khalen looked down at me. "Over 300. No one really knows his exact age."

I shook my head, having difficulty taking this all in.

Living so long was unheard of. How could they do that without attracting attention? "Why is he sick?"

He pursed his lips. "According to him, he's fulfilled his contract and it is his time to return home."

"And what's your take?"

He squeezed my hand. "I think he's tired and done here on Earth."

We followed the fire pits to the opposite end of camp, and then veered right into a thick forested area. The path was narrow and littered with debris. Khalen pulled me behind him and ensured that nothing would trip me. Maiyun followed close behind. It was so dark that I couldn't see a thing.

We reached a small cabin at the end of the path. "Gregg and Ro like seclusion," he said.

He opened the door, and then proceeded to light candles. "There is no electricity," he explained. He led me over to the bed, and placed my bag on the floor. "I'll build a fire."

Even with the firelight, I could not see well.

"Come." He took my hand. "I'll show you around." The place was small, with no dividing walls, and very little furniture. He showed me where to find the bathroom and the small kitchen. "I'll come by in the morning with fresh eggs and milk." He led me back to the bed.

"Thank you," I whispered. I could not see his face, but I could feel the heat of his eyes resting upon me.

He squeezed my shoulders. "Yeah," he groaned. Without

another word, he turned and left.

The heat of the fire quickly warmed the small space. It was quiet here and strangely isolated. I reminded myself that it was I who had asked for this.

Chapter 19

To come to a conclusion is to accept the fallacy that there are no other choices to consider.

~ K h a l e n ~

Leaving Skye in such a remote cabin did not sit well with me, but I knew she would never agree to stay with another family. I would go back and check on her later this evening when she was sure to be asleep.

At the moment, I felt the need to check on Shanuk. His time was growing close; we could all feel it, especially Case. Beneath his tempered steel exterior, there was pain that could not be cured with a mere touch.

After Shanuk's wife died, his health declined severely and there was nothing any of us could do to turn him around. He joined this clan years ago when the Squaxin tribe still occupied Harstine Island. Now the tribe merely owned several acres and rights to harvest the natural oyster beds along the shoreline of this and other neighboring islands. Case left for England to study metaphysical psychology. It was there that he met Eve. They started their own clan in Eastbourne, and were eager to return there soon.

I knocked on my father's door and waited for the okay to enter. My mother, Eve, opened the door and smiled at me. "Were your ears ringing, my son?"

The smell of fresh-ground wheat, cardamom, and rye greeted me. Mother took great comfort in providing the clan with bread every day, and she never failed to fulfill that duty with love and appreciation.

Her comment was her way of saying that I was the topic of discussion. I looked across the room to see my father and grandfather sitting on the couch. Shanuk looked weak, but happy. His deep blue eyes sparkled with a spectrum of subtle colors.

"Khalen," he said, his voice shaky, yet deep and rich with authority. "Come sit." He pointed to the empty chair across from him.

I took his cold hands in mine and bowed my head with respect before sitting.

The old man smiled, displaying a brilliant set of teeth that should not have belonged to a man his age. "I hear your young woman is doing quite well."

I nodded. "Better than expected," I added with an un-merited sense of pride.

He nodded. "Hmm." His eyes narrowed a bit as if he were reading my deepest thoughts. There was no use in try-ing to block a man of his stature. His skill outweighed mine tenfold. In comparison, he made Case look weak and new in skill. Shanuk could kill with a mere glance, yet his spirit was as gentle as a summer breeze, and as genuine as God's abundant love. Even in the midst of violence, Shanuk remained in control.

I remembered once when I was feeling cocky with my new skill of telekinesis, anger got the best of me, as it often did in my youth. Shanuk grounded me for a full week, giving me time to reflect my poor decisions. In response, I flung a steel statue at him with the intent to harm. Shanuk shattered the statue before it made contact. At that moment, he could have rebutted with deadly force, but he simply smiled and walked away.

"She is a good mate for you," he finally said.

I shook my head. "No."

"Don't allow your fear to alter your path, Khalen. You cannot rule this clan alone. You need a strong woman by your side, just as every man does."

The thought of taking another mate turned my gut. "Not possible," I managed to say. "Not again."

"Valerie was not right for you."

Shanuk and Case had tried to warn me years ago when my attraction to her was evident. I didn't listen.

"Skye deserves someone better," I said.

Shanuk looked as if he was just about to call check mate in an intense game of chess. "Yes, perhaps Aidan is a better choice. They show interest in one another."

My knuckles turned white. I stood, trying to keep the growl from escaping my chest.

Case and Shanuk laughed. "You fight your own spirit,

son," said Case. "How long can you continue the battle before she moves on? And, if she decides to move on, are you willing to let her go?"

"If it is her choice, yes," I grumbled. The truth, however, was that I could not allow her to leave any more than I could allow Aidan to advance on her. Both my father and grandfather knew it.

"Khalen, sit," Shanuk demanded.

I did as he asked.

"She is not Valerie. Skye will be tested, you cannot save her from that. Your father and I have faith in her and so should you."

His expression grew more serious as he held on to the silence. "If she is the one," he added. "The Shadows will want her."

The "one," meaning she was the woman of legend. The legend that had no root, or point of origin.

"With the right man," Case added. "Her children will mark the beginning of hope for our kind."

"And with the wrong man?" I asked.

"Destruction," said Shanuk.

He reached for my hand and squeezed it. "This life is hard—full of pain and difficult choices. It is also a life of purpose that must be fulfilled."

"Take her as your own," said Case. "Before it's too late."

My insides twisted and churned like an angry sea. "You know what must happen if I take her now and she is turned."

I seethed with anxiety for her.

They all knew. Like Valerie, Skye would have to be killed or the entire clan would be at risk. Once the union took place, Skye would be connected to the clan, making them susceptible and easily turned. She was the link the Shadows had been waiting for.

"And if they claim her first?" asked Case.

"Ugh," I screamed. "I need more time!"

Shanuk's grip on my hands grew firm and almost painful. "We are out of time, Khalen."

"It must be her decision," I said. "She will have to know the consequences."

In truth, I could take Skye against her will and the union would be complete, but that type of union was not practiced by the Protected ones as much as it was by the Shadows, where women were nothing more than property to be owned.

Shanuk nodded and released my hands. "Understood."

I spent the rest of the evening with them, and then headed back to the cabin to check on Skye. On the way, I stopped by my yurt to grab the soft blanket she loved to snuggle against. There was nothing soft for her in Gregg and Ro's place.

As I approached the cabin, the hair on my back stood. I felt a coldness that was not a part of the evening chill. The dim light of the cabin's fire flickered in the darkness. Through the door, I heard Maiyun's low growl. I opened the door and peered inside.

Maiyun's hackles were raised, but she seemed relieved to see me. "Yeah," I told her. "I felt it too." I patted her head reassuringly.

On the bed, Skye lay on her side with her legs curled up. Her feet, of course, were uncovered and her clothes lay sprawled on the floor. I unfolded the soft purple blanket and draped it over her shoulders. She immediately stroked the softness of it and pulled it up to her face. Her furrowed brows softened. I fought the urge to brush her soft cheeks, pink and bright from the coldness of the room. It was no use to cover her feet. They were warm to my touch. How they managed to stay that way when they were always uncovered was a mystery, just like the woman they belonged to.

The fire had dimmed down. I stoked it and added a few more logs. Maiyun retired to her bed next to Skye, content to have me in the room.

I thought about what my father and grandfather asked of me. In my gut and in my heart, I knew they were right. Fear kept me from taking her. If things went wrong, I could not bring myself to take her life, though that is exactly what I would have to do to protect the clan.

Shanuk said she was strong and would not be turned so easily. This I knew was true. If she was the woman the legend spoke of, her children would be a valuable asset. I was sure that the Shadows knew this as well. If I claimed her first, they would not be able to sire her children, but they could unite with her and gain control of our clan. Either way, she was valuable—too valuable.

I twisted a branch in my hands until it was nothing more than shredded fibers. I tossed it into the flames and watched it burn.

Skye moaned and jerked. She was having another nightmare—the same one as before, about the Shadows, no doubt. Like her, I had been dreaming about the fearsome clan of Seattle for several weeks. That clan had been severed from Damon's branch for years. What interest could they possibly have in Skye?

Unlike Damon's clan, the Seattle clan had taken to vampirism to increase their powers, or so they thought. It was a disgusting ritual that found its roots in the darker side of witchcraft. Despite their crude habits, they were a dangerous lot.

Skye kicked violently and shouted some inaudible plea. I walked toward her and placed my hand over her forehead. She whimpered and relaxed beneath my caress. I wanted so badly to hold her and keep her safe, but with me she would never be safe. My gifts were strong, but tethered by precarious thread that could be severed with a sudden burst of anger. If I allowed Skye into my heart and bound her to my soul, what possible hope would she have if I ever lost control?

I ran through the various solutions to my problems until the sun peeked through the trees. Skye would awaken soon. It was time for me to leave.

Chapter 20

*B*itterness *is hard to swallow but it calms an angry stomach.*

~ S k y e ~

Khalen arrived early that morning as promised with fresh eggs, milk, and bread. I awoke to the smell of coffee with caramel. He placed a steaming mug of the sweetened joe with goat milk on the end table beside the bed. Bacon sizzled on the stove and the fire had been stoked and fed.

My vision was fuzzy as it adjusted to the sunlight streaming in through the windows. I sat up, and then remembered that I had no clothes on. Quickly, I grabbed the blanket and covered my chest.

Khalen laughed and handed me my shirt. "Honestly, Skye, I am a doctor."

I waited for him to turn before donning my shirt. "Right now," I said, "I'm not your patient, so please allow me some semblance of dignity."

He walked back over to the kitchen across the small room, and tended to the bacon.

I quickly grabbed my white capris and slid them on

under the covers. My hooded sweatshirt was next. I noticed there was a soft and fuzzy blanket on the bed that was not there last night when I fell asleep. It smelled like Khalen's place and I smiled.

He must have noticed. "I brought that over last night when I realized that Gregg and Ro did not have any soft blankets."

"Thank you." I sat back and took a sip of coffee. It had a hint of coconut. "Hmm, this is good—creamy."

"I added coconut milk along with the goat milk."

I took another sip. "I like it."

He smiled. "You sleep better when you have something soft against your neck," he said, as if in deep thought. "You dream less, too."

I frowned, wondering how long he had stayed with me after delivering the blanket. "Did you get any sleep at all?"

He flipped the bacon over then cracked four eggs in another pan. "Some."

I took another sip of my coffee. Maiyun was by Khalen's side, waiting for the next tidbit he tossed her way.

I shook my head. "You are undoing all my training," I said. "She is not allowed in the kitchen when I cook."

Khalen raised his brow. "You're not cooking."

I stood up and padded my way toward him. "Do you need any help?" I rummaged through the cupboards looking for plates.

"No," he said.

I found the plates and began setting the breakfast

counter. The coffee press was empty, so I filled it again with the hot water still boiling on the stove.

Khalen shook his head and smiled. "Have you always been this willful?"

I carefully placed the silverware on the napkins. "Meaning?"

"I said I didn't need help and yet you ignore me."

"I'm not ignoring you. Not needing help doesn't mean don't help."

He rolled his eyes and took the plates up from the counter. "Sit, Skye." He refilled my coffee and waited for me to comply before handing it to me. "Are you always so commanding?"

He laughed. "Well, you know my father, and have yet to meet my grandfather." He looked up between dark eyelashes that gave him a byronic appeal.

No arguing with that. Case himself was commanding. I could only imagine what Shanuk was like. Although he was not too intimidating at the hospital, presuming that truly was Shanuk. A part of me still thought he was just a figment of my drug-induced imagination.

Khalen served up breakfast, and then came around to join me. I closed my eyes to pray. He held my hands in his and said a prayer of his own.

"Great Spirit, you know what is best. I ask that you put your hand on us and make your wishes known. Amen."

"Amen," I said. "Interesting request, Khalen. Care to explain?"

"No." He took a sip of coffee and stared across the kitchen at apparently nothing.

"Okay." I noticed that he had only fried up egg whites for me. I didn't care for the yolks, but he didn't know that, at least not from my telling him. He also seemed to know that I loved cayenne pepper sprinkled on top, and extra-crispy bacon. Even my toast was light and warm, with a spread of coconut oil and Marmite—a yeast extract that many Americans have never heard about, let alone eaten. Either he was incredibly observant, or he read my mind.

For what seemed to be several minutes, we ate in silence, which I appreciated.

"I hope you don't mind," he finally spoke.

"Not at all," I replied.

He frowned. "How do you know what I'm referring to?"

"Well, I figured since you so often read my thoughts without permission, I figured that clan etiquette allowed me to do the same." I met his intimidating stare and tried hard not to blink first. "You were wondering if I'm offended with you invading my space, and making me eggs the way I like them, cooking my bacon to my satisfaction, and even dressing my toast with perfection," I guessed. There was absolutely no way to read his thoughts when he was so guarded all the time, but I wanted to give him something to think about either way.

Though still quite guarded, he looked genuinely concerned. He pursed his lips. "Your mind reading leaves something to be desired." He sipped his coffee, expecting me to question his comment.

I sipped my coffee in silence and continued to enjoy my meal. I could feel his eyes on me, now and then, looking away only when he thought I would turn my head.

"Would you like to return to work soon?" he asked.

I nodded. "I miss it a bit."

"I have to go in today, but I will take you with me on Tuesday, if you're up to it."

"Yes, that would be great. My training is complete, then?"

He frowned. "No, but it's as far as Case is willing to take you for now."

"So I can move back to my apartment?"

His knuckles turned white. "If you so choose."

"It is my home," I added, quietly.

"So is this," he mumbled. "You are one of us." When his eyes met mine, there was something different about them. They were deep green now, like the Caribbean waters.

I hadn't really thought of myself as being part of a family since my own passed on. The thought of being a part of one now made me a bit apprehensive. I had held my friends at a comfortable distance for so long, I wasn't sure if I could be close to anyone, even if they were considered family.

"I'm sure Gregg and Ro would not appreciate my extended stay in their cabin."

"Would it be so intolerable for you to stay in mine?" His words had an edge to them.

"Intolerable, no. Improper, yes."

"Improper?"

"Yes," I explained. "I'm old-fashioned in that sense. Although I do enjoy your company, it is not appropriate for me to live with you."

He laughed. "And what would make it appropriate?"

I frowned and fumbled with the edge of the rust and green placemat that was fraying on the edges. I didn't want to mention marriage. That idea was preposterous and not anything I was ready for anytime soon. "For us to be related," I said. "Like brother and sister."

His brow arched. "Brother and sister?" The deep green in his eyes faded to a murky gold. He stood and gathered the dirty dishes. He laughed and shook his head. "An impossible relationship."

I suddenly felt a chill in the room, as if the temperature had dropped several degrees. It was clear he didn't like my solution.

"I'm open to hearing your thoughts," I said.

Again, he laughed. "You don't want to hear my thoughts right now, Skye." The edge in his voice grew sharper. I shrank back.

As he busied himself in the kitchen, I gathered my things and then ran my brush through my hair. I planned to leave it down today, and perhaps go for a walk.

Khalen put away the dishes, and then left just as quietly as he came. When I finished brushing my teeth, he was gone and the coldness went with him.

I strolled outside with Maiyun beside me. She confidently led me toward camp. I was drawn toward Khalen's thinking log by the water. There was a small fire crackling, and a very old man sitting on the log, bundled in a blanket.

"Skye," he said, his voice frail but deep and commanding. "Come sit with me."

Maiyun led me to him as if obeying some silent command. When I saw the man's face and unbelievable eyes, I gasped. "It's you." I was sure it was Pastor Mark, the same man who visited me in the hospital. There was no mistaking his eyes, or the shape of his strong face. He looked much older now, and perhaps a bit sad. I sat beside him and touched his frail arm. "You came to me in the hospital."

The old man nodded. His short silver hair glistened with sunlight. "I did," he said.

"Why?"

"I needed to know if you were the one the legend spoke of. I felt your presence and it drew me to you."

I shook my head. "I am no legend, sir, I assure you." I thought for a moment of the young pastor who visited me that day. It surely was not this frail old man. "How did you get to the hospital?"

He smiled, displaying the same brilliant set of teeth Pastor Mark had. "The spirit knows no bounds," he said. "I was merely there in thought."

"That's why no one else saw you?"

He nodded. "We don't have much time, Skye, so I'm afraid I must be blunt with you." He reached over and took my hand. "You are the one the legend speaks of, and you are pivotal to what will come."

I started to open my mouth, be he silenced me with an open hand.

"The Shadows will come for you. That is evident. You will be tested severely. Your outcome will determine the direction our kind will take, so be wise, my dear. Don't underestimate the Shadows. They are crafty and very gifted."

My stomach turned as if it were caught in a tornado. My head filled with clouded thoughts, and fear began to grip me. "I'm not the one," I whispered, shaking my head.

His dark blue-green eyes studied mine and peered down into the depths of my soul. I was vulnerable in his presence. Shielding him was useless. Instinctively, I knew it.

"It is never useless," he claimed. "Once you believe another is stronger than yourself, you have already lost the battle. Remember this, with God, all things are possible. If you forget that truth and rely only on your own power, you will fail."

He gripped my hands firmly. His were cold. "Case will collect me soon," he said. "Forgive my haste and my rudeness. I am Shanuk, Khalen's grandfather. We have asked him to take you as his mate."

My eyes widened. "His mate?" Suddenly, I felt like property about to be sold.

Shanuk nodded. "Yes, but he will not do so without your consent."

Again, I tried to speak, but his hand stopped the flow of my words.

His eyes grew dark. "It is imperative that this union take place, and soon."

This time, I did speak, breaking his barrier of control. "I am not property, sir, and I am certainly nobody's mate."

Case came toward us, and then quietly sat next to me. If I had any sense at all, I would bolt and run as far from this place as possible. Ridiculous notion, I reminded myself, especially when Shanuk could project faster than I could ever run and Case could disable me with a simple thought.

"Spirians" are different from humans," Shanuk explained. "We are caught between the physical and the spiritual realms. When we join, the union binds us. We truly become one spirit with two physical bodies."

"And what makes you think Khalen wants this union to occur?"

"It is not his choice."

I started to stand. Case pulled me back down. "Khalen took a mate several years ago," he explained. "Her name was Valerie. She was Ian and Aidan's sister. A fiery lass with strong gifts. She was seduced by the Shadows and was easily turned. This created a gateway between us and the Shadows—a very dangerous and destructive gateway. Because Khalen and Valerie were joined, the Shadows and Protected ones were also joined." He gripped my hand. "Khalen had to kill her to save the clan."

I tried to swallow the bitter fluid in my mouth, but my throat was paralyzed. My dreams were making sense. Valerie was the redheaded woman, and I was Khalen, but who was her lover? I shook my head with frustration. "He's worried that if I turn, he must kill me as well."

Both Shanuk and Case nodded.

"Once you are joined with Khalen," said Case, "the Shadows cannot unite with you unless you choose to join their kind. If you and Khalen are not joined, the Shadows will take you by force. They will not ask your permission."

"Joined?"

Shanuk pulled my chin toward him. "Your child will determine the direction of this clan, which expands beyond this camp you see here."

I laughed. "My child? I cannot get pregnant," I said. "My eggs were exhausted years ago."

"Like I said," Shanuk explained. "It is different for our kind. You cannot bear the child of a human. You are not human."

"I'm 45 years old."

He shrugged. "And I'm over 300. Age means nothing to the Protected and Shadows alike. We are more spirit than human. Spirits do not age. It is only our physical bodies that age."

I shook my head, having a very difficult time believing the words coming out of their wisdom-endowed mouths. "Khalen is a train wreck waiting to happen," I said. "He doesn't know what he wants. One moment, he's hovering over me like some overprotective brother, and the next, he's pushing me away as if I had the plague. I'm confident in saying this union won't work."

Case squeezed my hand, painfully reminding me of my pitiful stature in this camp. "Skye, you must offer yourself to Khalen, or he will not take you as his mate."

"Wife," I corrected. "I am nobody's mate."

Case rolled his eyes. "Wife," he confirmed.

Chapter 21

*T*houghts are powerful things. They can create or destroy.

There was much for me to think about. Maiyun and I strolled around the camp. Aidan and Ian caught up with us by the stream that marked the border of our land. I really was not in the mood for idle conversation, or for their playful advances.

"Your mind is heavy, lass. What weighs upon it so?" asked Aidan. He draped his heavy arm around my shoulders. He looked dashing in his faded black jeans and white pullover sweater.

I told him what Shanuk said, and about Case's request.

"Khalen doesn't need your permission, ye know. He can take you anytime he likes. His stature gives him that right, which is why no one challenges him."

My eyes grew wide. "He wouldn't dare."

Ian's level stare told me otherwise. "If given no choice, he would for sure."

He too looked good in blue jeans. His dark green, button-up shirt made his eyes light up like the aurora borealis.

Why these two men were still available eluded me.

"His father and grandfather have requested that he join with you. He cannot do otherwise."

"So," I said. "It is not his choice to join with me, but his father's?"

Aidan shook his head. "No, missy. Khalen likes you sure enough. Ye saw a bit of his possession in the field after our flight."

"Then why doesn't he say anything to me? Why not just come out and ask me?"

"That is something to ask him, don't ye think?" said Aidan.

Ian looked as if he wanted to explain something, and then bit his lower lip. What he wanted to say was as clear as the pain that clouded his eyes.

"I know about Valerie," I said.

Both of them became uncomfortably quiet. I wasn't sure if it was because they vowed to keep Khalen's secret, or that the truth of the ordeal was too much to recount. Either way, I wanted to change the subject. "Why haven't either of you married?"

They both laughed.

Ian's expression resembled a young boy's after successfully snatching a fresh baked cookie from a forbidden cookie sheet. "Why settle for one lass when so many are available?"

I jabbed him hard in the ribs with my elbow. He pitched sharply away from me, laughing.

"Ugh," he grabbed his ribs. "Was it something I said?"

I looked over at Aidan, who was clearly enjoying his brother's comeuppance. "And how about you?"

Aidan's mischievous smile matched the fire in his playful eyes—all charm and no sincerity to back it. "I'm still waitin' on you, lass."

I laughed and rolled my eyes. "Both of you have much to offer. I'm honestly curious."

He bent down and picked up a stick. "I haven't found the right one," he said matter of factly. He tossed the stick. It whirled into the air, scaring a flock of birds into flight, and then bounced off a tree with a thick dull thud.

"Hmm." It was clear that I would not get a better response than that, so I gave up the battle.

"A Spirian union is permanent," Ian finally offered. "There are no divorces, or change of heart after the fact. The mate you choose should be your second soul, one that completes you. They are not easy to find."

I thought about Khalen. He and I were opposites, for sure, like fire and ice. There was also something deeper, though, something I never felt with Derrick. I was drawn to Khalen in a magnetic sort of way. It was a force I couldn't deny, despite how he infuriated me at times. We were connected, and when he touched me, it charged my soul, like thousands of electrons rushing to my core and filling it with brilliant light. I never felt that with Derrick, as much as I loved him. I was not convinced, however, that I affected Khalen the same way.

Maiyun whined, then backed up a few paces, looking intently into the dark shadows of the forest. The brothers peered ahead as well, their bodies stiff and alert. "What do you see?" I asked.

Aidan scanned the thick trees and brush. "We best turn back." He tightened his protective hold on me as we turned around.

Ian stayed a few paces behind.

"Nice day for a stroll," a voice called out from the trees. It was a man's voice, but there were others with him. I could hear their steps.

"We were just leaving," said Ian. He pressed his hand against his brother's lower back, prompting him to continue retreating.

"No cause to leave on our account, Ian, my boy." A man with short brown hair stepped out from behind the trees. Two blonde women stood beside him—tall by my standards, but still a foot shorter than the man accompanying them. They were the ones who demanded to see me at the center. I was sure of it.

"What do ye want, Talon?" asked Aidan, in a phlegmatic tone.

"A bit of conversation is all," the man said. His words were thick with a mixed accent of British, Irish, and a hint of Scottish.

Maiyun growled and lowered her head. I scratched her neck, more for my comfort than hers, but her ears remained flat against her large skull.

Talon approached us. The women stayed behind, clearly wary of Maiyun's warning. A chill charged the air.

The hair on Aidan's arm rose in response and brushed my skin. "Best stay where ye are, Talon. She doesn't take well to strangers."

Talon smiled, "The woman or her bitch," he said through clenched teeth.

Maiyun's growl deepened.

The two women stepped back further into the tree line.

Talon stared through Maiyun; the muscles twitched and tightened in his jaw. "Who's your woman?" he asked, nodding in my direction.

"She belongs to Khalen," Aidan said.

I felt my muscles tense and anger rising up from my gut. I belonged to no one, I wanted to say, but kept my words choked in my throat.

Talon's inquisitive expression indicated he knew more than just the mendacity of Aidan's words. "They are not joined," he said with surprising authority.

Aidan shifted his feet. He looked to me like he intended to lie but then thought better of it. "Soon to be," he said.

"Why are you here?" Ian asked. The red flush in his skin betrayed his impatience. It was clear he did not like where this conversation was heading.

Talon focused on him and smiled. "This is neutral land, is it not?"

"It is," Aidan responded, "but that was not his question."

Talon turned his attention to me. His eyes scanned me

up and down twice. The sneer on his lips conveyed his assessment. "She's rather plain to attract the likes of Khalen, don't you think?" Then, as if not humiliating me enough, he pointedly looked at my feet. "Does she not have shoes?"

Both Ian and Aidan answered simultaneously. "She doesn't like wearing them."

Talon scoffed. "How quaint."

Ian started to say something, but Aidan stopped him with a glance.

Talon rubbed his smooth chin as if thinking something through. "Khalen would not have interest in her. Unless," he paused, "her value lies more in her gifts?" He cocked his head with curiosity and stepped toward me.

His probing thoughts sent chills up my spine as if he were tapping my soul, seeking the answers he needed to confirm his suspicions. Maiyun moved between me and Talon, bristling like her wolf forebears, intent and fierce. Talon ignored her as if she was not worth his while to contend with right now. Maiyun's fight stance was not something ordinary people would disregard, yet this man showed no fear, absolutely none. Now, Maiyun's hackles rose, making it clear that she was not going to relinquish her position. She lowered her head and bared her teeth. Her growl reverberated throughout her body, shaking my leg.

Talon focused his black eyes on Maiyun. His intent was clear and my protective response was just as swift. I willed a shield to spring up between us, but his intention only grew stronger.

Clearly he was testing me, scanning for a chink in my armor. I funneled my energy into keeping him out, but the humming in my mind was dizzying. In desperation, I thrust my energy recklessly outward.

Talon flew back and slammed against a tree as if he weighed no more than a paper doll in the wake of a wind storm. His hair was disheveled, his gaze slightly vacant. He slid down to the ground like thick oil descending a smooth wall, stunned.

I stared at him, unable to move.

The two women gaped, their eyes wide with disbelief. They said nothing. The taller one made a move to help Talon steady himself, but he made a dismissive gesture that stopped her short. His eyes were sharp and dark as obsidian.

"Skye," he said darkly, his voice a low rumble. The vibration of his tone made my bones quiver. How did he know my name?

"You've broken the treaty," he added. An ominous smile spread across his face.

"You provoked her," said Ian. "You shouldn't be here."

Talon waved his arm. "Neutral ground," he said, still smiling. "She attacked first."

My eyes narrowed. "You were going to hurt my dog."

Talon looked smug and pleased with himself. "Gifts, indeed," he said, rubbing the back of his head.

Aidan grabbed me and led me away from the threesome before I said anything more.

Ian stayed behind. He caught up with us later after we entered the camp.

"Blimey," Ian said, panting with excitement. "Did ye see that?"

"Yes," said Aidan. "I saw it. Case will not be pleased."

"He was trying to hurt Maiyun," I said, still a bit fuzzy and rattled.

"We were on neutral ground," said Ian. "He would have thought twice before using his gift on us or her."

"Well, the treaty has been breached, now," said Aidan, "and there will be hell to pay for it."

"Why?" I asked. "I was only protecting my dog. I know nothing about the treaty."

"It does not matter," said Aidan. "You gave them an excuse to request council." He turned me to look at him. "They have the right take you from us."

"No one has the right to take me anywhere," I said.

Aidan's face grew firm and grim. "They have the right to kill you if they see fit," he said.

I shook my head. "No, I can't believe that."

Aidan grabbed my shoulders and gently shook me. "This is a different world, Skye. Human rules and etiquette do not follow suite here. Accept the way things are, or perish trying to fight them."

The darkness in his eyes was frightening, but not as much as the words he spoke. "I won't give in to them," I said. "They may destroy my body, but I'm keeping my soul."

"I don't think they want your soul," said Ian. "They want you."

"Case will not allow them to take me," I reasoned.

Ian patted my hand. "He won't have a choice."

Chapter 22

Fear is a prison to the soul; it lives in a dark place where demons reside. Only faith provides the means for escape.

Aidan and Ian explained what happened to Case. The look on the old man's face was more than concern, there was fear mixed with anger. When he glanced in my direction, my soul shrank and I wanted to melt into the soft earth beneath my feet. Case ducked into his yurt, as Ian and Aidan were sent away.

Aidan mouthed the words, "It'll be okay," as he passed by me.

Ian simply touched my arm with compassion, and then followed his brother.

I felt like a prisoner about to walk the lonely green mile on my way to execution. More than anything, I wanted Khalen to be here. Somehow, he made sense of things. I felt safe in his presence. Now, I just felt vulnerable.

Finally, Case opened his door. "Skye, come inside."

My legs felt shaky, my heart heavy and constricted. I followed him through the entrance and saw a very grim-looking

Shanuk gesturing for me to sit across from him. Maiyun curled up next to me and laid her head on my foot.

The old man was wrapped in a wool blanket, yet he was shaking as if he were freezing cold. "Tell us what happened, Skye."

"He was going to hurt Maiyun," I said.

Case, sitting next to his father, narrowed his eyes, not in anger, but with curiosity. "How do you know this, Skye?"

"His intent," I said, shaking my head. "It was violent. He meant her harm."

"How confident are you with that assumption?" asked Shanuk. His voice was shaky and tired.

"Very confident," I said. "I feel people's intentions. I always have, since I was a young girl."

A smile swept across Case's face. "So you know when someone is lying?"

I nodded. "Absolutely."

"It was a trap," said Shanuk. "They baited her."

"We can't prove it," said Case.

"He knew my name," I added.

Case looked down and shook his head slowly. "News travels fast."

"What will happen?" I asked.

Both of their faces grew pale and grim. Shanuk stared down at the floor.

Case took a deep breath and closed his eyes for a moment. "They will come for you," he said.

"Should I leave?" I swallowed hard.

Case shook his head. "There is nowhere for you to go, Skye. You must face them."

Shanuk shook his fist. "We knew this day would come. Now we are out of time."

Eve opened the door, her face pale. "Case. It's Traeger. He is requesting a council."

Case pounded the arm of the old couch. "Damn Shadows. They waste no time." He stood and followed her out the door. He looked back at me. "Stay here."

I moved over to sit next to Shanuk. He reached out and took my hand. "You will be fine," he tried to assure me.

"I don't feel fine," I whispered. "I feel as if I have ruined everything and have placed you and the clan at great risk."

"There are no mistakes, my dear. God orchestrates things perfectly, despite our best efforts to control them."

"Will He be with me?" I asked.

"If you allow Him to be," he said. "Simply ask for His protection, and have faith that He will follow through."

I nodded. Having faith is harder than it should be, sometimes. "I don't want to be a Shadow," I said.

"I know." His smile was warming, but still I felt fear in the core of my soul.

Case entered the yurt, followed by two men. The older one looked identical to Khalen, but with short hair and a sparse beard shadowing his face. He even moved like Khalen. Images of the redheaded woman's lover flashed in my mind. This man was the other person in my dream. My face felt cold and drained of blood.

"Shanuk," he said, nodding in the old man's direction.

The two men sat on the couch, across from the one Shanuk and I occupied. Case pulled up another chair for himself.

"Skye," he said. "This is Traeger," pointing at the older man. "And Seth, his son." He then looked at the two men. "Traeger, Seth, this is Skye Taylor."

Seth looked indifferent. His resemblance to his father was evident, though he lacked the strong jaw line and hazel eyes. Seth's eyes were more brown, and his hair more blond. He looked to be around 30 years old, which may have meant he was near 60 in physical years.

Traeger smiled, making me feel like dessert. "Khalen always did have great taste in women." His voice lacked the silky undertone of Khalen's.

I frowned, and then looked over at Case. His eyes pleaded with me to keep silent.

"Skye," said Traeger. "Tell me what happened today, with Talon."

I took a deep breath and closed my eyes for a moment, trying to escape his entrancing stare. I wasn't sure how much I should tell him, so I chose to keep it short and direct. "He and his companions approached us," I said. "My dog, Maiyun, growled in warning. The women stayed back, but Talon came forward. He focused on Maiyun. His intent was to harm her."

Seth suddenly looked interested but said nothing.

Traeger sat upright like a snake about to strike. "His intent?"

"That's what I said."

Maiyun moved closer to me, her ears alert and focused on Traeger. She did not trust the man, but knew there was no immediate danger. I scratched behind her ear to offer some assurance.

Traeger thought about reaching over to pet her, but quickly reconsidered when she changed her posture. It was subtle, but he certainly picked up on it. He noticed my response and smiled.

"You read intentions," he said, sounding much too pleased.

I tried to decipher Case and Shanuk's response, but they were solemn and not offering much in the way of direction.

"Talon baited her," Case interjected. "He broke the treaty first."

Traeger laughed. "You disappoint me, Case. Both of us know that intention does not count as a breach in treaty."

"She was protecting her dog against an attack," said Case.

Traeger sat back, a slight crease cresting his trimmed brows. "A potential attack."

"He was going to hurt Maiyun," I said. "I was not going to wait for it to happen."

He looked at me as if I had made the worst mistake ever. His eyes were dark, like molten chocolate with slivers of green. "Woman," he said, his voice smooth and calculating, "you drew first blood."

I wanted to remind him that my name was Skye and not Woman, but thankfully thought better of the idea. Instead, I raised my chin and met his piercing stare. "I shielded him back, nothing more."

He looked away from me as if dismissing my insolence. "Case, she will come with us."

"On what grounds?" he asked.

"I believe you know the answer to that question, as does your dying father."

Shanuk smiled at that bit of arrogance. "I'll live long enough to see this out," he said. His voice had found a strength I had not heard in it before. "Take her," he commanded, "but, respect her choice." There was power in that last statement and Traeger knew it.

He glared. The energy in the yurt increased tenfold. My heart raced with it, and my lungs labored against the added pressure. Traeger had no intentions of challenging the old man, dying or not, nor did Seth. It was clear who held the power in this room and it remained undisputed.

Traeger nodded. "Understood." He reached for my arm and Maiyun growled. "The bitch stays," he commanded.

Case held Maiyun's collar. "We'll take care of her, Skye."

Traeger's grip on my arm was unyielding and painful. I fought the urge to cry out, not wanting to offer him any satisfaction. His strength was harsh and commanding. I did my best to keep pace with him, but still felt the humility of being dragged like a disobedient mongrel. He shoved me next to Seth in the back seat of his black town car then slammed the door. The driver waited patiently for Traeger to settle into the passenger seat before setting the car in motion. Seth curled his long fingers around my arm, making it very clear that I was imprisoned with no chance of escape. The doors locked as we drove away.

Chapter 23

The illusion that we, as mere humans, are in control, is a poor excuse to assume command of the masses. The only thing we control is our own actions; the rest is up to God.

~ K h a l e n ~

Something was wrong. I could feel it deep in my gut. As I drove into the camp, the place was void of activity, empty. I parked the car and planned to head straight for Skye's cabin.

Case waited for me. His face and eyes were void of emotion. Something was wrong—very wrong.

"Where is she?" I demanded.

"Come with me," Case said.

"What happened?" I was not in the mood for mysteries.

Case turned toward his yurt. I reached out and grabbed his arm. It was a mistake and a very disrespectful one at that, but one of pure reaction. "Father, please, tell me."

"Inside," he commanded then jerked his arm away making it very clear that he was still in control. I felt grateful for still being able to stand after my careless attempt to stop him. Like Shanuk, Case could have flattened me where I stood with a simple thought, but he didn't. He knew my actions were driven by emotion. That was still no excuse and I knew it. That subtle realization was probably the only thing that saved me from a painful and memorable reprimand.

He and Shanuk recounted the day's events in grueling detail. My stomach twisted. I should have stayed at camp and kept her safe.

"What were Ian and Aidan thinking?" I asked, fighting the urge to castrate them both. "They know better than to take her from the grounds."

"Khalen," Shanuk said. "This was bound to happen. You know that."

My fists tightened; the knuckles turned white against the intense pull of my skin. My thoughts swam like cresting waves of water, heavy and full of destruction. "Where is she?" I demanded. I knew the tone of my voice was out of line, but now I didn't care. My elders' wrath would be a welcome distraction to the anger that coursed through my veins.

"With Traeger," said Case.

That name burned like acid in my ears. "No!" I screamed. My mind was numb with rage. With a wave of my hand, the pictures flew off the walls, the windows shattered and the lights exploded.

"Khalen!" Shanuk commanded. "This won't save her."

I dropped to my knees, cursing my very existence. My twin, the malediction of my life, had taken Valerie from me, and would soon consume Skye.

"She is strong," said Case. "Have faith."

My faith was weak, right now, if it even existed. Traeger nearly destroyed me when he turned Valerie. Now he returned for something even more precious and there was nothing I could do to stop it. "I must get her back."

"Not now," said Shanuk. "The time will come."

My gut churned. "They tricked her, Grandfather. The treaty is broken."

"Be patient," he said, his voice strong and direct. "Your time will come—trust me."

It was hard to not trust him. His wisdom had centuries of proof to bind it. He had strong foresight, and I could not deny that. I found peace in it, but still I wanted to claim what was mine. "I will not allow Traeger to take her."

Shanuk smiled reassuringly. "She makes that choice on her own, Khalen."

Case placed his hand on my shoulder, both as a comfort and as a warning. I had gone too far tonight and he had allowed it to a point, and that point had been reached. "It is in God's hands now, Son," he said. "Stay connected with her. Offer comfort. Traeger is counting on your anger to rule your actions. Do not give him what he wants."

Chapter 24

Either by blood or inheritance, the bond between souls is permanent even if it is unwarranted.

~ S k y e ~

We drove for an hour and a half. I recognized the Lucky Dog Casino as we passed it, and so I knew we were near the small town of Hoodsport. You could easily drive right past it without knowing you'd been there.

We reached a gated driveway. It was too dark for me to see any detail, let alone read signs. The driver pressed a series of numbers on a keypad and waited for the long, black, wrought iron gate to slide open. We drove along a winding path that ended in a circular drive. The driver pulled up under a portico and parked the car.

Seth's death grip remained firm on my arm. Where did he think I was going to go? It's dark, I'm blind, and the nearest town is at least five miles away. He opened his door, and then drug me across the seat—a true gentleman.

Apparently he hadn't led many blind people about. I tripped on three stairs, and nearly banged full on into the edge of the doorjamb. Clipping it with my arm was painful enough. The entranceway sounded huge. The lighting was very dim, and insufficient for me to see.

We continued down a long hall with a strip of carpet running through the center of the hardwood flooring. Seth shoved me into a room on the right then forced me into a hard wooden chair.

"Ah," said a very deep voice. "Face to face with the legend at last."

I really wished people would stop calling me that. It was silly, really, like comic book stuff. I was anything but a legend. An unfortunate blind woman who fell into an invisible quantum hole to Crazyville would be more accurate.

"What is your name?" asked the deep-voiced man. I could not see his face, just a shape of someone who resembled Frankenstein waking from a long sleep. His face was rectangular, and his dark hair fell in disarray around his head.

"Skye," I said. My voice betrayed my apprehension. My hands were cold and slightly damp.

"The winged one," he mumbled.

It was the Scottish translation for my name. Not many people knew that.

"You broke the treaty, Skye. Why?" he asked.

"I didn't know about the treaty, and Talon was intending to hurt my dog."

"Who are you paired with?" he asked.

I frowned and shook my head. "Paired?"

He sat back and cocked his head. "Who is your mate?"

"Khalen," I lied, and prayed that the shield I formed around myself was sufficient to hide it.

"She lies, Damon," Talon said. I didn't know he was in the room until now. "Their union has not yet taken place."

I could almost hear the deep-voiced man smile. There was a glimmer of white on his face. "Fascinating." He was silent for a moment.

I made my shield stronger until it hummed all around me.

"Hmm," he said. "Case has taught you well. Your shield is strong, but not strong enough."

"Ah!" I cried as a bolt of electricity pierced my gut, making me curl forward. It's only an illusion, I told myself. Ignore it. My body was shaking now as I focused on finding my ground. The pain eased. Father, help me, I silently prayed.

"I don't take lightly to lies, woman. Understood?"

I nodded. It was hard to breathe and I felt as if I had just been winded with a sharp upward blow to my diaphragm.

"Seeing you have broken the treaty, we have first rights with you."

Traeger cleared his throat. "On one condition, Father."

"What condition?" he said, emphasizing both words.

Traeger stepped toward his father. "It must be her choice." He said it softly as if the words were meant for only Damon's ears.

His heavy fist slammed down upon the solid wood desk.

"By whose demand?" Damon's question slithered from his lips like venom milked from a snake.

"Shanuk's."

The old man's eyes grew wide, his breath expanded his already broad chest. "She is a woman, she does not have a choice. I will not honor such a condition."

"I gave him my word," said Traeger. "The condition will be honored."

"Stupid boy!" the man yelled, causing the walls to shake. "Why would you honor such a request?"

"Once Skye sees the truth of things, she will accept her position willingly." There was poison within those words. The sound of them left a bitter taste in my mouth. His intention was vague, but confident nonetheless.

The old man stood and paced behind his chair. "I leave her in your charge, Traeger. Do not fail."

Traeger nodded then lifted me from my chair. "Come," he said. "You will share my chamber."

My stomach, still aching from the powerful blow, churned with the thought of sharing Traeger's chamber. He resembled Khalen far too closely and was not short on charm. There was something about him that drew me in and it frightened me. "I don't suppose I have a choice in the matter?" I was trying to sound calm and unaffected by his closeness, but the tremble in my voice betrayed me.

"No, you don't." His grip tightened around my arm. He led me up two flights of stairs, then down another long hallway. We entered a room on the left. He turned on the lights, but they did little to help me see.

I wondered how much he knew about my vision impairment. If he believed in the legend, he already knew I was blind. I was certainly not going to offer any more information than was absolutely necessary.

He guided me toward the bed then sat me down. "If you choose to run," he warned. "I will sever your tendons."

"Where do you expect I'd go?" Not to mention I could heal the tendons with merely a thought.

He huffed. "Women don't always think rationally when they are scared."

I fought the urge to demonstrate just how irrational a woman could be when pushed beyond her limits of feminine control. "I have nothing to fear, I assure you."

"So long as you obey, no."

The word "obey" played upon my nerves like an amateur's trumpet. "Well then, you might as well kill me now, sir, because I have never been one to obey."

"You will learn."

His careless choice of words dissolved his charming façade and weakened his alluring spell on my soul. My confidence returned. I didn't know whether I should feel sorry for the man, or do as he suggested and take a chance at escaping.

He would not kill the so-called legend. According to Shanuk, the pivot of mankind's future rested in the birth of my child, or rather who sired my child. The whole thing was ridiculous, and made me feel like a brood mare pining for the winning stallion. Honestly, how could the direction of all mankind be influenced by the birth of one child? Not to mention I was clearly barren.

He walked toward the right side of the room. In this light, it was like looking through water in dim light. Everything was fuzzy and shadowed.

"Would you like something to drink?" he asked, the alluring calm back in his voice.

"Warm goat milk and cinnamon honey, please."

He laughed. "Your choices are wine, brandy, or sherry."

"Nothing, thank you." I didn't want to let my guard down and dull my senses with alcohol. That was an advantage I was not willing to give him.

He poured himself something, and then came to sit next to me on the bed. By the smell, I guessed his choice was brandy—B&B to be exact.

"I'm curious," he said, "about what Khalen has told you."

I shrugged. "Not much, really."

He cupped my chin and turned my head to face him. "You're a terrible liar, Skye. Perhaps another reminder is needed to make you heed my father's warning?"

I bit my lip, curbing my instinct to sharpen my tongue and say something inappropriately sarcastic. "Khalen calls you Shadows."

"Yes," he drawled. "I am aware of that."

"He said you suck the light out of people until they have nothing but darkness left in their hearts and anger in their soul."

Traeger laughed. "And does my soul look angry to you?"

I studied his aura for a moment. Its vibration was low and the colors were dull and lifeless. He kept it close to his body, which typically meant he had something to hide or protect. "No, it looks sad and suppressed."

"Sad," he said with a deep roaring laugh. He waved his arm. "I have all this, and you think I'm sad?"

"Well, I'm not exactly sure what all this might be, but I'm quite certain your soul is sad."

"Hmph." He took a sip of his brandy, and then swallowed without even taking the time to savor the drink.

"Benedictine is best appreciated when allowed to rest upon the tongue," I offered.

"And how, pray tell, do you know what I drink?" He adjusted himself on the bed to face me more directly.

"Forgive me. I'm assuming you drink B&B, brandy and Benedictine."

"You are correct. Blindness has gifted you with amazing senses."

He was either stating the obvious, or fishing for information. I remained silent. I felt the heat of his scrutiny and the weight of his stare.

"You're rather plain-looking," he commented.

"I prefer to think of myself as practical." His rude comment was not enough to rile me. I knew I was no beauty queen by any measure.

"I see what my twin likes in you."

My expression must have changed and he was quick to read it.

"Oh ho ho," he chuckled. "You didn't know?"

I said nothing. Traeger's close appearance to Khalen should have been a clue, but one that had obviously evaded me.

"Khalen was always good at keeping secrets. I suppose he never told you about his dark side, either, eh?" He took another sip, this time allowing the burning liquid to rest upon his tongue.

Doubt began to creep in my thoughts, and Traeger's energy field grew, feeding on the negative emotion he had spawned. He smiled.

"The Protected," he growled. "They think they're so good, so pure." He laughed. "Khalen tries to drown his blood in their light, hoping it will save him from himself."

Khalen had always been difficult for me to read. His intentions were muddled most of the time, rarely distinct. In my heart, though, I knew he was no Shadow.

Traeger's eyes met mine. He was reading my thoughts. "You're wrong. He is one—my twin, Damon's son, by blood." He moved closer to me. "You've felt his anger, his hate. It makes you feel uncomfortable, edgy and unpredictable." He traced his finger down my spine. "You have felt the coldness of his anger, have you not?"

I remembered the cold I felt in his presence this morning and how that coldness followed him as he left my cabin.

Traeger was trying to make me feel those things now, I

thought. The more he spoke of them, the stronger his vibration became. He fed on negative thoughts and feelings.

"It won't work," I told him, keeping my thoughts pure. I focused on the good in Khalen, the kindness he showed others as well as me. I brought forth the memory of how I felt when he was near me. "I feel nothing but love for Khalen."

Traeger's energy shrank back, his eyes moved away. "You're a fool."

I shrugged. "Perhaps, but I like the way I feel when I'm around him."

He shrank back further like a snake avoiding a sandstorm.

"My skin tingles with his touch, and my heart—"

"Enough!" he roared. "No more of your lies."

The shocking pain he cast my way could not penetrate my shield. He was not as strong as his father. "You know it's the truth I speak, and it makes you weak," I claimed.

The anger that stirred in him swirled about us like dark clouds in the wake of a hurricane. This time, his pain penetrated my barrier and shoved me off the bed. I landed on the hard wooden floor with a heavy thud. The electrical shock was intense now, almost debilitating. Fear took its hold on me and I was caught in Traeger's web. It took all my strength to not cry out and plead for mercy.

"Your insolence is undesirable," he said.

The more I feared him, the stronger he became. His eyes glistened as he watched me writhe on the floor.

"Khalen is a predator," he said. "A killer. He can take a life with absolutely no effort at all. It is his natural gift. He started with small animals, then large ones. He took our mother's life when he was seven. Then, later, he took the life of his mate, Valerie." He walked toward me, his shiny black boots inches from my head. "Years of medical training will not erase what he really is."

His words jabbed at my gut like tiny daggers launched from a cannon. I could feel myself shrinking in the darkness, my hope slipping away.

"Fill yourself with the light," I could hear Shanuk say in my head. "Stay focused on the source."

Traeger continued to talk, but I tuned him out. Instead, I thought about Maiyun running and playing with seagulls on the beach. I imagined the sun on my face, the wind in my hair, and the soothing sounds of nature. I invited the light into my core and imagined it spreading throughout my body, removing the pain and sludge coursing in my veins.

I thought of Khalen and the gentle way in which he helped people. He became a doctor to cancel out the monster inside. It was clear how much he struggled against his underlying nature, but he chose to ignore it. How difficult that must be for him.

"Khalen is stronger than you," I said. "Stronger than your father." The words flowed through my lips like silk in the wind, as if I were not the one speaking them. The pain was gone now and I could feel myself glowing with hope and peace. I was protected.

"You're a simple female," he said. "Easily swayed to believe anything. He is strong, yes, and is even able to fool the great Shanuk. Even Case cannot see his true intentions." He finished his brandy then set the snifter onto the end table. I could hear him walking around. I chose to stay seated on the floor.

"He will take you as a mate," he continued. "Then he will allow himself to be the man he was born to be—dangerous. Even you cannot see through his intent, because he has you under a spell of illusion; that's another one of his great gifts." He laughed. "As a boy, he had me do things I would never dream of. I honestly believed that he loved me." He shook his head. "I was his fool, as you are now."

If there was truth in his words, it was self invoked; something he chose to believe. My heart was not convinced, but I decided to play along to see where his emotional ride would take me. "And why would he waste time with me?"

"You are the legend, the woman who is blind but can see. Your child will possess gifts that will make Shanuk look weak. Khalen's family can rule mankind."

"And that's what you think he wants?" I stifled a laugh.

He grabbed my arm and hauled me onto the bed. "My brother likes fine things: good wine, expensive clothes, comfortable accommodations. Do you really think he's satisfied living in a glorified tent?" My arm ached in his unyielding grip.

Khalen's attraction to the finer things in life was definitely evident. His attraction to me, however, was not in line with his penchant for finery. I was anything but the epitome of class. I was simple and plain.

Traeger's clever choice of words had me thinking—only it was in the wrong direction. I had to stay focused and not allow this man to sway my heart. The evidence, however, was disturbing. Khalen did have anger issues and I wasn't sure how strong that side was, or if it were merely sleeping. What if Traeger was right? What if Khalen was fooling Case and Shanuk to infiltrate the clan in the most destructive way, just as a Shadow would strategize?

What if Khalen really wanted to be a Protected one, but his Shadow side came through one day. How dangerous would he be? How much control did he really have?

"You see the truth of it, don't you?" said Traeger, leaning over me. Slowly he pushed me down onto the bed, his face inches from mine.

"I see many possibilities," I said, turning my head away from him. His hand caught my chin and pulled it back. His warm breath brushed against my face. It smelled of sweet brandy.

"As you mentioned," he continued. "My brother is much stronger than I and my father. So you see, it makes sense for you to choose me as a mate over him."

"Comparing fire to dynamite is not a very persuasive argument," I said. "I will not couple with a Shadow, nor do I choose to have a child with one."

He laughed. "Shanuk has given you a false sense of control. He will not live forever, you know."

"Long enough to see this through," I added.

His grip on my chin tightened. I wasn't sure what exactly would happen if Traeger ignored Shanuk's request to let me choose, but it must be something severe because it caused Traeger to pull back against his will.

"You will stay with the women tonight," he growled. He grabbed my arm and hauled me down to the basement where a large group of women had retired for the evening. Their conversations hushed when he opened the door.

"Katie, Marie, come," he commanded. He shoved me into the dark room. I felt two women brush past me. "Remember my warning," he said.

Chapter 25

*N*o *amount of darkness can quench the light of a single candle.*

The door slammed shut. There were no windows, no trace of any light at all, not even a single bulb. I could hear some of the women whispering. They were all very curious, but afraid to talk.

I introduced myself. "I'm Skye."

A frail hand touched my arm and a soft voice spoke. "I'm Sarah." I could tell her hand was disfigured when I touched it, and she pulled it back.

"What happened to your hand?" I asked.

"Talon crushed it," she said. "I did something wrong, but he never told me what it was."

I reached for it again. "I can help," I told her. "Let me help you." She relaxed her hand into mine.

The bones had been broken and were severely disfigured. She must have been in horrific pain. I asked the Father for help, then closed my eyes. I felt the bones shift and crack beneath my touch. The woman gasped. I controlled the pain and continued with the healing. My hands grew hot. I pushed the heat to the earth and imagined the healing blue mist that Shanuk had gifted me with. I imagined his brilliant teeth shining down on me. Within minutes, the woman's hand was healed.

"Oh," she cried. She pulled me close and hugged me. Her warm tears trailed down my neck. "Thank you," she whispered. She turned to the others in the room. "It doesn't hurt anymore," she cried. "My hand is healed."

The other women gasped and whispered more loudly among themselves.

"Come," said Sarah, leading me across the dark space. "You can share my blankets."

"Why is it so dark in here?" I asked.

"To keep us quiet," another voice spoke. "We are not supposed to talk."

I could feel the other women come closer. They all started telling me their names. I was in desperate need of a bathroom, but the timing to ask about one was not right. Sarah guided me down onto a soft mat with blankets.

"What's in this room?" I asked. "Any furniture? Facilities?" I was hoping she would take the hint.

"There is a large mat in the center of the room. That's where we sleep when our mates do not come for us. There is a bathroom in the far right corner of the room."

"Perfect," I said. "Can you show me?"

She helped me up, and then led me toward the back wall. We followed it to a door. She opened it, then showed me where the toilet and the sink were. "There is no shower or bath," she added sadly.

"Any lights?" I flipped a switch but nothing happened.

"Women do not need light," she said. "That luxury is reserved for our mates."

"You honestly believe that garbage?" I asked. My answer was silence. "How long have you been here?"

"Since we were very young," said Sarah. "We were paired with a mate before we could talk."

I rolled my eyes. "Good grief."

I reached in my pocket and retrieved my pocket knife. There was a very bright LED light on it that provided enough contrast for me to see shapes. I turned it on and the women gasped. I entered the bathroom and closed the door.

There were no windows and the air smelled stale. When I exited the bathroom, I used my penlight to cast light on the ceiling. There had to be a light fixture somewhere. But the light was not strong enough for me to see.

"What are you looking for?" asked Sarah.

"A light fixture."

She took my penlight and shone it in five places in the ceiling. "There are no bulbs in them."

"There are some in the hallway," I explained. "We only need one."

"No," she cried. "We cannot leave the room. They lock the door."

I walked over to the door with little effort.

"You get around well in the dark," said Sarah. "I have to find a wall and follow it over."

"I'm blind," I explained. "Once I get my bearings in a place and know where things are, I can negotiate my way quite easily. Walls are the easiest because they reflect sound flatly. Since there is no furniture here I have nothing to bump into save you ladies. Your brilliant auras are easy to see, so I can avoid you easily enough." That was my condensed version of Blind Mobility 101.

"You're blind and gifted?" she asked.

"Well, mostly blind. I see better in bright daylight."

"So do we," someone giggled. The other ladies chimed in.

I felt the door knob and immediately knew that it was a simple privacy lock, one that was easily picked. I opened my pocket knife and swung out the tiny flathead screwdriver. I slipped it into the hole, found the locking mechanism, and then gently turned it. The door opened.

I did not sense anyone near, so I proceeded to step through the door. I motioned for Sarah to follow.

She did so, hesitantly. The other ladies whispered excitedly among themselves.

"We need to find a light bulb," I whispered.

"I know of one that won't be missed," she said. She took my hand and guided me down the long, narrow hallway. There were several closed doors along the way. When we reached the seventh one, she opened it. The light bulb was screwed into a fixture that was just inside the door on the wall to the right. She reached over and unscrewed the bulb from its socket. "I have it," she whispered, closing the door quietly behind her.

We padded our way back to the room. I took the bulb from her hand and carried it off to the bathroom. The ceiling in the room was much too high to reach and we did not have a chair to stand upon. The bathroom fixture was much more accessible. "We'll have to remember to remove it come morning," I said.

I installed the bulb and flipped the switch. The ladies all giggled. A few of them grabbed the edge of the sleeping mat and hauled it closer to the bathroom.

The light was not sufficient for me to see their faces, but it certainly did a lot for their energy. Each of them shone brighter and stronger as they talked among themselves.

We all sat on the sleeping mat and chatted. I heard horrific stories about their mates. These ladies were prisoners—the sludge, they called themselves. None of them had gifts like the others, and therefore, they were expendable and used often to vent aggression.

I felt sorry for the two girls who were called to go with Traeger this evening in my stead.

"You're gifted," said Sarah. "Why would Traeger send you down here with us?"

"I made him angry."

She shook her head. "The gifted ones never share space with us."

"Perhaps he was trying to make a point," I said.

As the evening progressed, the women fell asleep one by one until I was the only one left awake. I turned off the light and sat in meditation. I contemplated what I had learned about Khalen. Case and Shanuk had very strong instincts. If Khalen had ill intent, the two elders would know about it, I was certain. I wished I had the gift of communicating with them, to let them know I was all right.

What if, I thought, I was not the main reason for this fiasco? What if this was about Khalen, and not myself? I played it out in my head, turning the thought over in my mind. I wondered if any of the ladies knew about Valerie. Seeing they were literally kept in the dark most of the time, I seriously doubted it. Most of them couldn't hold a decent conversation, let alone have valuable information.

If Khalen really was a predator, he is far more valuable to this clan than I am. I was more like a pawn in this game. Insignificant, just like the ladies in this room, or so they were made to believe. The only draw to me was Khalen's interest.

I shook my head. No, that didn't make sense. Khalen kept his interest in me at bay. Case and Shanuk seemed more interested in our union than Khalen was. Though, I thought, he did react rather possessively when Aidan placed his arm around my shoulder. I breathed deep, and tried to clear this clutter from my mind. Nothing made sense tonight. Exhaustion had a way of clouding the truth. I needed to get some rest.

Chapter 26

Revenge is sweet, but like most sweet things, it comes with a price.

~ E m b e r ~

Tonight was the night. Those bastards on Timothy Drive would pay for what they did to my son. Pete was a good boy, with a decent heart. The Rogers preyed upon him like vultures on a weakened yearling.

After my husband, Ted, was killed by the Shadows five years ago, Pete had fallen into a deep depression. I, too, had fallen deep in despair and was blind to what was happening to him and his younger brother. I had a hard time letting go of Ted, and an even worse time letting go of my anger toward the Shadows who killed him.

Khalen took us in and offered us shelter and a home. He promised we would be safe. I felt safe. As my heart healed, my boys healed too. They found solace in friends. Unfortunately, Pete's so-called friends were nothing but low-life druggies looking for their next victim.

He came home one night, high on meth. We almost lost

him. It would not be the last time he returned home in that condition. Khalen was concerned and confined Pete to the camp. After weeks of nursing him through withdrawals, he finally started acting like himself. He was happy and eager to contribute to the clan's way of life, until now.

His anger was back and he was eager to return to the Rogers' house. I asked Khalen for help. Pete would not try to pass beyond the barriers of the camp against Khalen's will. He had made that mistake once and he was not about to repeat the error. When Khalen stated an order, that order was obeyed. To go against him brought certain pain beyond anyone's tolerance. In some respects, he was much more strict than Case in the form of retribution.

I, on the other hand, was not bound to the camp, and was also eager to pay the Rogers a visit. Since the night of Pete's return, I had been saving something special for the Rogers. Something they would not soon forget.

Oysters, clams, and shellfish have a very distinct odor as they decompose over time. It is the type of odor that lingers with a person for many days, if not weeks. If allowed to bake in the sun for several days, and then placed in an airtight bag, the aroma intensifies to something akin to corpses rotting in a warm area with little to no airflow.

I patted the neat little packages I had wrapped up special for the Rogers. They would soon receive a special delivery of unknown origin—a gift from a friend, you might say, a small token of my appreciation. A wicked smile stretched across my face.

I had used small Godiva Chocolate boxes to whet their appetite for what lay hidden inside. I then wrapped them up in a plain brown wrapper to make them just interesting enough to spark their enthusiasm. For fun, I drew red hearts on the packages. They looked alluring, I had to admit.

Case and Khalen were too wrapped up in their own drama of the day to even notice me missing, I was sure. Tonight was the night I would deliver my gift. I knew from days of spying that it was pool night at Spencer's Grill and the Rogers never returned from it until early morning. Their darling children were staying at Grandma's for the night. Everything was perfect.

I parked at the end of the street, a good distance from the house. Staying in the shadows, I crept my way up to their yard and listened for the two Rottweilers they called pets. I knew better. They were vicious guard dogs, trained to kill anyone who dared to venture too close. Tonight, however, they were secure in the back yard. It was a clear night, crisp and dark with the help of a new moon.

I slowly walked up to the front porch. My delivery mechanism was in clear sight. The mail slot in the door was just large enough for my little packages. Quietly, I slipped the first package through the slot. It fell with a muffled thud to the hand-polished Jerusalem tile. I still remember the enthusiasm that Roseanne had shown during one of my visits. She was very proud of her home and made a point to show me every one of her luxuries. At that time, I hadn't known that she and her charming family were drug pushers.

The Rogers house was decked to the gills. What they lacked in morals, they certainly had tenfold in the luxury department. Dealing drugs had proven profitable for them. My stomach lurched with the thought of how many children they had hooked on meth and other nasty stuff. As a bitter taste rose in my throat, I stuffed another package through the door.

The dogs were unusually quiet, I thought. They typically barked at anything that came close to the property. I heard nothing. In fact, the entire neighborhood seemed quiet. I slipped another package through the door, then heard a swoosh sound.

Feeling a bit creepy now, I quickly pushed the other two packages through. The last one was snatched from my hand with a vicious growl. My eyes grew wide as I pulled my hand back quickly. The dogs were in the house.

I heard more growling and aggressive snips. One of them banged into the front door, making it vibrate with thundering protest. More fighting occurred. I quietly opened the wide mail slot and peered inside. Both dogs were pulling and tugging at one of the packages. The slobber-sodden paper gave way and the package ripped in two. The contents spewed all over the dogs and splattered the heavily textured walls.

I closed the mail slot and covered my mouth. I never imagined anything like this. I heard the dogs grab another package and run into the living room. I ran toward the side of the house, hoping to get a look inside. The drapes were closed, but I heard more tearing, lapping, and the distinct sound of dogs rolling with delight. One of them got up and shook. I could hear faint splats of liquid hitting hard surfaces.

That thick, white plush carpet would be hell to clean, I was sure. The large flat screen TV wouldn't fare too well, either. I hurried back to the mail slot to peer inside. The dogs had taken all the packages. I closed the slot and grabbed my stomach as I witnessed the female lapping up the mess. Thank God my stomach was empty. The aroma was everything I hoped it would be.

I turned to leave and nearly jumped out of my skin when I saw Case standing right behind me. I straightened and put on my most innocent smile.

"Case, you scared me."

"Uh huh," he replied. "I'm sure I did. Care to tell me what you are doing here?"

The dogs growled furiously at each other as they tore another package into pieces, followed by a splash. It was no use lying to Case.

"I came to deliver some packages," I explained.

The dogs ran from the kitchen, slipped and rammed into something hard. The vibration was quickly followed by a loud crash of glass and metal. I cringed.

"Ow," I said. "That's gotta hurt."

Case grabbed my arm and hauled me toward my car. "Go straight to camp," he said, "and wait for me outside my yurt. Understand?"

I nodded, knowing full well that I was in more trouble than I had ever been in during my entire teenage life. Now, here I was in my 40s and about to be scolded like a young child all over again. With any luck at all, I would be allowed to stay at the camp and not be ostracized. There would be ramifications, I was sure, but in truth, today was definitely worth whatever penalty Case would dole out.

I sat in my car and contemplated the notion of grabbing my kids, my few belongings, and finding another place to live. That would be the wrong choice, for sure. Case would find me either way. There was really no escaping this punishment. It was best for me to just stand up to it and pray for mercy and understanding.

As agreed, I returned to the camp and sat waiting for Case on the foot of his steps. Eve came out and placed her hand on my shoulder for reassurance. I squeezed her hand in acknowledgment and appreciation.

Case came walking up the path. I was curious why he did not ask for a ride back. The scowl on his face convinced me he needed the time to think and cool down. My stomach felt as if it were twisting. I had never felt the wrath of this great man, but had witnessed the effects he had on others who had. Those effects were not pretty.

He approached me and swung his hand toward the front door. "Inside," he said.

I stood and ascended the short set of stairs. The front door opened before me.

"Sit," he instructed, gesturing toward the couch opposite

the one his father occupied. Shanuk nodded in greeting but said nothing. He looked so frail these days. His bony frame was wrapped in a thick wool blanket. Despite the warmth of the room, I could see him shivering.

Case sat beside him, and then invited Eve to join him.

Eve's black eyes pleaded with him to be kind and understanding. They were met with a cold and grim expression.

"You created quite a mess," said Case to me.

"That was not my intent," I countered hastily. I held my tongue as he raised his hand in warning.

"Whatever your intent," he said, "I'm sure it was not to do good."

I lowered my eyes, unable to counter that accurate assessment. I felt like a child in this room, yet I was an adult. Compared to Case and Shanuk, however, I was a child, not only in body, but in spirit as well.

Eve looked at me, pleading. I knew she wanted an explanation, but she would not thwart her husband's interrogation. She would remain silent until asked to speak. Given Case's current state of emotion, I couldn't blame her. I, too, found it hard to speak.

Shanuk sat quietly waiting, feigning disinterest. His eyes were hollow and dark. He almost looked preoccupied.

"Come morning," Case said. "You will confront the Rogers and confess your actions."

My heart pounded loudly in my chest, yet my face felt numb and cold as if it were deficient in blood. I nodded, lacking the air to voice any words. With any luck at all, the angels would call me home tonight and spare me the humiliation of apologizing to the drug dealers who provisioned my son with meth. The mere thought of it filled me with rage.

"I'm not sorry for what I have done," I said in a small voice.

Case sat back, his hand on his chin. "I'm curious," he said, "about what you hope to gain from this feeble attempt at vengeance."

"Satisfaction," I said, my chin high and my eyes bright with courage. "To give back some of the joy they have been so graciously sharing with our youth. To let them know how much their efforts are appreciated by others, especially me. I was intent on leaving them a gift that was just as pleasant as the gifts they hand off to others. I was not counting on their miserable mongrels tearing the packages to smithereens and making an awful mess. That," I said, "was God's doing."

Case did his best to hide the smile tugging at his lips, but finally lost the battle when Eve burst out laughing.

"God, almighty," he said. "I'd hate to see their faces when they return home." He sobered up a bit and tried to look serious. "If they come here, dear Ember, you will confess and offer to help clean up the mess."

"Then I will pray that no one saw me," I said. "I'm sure that God has at least one more favor up his sleeve for me."

Now Eve and Shanuk joined in on the laughter; clearly they'd been reading Case and Ember's thoughts. The old man had tears rolling down his eyes.

"Oh ho ho," Shanuk laughed. "St. Timothy will have a coronary when he goes to turn on his precious flat screen."

It was a private joke among the clan members. Mr. Rogers prided himself on being the model citizen of the Island, but in truth, he was the heart of the problem—the germ that spawned the disease. He literally called himself St. Timothy and quoted the Bible as if he were the original author. It was pathetic, really. The man couldn't see the forest for the trees.

My heart suddenly felt lighter, yet there was still that edge of doubt that lingered in my mind. What if someone saw me, or Case? My destiny was in God's hands now. Having felt the brunt of his sense of humor, I knew he had one, but would he understand my need for justice? That was yet to be seen.

As if reading my mind, Shanuk added, "Vengeance rarely comes without a price, my dear."

I nodded, not really understanding what he meant, but trusting it nonetheless.

Chapter 27

Ego rules the spirit with dagger-fisted hands. Pain and scars are often left in its wake.

~ S k y e ~

If morning came, I wouldn't know it. The room was still very dark, having no windows to provide any light. I couldn't tell what time it was. The lock on the door rattled.

A man peeked inside. "Wake up, ladies. Breakfast in five minutes." He was a young man, perhaps in his 20s.

The women scrambled up from their sleep, each taking turns at the bathroom. I was the last to follow suit. I remembered to remove the light bulb and tucked it neatly under the sink basin. It would not be noticed unless someone glanced under the sink. Since there was nothing stowed in the cabinet, there would be no reason for someone to open it.

"Come on," Sarah said urgently. "They're not patient."

The door opened and the women followed the young man with short-cropped hair down the hall. No one spoke. Sarah led me by my hand. We entered a large dining hall and sat at a table that had an impressive spread of lumpy oatmeal, toast, and fresh cut fruit. I was famished. Bread and water would have been inviting.

We sat at the long table. The ladies all had their heads bowed. When the young man noticed mine was held high, he walked over to me and grabbed the back of my hair. It felt like hot coals raking my scalp.

"I heard about you," he said. "Your master wants you to join him in his chamber."

"I have no master," I countered.

His grip on the back of my hair tightened, causing my eyes to water. He forcefully led me back to Traeger's chamber.

Traeger smiled. "Slept well, I trust?"

I smiled back. "Better than I have in weeks," I lied.

The lie amused him this morning. He gestured toward the bathroom. "There are clean towels and clothes for you in there. Breakfast will be ready when you are done getting cleaned up."

I walked passed him. He smelled of bay rum. I closed the door to the spacious bathroom. The lighting was strong enough for me to see what horror reflected back to me in the mirror. My hair was in complete disarray and my eyes were dark and swollen as if I had cried myself to sleep. I hadn't remembered doing so, nor had I remembered any dreams.

I turned on the shower. It was already warm and smelled of bay rum, just like Traeger. Another bar of soap rested on the rack in the corner. It was freshly opened and smelled of lavender and ylang ylang. I chose that one over the bay rum.

The hot water showered over my tangled hair and dry skin. I took my time, as I did with most things, and relished my moment alone. I wondered how Maiyun fared in my absence. She hadn't been away from me since the accident.

My thoughts also turned to Khalen. He must be in fits about now. I wondered how Case and Shanuk broke the news of my absence to him, and could only imagine how he responded. In a vibratory sense, I could feel him with me. I just wished I could hear his voice.

I shampooed my hair, and then allowed the conditioner to soak in while I tended to the rest of my body. The towels Traeger left for me were thick and soft. They smelled fresh like white sage. There was even a pink toothbrush waiting for me on the counter.

When I stepped out of the bathroom wearing the rayon yellow dress he left for me, I felt a little awkward. He provided no undergarments. Although the dress did cover everything sufficiently, it still felt odd by itself. The hem fell just below my knees and the simple rounded neckline was conservatively high. The material was thick, warm, and loose enough to provide some semblance of cover. The three-quarter sleeves ended with flaring lace—a bit fancy for my taste, but attractive nonetheless. There were a pair of stockings and impractical shoes in the corner. I chose to ignore them.

As promised, breakfast was enticingly spread upon the table near a bay window that overlooked the Hood Canal. Traeger stood and slid a chair out for me.

"That dress suits you," he said. "I will have to provide you with more of them." He was clean shaven and very much like the image of the man in my nightmare. Like Khalen's, his eyes were hazel with more brown than green. He did not have the golden flecks in his irises that Khalen had. They traced a scrutinizing line from my head to my naked toes.

"I believe you have forgotten something, my dear."

I glanced down, following his gaze. My appetite shrank. "How long do you intend to keep me here?" I asked, trying desperately not to sound too concerned.

"Where are your shoes?"

I swallowed hard. "Where I left them."

He walked toward the bathroom, gathered the stockings and shoes and tossed them at my feet. "You will don them," he said.

"I don't like shoes," I replied.

His eyes narrowed. "I won't—"

"I want to go home," I interrupted, and then scattered the shoes and stockings under the bed with my foot.

He pursed his mouth the way Khalen did when deciding how to word his thoughts. "Are you in a hurry to leave?" he asked, serving me two fried eggs, sliced ham, and toast with butter.

My heart pounded in my chest, expecting the worse. I

took a deep breath trying to remain calm. "I would like to return to work," I said, helping myself to a banana.

He poured me a cup of black tea, then remained quiet when I closed my eyes to pray.

"Amen," he said.

I looked at him and glared, wondering if he was mocking me.

"The Father loves us all, does he not?" he said.

I nodded.

"Why is it then that we Spirians choose to fight among ourselves?"

"Ego," I said. "It gives us a false sense of power."

"And with power," he continued for me, "comes the desire to rule."

"Exactly," I confirmed, separating the whites from the yolks.

"Wouldn't it be preferable if the Protected and the Shadowed ones could respect one another and reside on this planet in peace?"

I nodded. "Yes, it would."

"Do you think it possible?"

"With God," I quoted, "all things are possible."

"We have God."

I looked at him with a questioning glance. "Do you? In your heart, I mean."

He couldn't answer me. I decided to answer for him. "If you did, you wouldn't be a Shadow."

"There will always be Shadows," he said, confidently.

I sipped my tea. "I'm not doubting that."

"Not all Shadows are bad," he said.

"And not all Protected are good," I added. "As Spirians, I believe we walk the fence between the two, constantly swaying out of balance, always struggling for control." I stared out the window allowing my thoughts to carry me away. "Afraid to fall, one way or the other, in fear of what might happen when we relinquish control." The words stumbled out of my mouth as if I were not the one speaking them.

He nodded. "And which are you, my dear—a Shadow or Protected?"

"Both," I said. "Life relies on balance to flourish. We cannot escape duality, no matter how hard we try."

He laughed. "So you are saying that good cannot survive without bad?"

"It can survive," I said, "It just wouldn't be considered good anymore. Without dark, light would cease to illuminate. Without sadness, happiness would lose its purpose, and so on."

He continued to chuckle and shook his head. "In the midst of chaos," he said, "peace arises."

"Exactly," I confirmed. The food, tasteless as it was, provided nourishment but that was all. I managed to finish my eggs and bacon, but left my half-eaten toast and the banana unpeeled.

"There is no reason for you to return to work," he said, bringing us back to the original topic. "I can provide for your every need, right here."

I pushed my tea aside. "Can you provide me freedom to leave?"

His eyes narrowed for a moment, clearly disturbed by my comment. "You broke the treaty. Your freedom is lost."

"I am lost to you, Traeger. Why waste your time on me?"

"I am patient," he said. "Either you will choose to accept me as your mate, or I will wait for Shanuk to die. By the looks of him, it won't take long."

This conversation was heading nowhere. I decided to kick it up a notch and do some fishing. "Do you believe Khalen will relinquish me to you so willingly?"

His energy shifted. His eyes grew darker with traces of green and gold. "I have no doubt he will come for you."

My suspicions were confirmed. It was Khalen they wanted, not me. I was simply the bait to allure the larger fish. "And when he does come, what will happen?"

"Our clans will unite," he said.

"Unite?"

"To have you," he explained. "Khalen must vow loyalty to Damon."

"And if he refuses?"

Traeger's eyes grew black. "Damon will kill you."

I swallowed hard and pushed back the fear that fed Traeger's black soul. "Is that what happened to Valerie?"

He smiled and his eyes glistened. "Ah, Valerie." He fumbled with a butter knife on the table, rotating it between his long fingers. "She was easy to turn. Damon gifted her with powers beyond her expectations. She loved the way they made her feel. After experiencing my affections, she no longer wanted to be tied to Khalen. She aborted his child."

He stood and paced in front of the window. "Khalen went mad when he found out. He blamed Damon for it. In truth, it was I who had turned that vixen. Ah, she was wild in bed." His gaze clouded with distant memories of the redhead. He looked damnably proud of himself.

My jaw tightened. "Did Khalen ever know it was you who turned her?"

His attention snapped back to the present. "Oh yes. Valerie made sure of it. She begged Khalen for her freedom, but that is not possible in our world." He turned his gaze on me. "You see, she and Khalen were paired, two souls becoming one. Unlike human marriages, our unions are for life. Death is the only means for separation, but to take a life means to die a bit yourself."

"Khalen heard my thoughts through her, and knew she had paired with us both. Our clans were united so long as she lived. He, of course, refused to grant her freedom."

"I thought he couldn't grant it? That it was impossible."

"We can take multiple mates," he explained, "but we cannot separate our thoughts. Khalen would always hear what she felt and thought. She was connected to him. The Protected take only one mate." He huffed and shook his head. "Such a waste."

Apparently, Traeger did not share the same sentiments as

Khalen on the matter of marriage. "So, what happened?"

"Khalen tried to force Valerie to return with him. She refused. When he picked her up to carry her out, she stabbed him in the back."

I remembered seeing the scar when I worked on him. It ran deep. In my dream, I had witnessed the act, though it was slightly different and lacked the details that Traeger's story provided.

"Khalen took her life before she could strike a second blow. In his present state of mind, he could have easily taken all our lives, but he chose to leave instead. No one heard from him for seven years."

So much happens in this world, I thought, and we live past it blind and deaf of the wake our actions leave behind. For so long, I had not seen where humanity was heading. It was clear to me now, clear as black without white. The battle between good and evil was seeking an end, but they were like oil and water, able to share the same space but always separate.

"Why is it important for the clans to unite?" I asked.

"Together," he said, "our powers will be unstoppable. We can determine the direction of this planet and perhaps beyond."

"Like Satan wanting to reunite with God," I said.

He smiled. "Perhaps, yes."

"God help us," I retorted.

Traeger turned me to face him. He stepped uncomfortably close. "You said it yourself, my dear. Good and bad complete one another. You and I make a perfect pair."

I stepped back, but his grip on my arm held firm. "I will not choose you," I said, my voice shaky but firm.

He slammed his mouth on mine. We shall see, I heard him think as his bitter tongue slithered inside me.

Chapter 28

If the road ends, step out of your vehicle and continue your journey on foot.

Traeger tore away from me. His back slammed into the wall. The door to the room flew open. Khalen stepped in, his eyes dark and menacing.

"Morning, brother," Traeger grunted, struggling to stand.

"Where's Damon?"

Khalen must have dressed in a hurry this morning, I thought. His wrinkled blue jeans and baggy sweatshirt were a far cry from his typical apparel of fine pressed slacks and silk shirts. A pair of brown suede loafers covered his feet. I would have never guessed he owned a pair.

Traeger rubbed the back of his head. "I'm sure your dramatic entrance has alerted him by now."

The energy in the room intensified as their father entered. He was slightly taller than his sons, and his hair was more grey than black. It was better groomed this morning than when I first met him. It fell neatly down his head and ended in a short stub at the base of his neck, tied with a black band. His dark green turtleneck was neatly tucked into a pair of neatly pressed black pants.

"Khalen," he drawled. "So nice to see you again."

Khalen nodded. "Damon."

Damon laughed, seemingly amused at his son's use of his first name. "Father will do," he corrected.

"No," said Khalen. "It won't do."

Damon slammed Khalen against the wall without touching him.

"I request council," Khalen choked.

Damon's eyes narrowed. He released his hold on Khalen. "Speak."

"Not here," rasped Khalen, rubbing his throat. "Downstairs, in the study."

Damon pressed the tips of his fingers together, his eyes narrowed. "Hmm," he growled. "You brought company."

With a thought, Khalen assured me all was fine. I heard his voice as clear as if he were speaking in my ear.

They're trying to trap you, I said silently, sending him the thought.

I know, he answered.

Traeger grabbed my arm, keeping a wary eye on his brother. "She tastes sweet," he said snidely, as we walked past.

He tastes bitter, I added. Khalen smiled, but there was still some concern etched in his eyes. Nothing happened, I assured him. He kissed me, that's all.

We headed down the curved stairwell, and traveled down a wide hall to a large room on the right. I was grateful to see that it had windows with plenty of sunshine pressing through.

Case stood in the far corner, examining a picture of a grey wolf on the wall. Shanuk sat quietly on one of the three black leather couches arranged in a horseshoe configuration. Ian and Aidan flanked him like two diligent guards. The room was furnished in rich cherry with brass trim. The dark Tigerwood floors were tastefully covered with rugs hand-woven in rich Native American patterns of blue, red and brown. The smell of old books and leather permeated the room.

Damon was the first to speak. "This visit is highly outrageous, Case. I don't remember extending an invitation."

Case turned slowly to meet his gaze. "We don't need one. It seems we have a bit of quandary, Damon."

Khalen removed his brother's hand from my arm, and then led me over to the couch. Stay calm, he warned.

I looked over at Shanuk, who looked tired and void of life. His beautiful blue eyes sparkled at me, but his expression was drawn. Stay by his side, he silently told me. I nodded.

He was referring to Khalen, ensuring me that I was to choose him over another. I looked over at Case. The intense concentration on his face made him appear as formidable as Damon on a bad day. I imagined they were testing each other's shield and power, but I couldn't be sure. The hum in the room was nearly deafening.

"Summon Talon and his two mates," Case requested.

Case looked at Traeger, who then glared at Khalen and disappeared.

"Please," Damon said, gesturing toward the couches. "Let us sit."

Khalen sat next to me and Case flanked him. Damon occupied the third couch by himself. He sat back displaying an amusing amount of confidence, considering his company, I thought.

Traeger returned with Talon and the two blondes. Traeger took his position next to his father. Talon and the two blondes kneeled on the floor. Each of them nodded to Damon.

"You have your council, Case. Now explain why you have chosen to invade my house." His voice was harsh.

Case and Shanuk remained calm.

"I believe Talon and his two mates have some explaining to do," said Case, glancing over at the young man and his women.

Damon glared at the threesome kneeling before him on the floor. "Well," he growled. "Get on with it!"

Talon glanced over at Case.

"We found your footprints," said Case. "Just outside the cabin where Skye was staying. When you heard Khalen return, you left."

Damon's eyes grew wide. "Is this true, Talon?"

"It is," he quietly stated.

"Go," Damon demanded. "Wait for me in my chamber."

He sighed and nodded at Case. "My apologies," he stated. "It seems we have broken treaty first."

"Sir," said Case, "your apologies should be directed at Skye, not me."

Damon slapped his hand on the ornate couch arm. "I will not!"

He stood. The door to the study slammed shut before he could reach it. He turned and glared at Case. "She is a woman," Damon sneered, and then he sat back down.

Though he was certainly a tiger trapped in a cage, he appeared eerily calm and calculating.

"No!" I shouted.

Khalen gripped my arm.

He's intending to harm Shanuk, I explained in thought.

"You are correct, woman," said Damon, "and there is nothing here that will change that."

The anger welling inside me made Damon stronger.

"Stop him, Skye," Traeger warned.

My shield grew stronger.

Shanuk raised his hand and dispelled my efforts immediately and my shield collapsed. "You will take my life, Damon, but that is all you will take. The war between our kinds will not end today but the odds will shift in our favor."

I felt Khalen tense. Case warned him with a glance.

"We shall see," said Damon. Then his eyes grew black

and empty. He looked at Shanuk, who smiled, then slumped against Aidan. A look of shock shrouded Damon's face as he gasped, then collapsed against his son.

"No!" shouted Traeger. He shook his father. "Noooo!" He looked around the room with vengeance. His eyes finally rested on Khalen. "Did you do this?"

Khalen shook his head. "No, Traeger, I did not."

"He took his own life," said Case. "When you take a life, you lose part of your own. Taking Shanuk's life was more than your father had to offer, so in turn, he perished."

There was sadness in his voice, but his posture didn't show it. The pain in his heart, though, was reflected in my own. Khalen must have sensed it as well. He placed his arm around me and offered a reassuring hug.

"This is not over," Traeger growled.

Aidan and Ian lifted Shanuk's lifeless body, and carried it out of the room. Case followed close behind.

"You are one of us," Traeger said to Khalen. "You cannot deny that which is a part of you."

"But I can ignore it," said Khalen.

Traeger grabbed his brother's arm. "He was your father."

"No," said Khalen. "He was not."

I took Khalen's hand in mine and gave it a squeeze. He led me back to the Escalade in silence.

Chapter 29

Visions are a prelude to what may come. They offer a chance to foresee a desired outcome.

When we reached the Escalade at the end of the drive, everyone disappeared, including Khalen. I was suddenly alone. I saw movement in the driveway, though I wasn't sure if my eyes were playing tricks on me. It was bright enough for me to see, but what I did see was most likely a figment of my imagination. This was not the first time I had seen something that wasn't real. The doctors called them ghost images.

I heard whispers. The voices sounded like Ian and Aidan.

"Don't move," I heard, but the words were muffled and indistinct. I couldn't be sure.

"You won't have her," I heard Khalen say. His voice came from the area where I thought I saw movement. I wandered over to investigate.

Voices echoed in my mind, but I couldn't understand what they said. My feet seemed to move on their own accord toward the alley where Khalen's voice resounded. Everything looked so familiar in the bright sunlight, I could see quite well. Nothing made sense, though. Where was Case and Shanuk? Why did they all leave?

The alley beckoned me forward. My feet felt heavy, yet they continued to carry me toward the narrow passage. When I saw the five figures moving toward me, my heart stopped. The elevated sound of my breathing reverberated in my ears as if I was plunged under water. Was I dreaming?

Three men and two women, all beautiful, with black hair and eyes as red as demons stood before me. They wore matching black coats with long split tails, like those I had seen on cowboys in old western movies. I knew what I would see when they smiled—sharp teeth like those of wolves.

"Wake up," I told myself. "It's just another dream."

One of the men approached me. His arm seemed to lengthen as he reached out to grab me. My feet held firm to the hard pavement, unwilling to move. My legs were heavy as lead.

Where was Khalen, Aidan, Ian, and Case? I called out for them, but nothing escaped my lips. This had to be another nightmare. I had to wake up.

The man grabbed me. His short dark hair glimmered like blue flame under the sun. His grip tore at my flesh. His bared teeth sparkled with a thick coating of saliva, inches from my throat.

A deep growl came from behind me. The man backed away, his pale flesh moist and his brows furrowed with alarm. His four companions looked equally concerned.

A shiver ran down my spine as two enormous wolves flanked me and then advanced ahead, moving toward the five figures.

Another hand grabbed my arm and pulled me backward. I was weightless in the strong embrace.

"Stay still and don't speak," Khalen warned.

We watched as the two wolves advanced toward my at-tackers. They stood, staring at each other as if having a mental conversation. The man who had me in his clutches just min-utes ago stared at me. Khalen's grip tightened. I imagined his stare in return was just as intense in forewarning.

The five figures turned and left, their long-tailed black coats trailing and fluttering behind them.

The two red wolves turned and came toward us. Khalen's grip relaxed.

My eyes widened then blurred as the two lupine figures slowly morphed into more familiar beings: Ian and Aidan.

"You're all right now, lass," Aidan said with a beaming smile.

I shook my head. "What happened? Who were they? Why were they trying to hurt me?" The questions streamed from my shaking lips. I had been powerless, barely able to move in the presence of those five formidable beings.

"Sean," said Khalen. "From the Seattle clan."

"Aye," said Aidan, confirming the statement. "Don't know about the others, though."

Judging from the intense looks on his and Khalen's faces,

I knew they were continuing the conversation in thoughts not meant for my ears. I tried tapping into Khalen's mind, but he kept me out. My eyes narrowed.

"Easy, lass," Ian said, placing his huge hand on my shoulder. "That was quite the illusion, eh?" he added, trying to distract my attention. "Not quite as thrilling as flying but interesting, nonetheless."

Khalen allowed him to escort me back to the Escalade. He and Aidan were not far behind, still engaged in mental conversation.

"What happened?" I asked Ian.

"They snared you into an illusion, lass."

He opened the car door and helped me into the front seat. Case sat quietly waiting with Shanuk's limp figure leaning against him. Case looked deep in thought, no doubt listening to what Aidan was telling Khalen.

Ian sat behind me.

"Who is Sean?" I asked, "and what does he want with me?"

"He leads the Seattle clan—a small but odd bit of birds. They drink the blood of their victims because they believe it strengthens their gifts, makes them stronger." He scoffed. "Sick bunch of buggers, they are."

I waited patiently for him to get to the point of my question, but it was too late. Khalen and Aidan entered the car and disrupted the conversation. Neither of them were talking.

My patience finally reached its end. "Would someone

please tell me why a clan of blood-sucking Shadows from Seattle want me dead?"

Khalen looked in his rearview mirror to glare at Ian in the back. I was certain that Aidan gave his brother the same kind of look.

"I never said they wanted you dead, lass," Ian said in defense.

"You didn't have to," I qualified. "I read intentions, re-member?" I leaned back in my seat and crossed my arms. "Sean's slobbering canines aiming for my throat was also a fairly good clue."

"Tell her," said Case. "She ought to know."

"She doesn't need to know," said Khalen. "This doesn't concern her."

That ironic statement had my blood rising like a ba-rometer in the sun. "Doesn't concern me? If not me, then whom, pray tell, does it concern?"

"The Shadows," he said through clenched teeth. "Of which you are not." His last statement was said with a harsh edge. His knuckles turned white as he drove the Escalade down the driveway and onto the street. His jaw clenched, forming deep grooves where his masseter muscles flexed.

"You're right, I'm not, but it was my throat Sean was after. I want to know why."

"We will discuss this later," Case said. He was warning me not to cross that line that I very much wanted to push right now. I was tired of being kept in the dark. It seemed everyone understood what just happened except for me.

Khalen emitted a coldness that sent shivers through my bones. He was angry and struggling for control. Perhaps Case was right. It was best to wait until later to talk about what happened.

Khalen reached over and covered my hand with his. It was warm and gentle as he offered reassurance and appreciation for acknowledging Case's warning.

I was willing to comply for now, but the subject would arise again, and soon.

Chapter 30

Sometimes, the needs of one outweigh the needs of many.

The entire camp mourned over Shanuk's limp body. The air was so thick with sadness that it was difficult to breathe. My own heart felt heavy and burdened with grief. I didn't know the old man well, yet I felt as if I had known him all my life. He was an inherent part of me now. I felt him near my soul as if he resided there permanently.

Maiyun hadn't left my side since I returned. She pressed against me as if I would disappear if she ever lost contact again. I felt comforted by her closeness. My fingers combed through her thick fur as I stared into the fire crackling in the pit.

As Case and Eve prepared Shanuk's body for the cremation, Khalen sat next to me by the fire. I wanted to ask him about what happened earlier today, but now was not the time. He needed some quiet reflection.

"I will tell you," he quietly said.

"You don't have to do it now," I replied. "It can wait."

"No," he said. "I should have told you sooner. You were

right, it does concern you."

I looked at him. He was serious, clearly troubled. His furrowed brows arched and relaxed as he tried to form the words that threatened to choke him.

"Traeger wants to use you as a link between our clans. The rest of the Shadows believe that will be their undoing. As it stands, you are a threat to their existence—their way of life."

I listened quietly, fighting the urge to scream. Instead, I swallowed back the exclamations in my mind like bitter pills.

"Sean and his clan want you dead. They have made it clear that you will be so one day, very soon."

My skin turned cold. My stomach felt hollow and it had nothing to do with the fact I hadn't eaten since early this morning.

He turned to look at me with concern etched in his emerald eyes. "If Aidan and Ian were not there, Skye, I would not have been able to break through the Shadow's illusion. I would have lost you, forever."

"Why was I not able to form my shield?" I asked.

"Your gifts do not work in the spell of an illusionist, just as I cannot reach you once they have you in their spell."

I contemplated that for a moment and thought I understood his gist. "And you feel that you cannot protect me?"

He nodded. "I do."

"Yet, somehow, you always seem to be in the right place at the right time to save my hide."

His brows furrowed with obvious confusion. "Explain."

"When I was confused in the Mexican restaurant, you were right by my side. When the Shadows tried to kill me with an embedded capsule, you saved me. When Traeger tried to kiss me, you came and stopped him. In my dream, when I was about to be bitten by some psycho, you pulled me away. And today, you were there again, at my side, in the midst of danger. Honestly, sir, if I were to choose my champion in this life, it would be you."

His face softened and his eyes grew moist. He closed them and brushed a soft kiss against my forehead. "I pray you have not chosen carelessly," he whispered.

"You know," I said, taking his hand in mine. "In many ways, I already feel joined with you, Khalen Dunning. I feel as if I have known you all my life and I'm comfortable with that."

He squeezed my hand and smiled for the first time today. "I am too."

"I'm curious," I said, "about why the Seattle clan feels as if I'm a threat to them."

He sighed. "Apparently, you have become Traeger's obsession. He believes he can have you."

I looked up at him, my brow raised and my chin held high. "And how, pray tell, is your brother's demented sense of confidence a threat?"

He brushed a finger under my chin. "You are a dangerous distraction, my love."

His endearment for me caused my stomach to flutter as

if it housed a thousand butterflies suddenly gaining a lust for freedom. "Am I?" I asked.

His eyes looked distant. "More than you know."

"Well then," I said, suddenly feeling up for the challenge. "Let's give them a ride they won't soon forget."

He turned to look at me, brow arched and a smile tugging at the corner of his mouth. "Meaning?"

I welcomed the thrill this little challenge presented. It had been a long time since I felt this young and reckless. I had to smile. "I'll show them just how dangerous I can be."

He narrowed his gaze. "I'm not sure I like the sound of that."

Case and Eve walked toward us.

"Son," said Case, "it's time."

Khalen squeezed my hand. "Meet us at my thinking log," he said, then stood to join his father.

I nodded.

Eve stoked the fire a bit, added another few branches, and then joined me on the log.

"You look troubled," she said.

I shrugged. "It's nothing, really. I have a clan out to kill me, a man who wants me but is not ready to claim me even though he's in direct competition with his evil twin, and a very special old man who just gave his life for mine. Just an average day, really."

Eve laughed. "Ah, the life of a Spirian. Isn't it grand?"

She flagged Ember over to join them. "This will take

your mind off things a bit," she said.

Ember smiled down at me. "Welcome back, Skye."

I patted the log beside me. "Can you join us?"

She sat down beside me and warmed her hands with the fire. She had a bit more color to her than I had seen for quite some time.

"How's Pete?" I asked.

She nodded, but her lips remained firm and straight. "Better. Those drops you gave him really help. Khalen is making him a tincture that should help him as well, but it won't be ready for another five days, he said."

"Pete must be having quite a time of it, I'm sure."

Ember chuckled. "Khalen has placed him on house arrest. He's not allowed to step outside the camp. I've never seen Pete so angry."

"It's probably the best thing for him right now," I said. She nodded.

Eve placed her hand on Ember's knee. "Ember, you must tell Skye about your adventures today. I'm sure she'd love to hear it."

Ember covered her face as if to hide some hideous embarrassment. She then told the story about her package delivery, and how the two dogs made a mess of everything. To embellish the story, Eve sent images of the entire scene to my mind. It was like watching a short movie.

The three of us laughed as we witnessed the utter horror on Ember's face as the dogs tore apart the packages. It was clear that malice was not her intent. Like she had told Case, that little addition was God's doing.

Jimmy, Ember's younger boy, came running toward us, holding his hand. He was crying.

The three of us stood.

Ember embraced him. "Jimmy, what happened?"

"I burned myself," he cried. "I picked up a stick and it burned me."

Ember looked at the blistering wounds on Jimmy's palm. "Oh, God."

"Khalen told me to find Skye. He said she could help me."

I led Jimmy to sit beside me and placed his hand in mine.

Maiyun offered her own kind of comfort by gently licking his arm. He patted her huge head and smiled.

A faint vibration emanated from my hands, and then grew increasingly stronger. The blue mist rose and the vibrations started to calm.

Jimmy's eyes widened, his mouth hung open. "It's gone," he said. "My burn is gone."

Ember looked at his hand and tears began to well in her eyes. "Oh, Skye, thank you."

"Wow," said Jimmy. "That's cool." He ran off toward a group of kids walking in the distance.

Ember rolled her eyes. "I'm afraid you're about to be inundated with a slew of aches, pains, and injuries that suddenly need relief."

For the first time since I entered this camp, I finally felt useful. Khalen had kept such a tight hold on me that I was unable to contribute like others in the camp. If I were to stay here, that would have to change.

"I don't mind," I said. "It feels good to work again. I miss it."

Eve smiled. "Ian says you give an incredible massage. I could use one of those at least once a week."

"Me too," said Ember.

"Hmm," I chimed. "I'm going to have to ask Khalen about bringing a massage table here."

"I'm proud to call you my daughter," said Eve. "Welcome to our family."

I frowned. "It's not official yet."

Eve squeezed my hand. "Men can be stubborn at times."

"And stupid," added Ember.

I stood. "I told Khalen I would wait for him at his thinking log. I'd best be going."

Eve and Ember gave me a hug.

"We'll talk again," said Eve.

I nodded and grabbed Maiyun's collar. "Good night."

Chapter 31

To sacrifice yourself to save another is by far the greatest gift you can offer, and one that is never forgotten.

The lake was still, reflecting the glow of the waxing sliver of a moon like a flawless mirror. Crickets chirped, breaking the croaking rhythm of baritone frog song. The bitter cold of the evening discouraged annoying insects, and for that, I was grateful. I wrapped my coat around me, still warm from the fire, and sat on Khalen's log. The quiet time offered me the much-needed solace I wanted. I imagined Shanuk sitting beside me, quietly reflecting on the day's events, his vivid blue eyes focused on the still of the water.

Maiyun sat next to me, her head resting on my thigh. She hadn't let me out of her sight since I returned. By the looks of her, she hadn't eaten much either. Her ribs were much too palpable as I stroked her sides.

The tall grass felt good between my toes. The recent downpour of rain had freshened the evergreens; the pungent aroma of pine, cedar, and hemlock was intoxicating. If it weren't for the bear skin that Case had draped over the log earlier today, my pants would be soaked through. I thought about the bear that had attacked Maiyun and Khalen, wondering what had happened to it.

I heard Case and Khalen walking up the path, talking quietly. They sat next to me. Khalen attempted to move closer to me but Maiyun refused to give up her position. He placed an arm around my shoulders and drew me to him.

I rubbed the bear skin between my fingers. "Khalen," I said.

"Hmm," he responded.

"What happened to the bear that attacked you and Maiyun?"

He was silent for a moment as if trying to think of the right thing to say. "She went home."

I pulled away from him so I could turn to see his face. The moon did not provide enough light. Still, he seemed much too satisfied with his answer.

"Home?" I inquired, "as in, with the Father?"

He tried to pull me back next to him, but I wouldn't allow it.

"Why is it important, Skye?" His hold on me tightened.

"Did you kill her?"

Case chuckled, clearly enjoying his son's interrogation.

Khalen pet Maiyun on her head. "She was going to kill your dog," he finally said.

I reached for his hand and squeezed it. "I understand. Thank you for saving her for me."

He squeezed my hand back, and then relaxed a bit. "You're welcome."

He pressed his lips to the top of my head as if fighting some internal battle.

"Hey," I said. "I know about what happened to your mom, and Valerie. Traeger told me."

He pulled away from me.

"You're not a monster," I assured him. "I know that, and so do you."

Case whittled on a stick he had picked up off the ground. "Traeger has his own agenda, Skye."

"He's not going to let this go, is he?" I asked.

"No," Khalen growled, still clearly angered by his brother's malicious tongue.

"Why did Shanuk allow Damon to take his life?"

Case smiled. "Because he knew it would claim Damon as well."

"So, an eye for an eye?"

Case shook his head. "No, Skye. Shanuk would never offer his life to take another. He did it to invoke change. Damon was dangerous and destructive. He provoked others to do his bidding and in turn, corrupted their soul. He was becoming too powerful."

"And now that he's gone?"

"Traeger will take over. Unlike his father, he wants peace between our clans, but there is still a darkness in him that is dominant and unpredictable. His power will continue to grow and his vindictiveness toward Khalen is strong. Only time will tell what direction he will take."

Case reached over and squeezed my hand. "You did well, my dear. Shanuk was right about you all along. You are strong and observant."

I squeezed his hand back and smiled. "I had a good teacher."

Case stood. "Well, Eve has dinner waiting for me, so I'd best get home." He nodded to Khalen. "Son," he said simply.

Khalen bowed his head not only out of respect, but also gratitude. "Father."

We watched him leave, and then I noticed that Khalen had removed his shoes and socks. He now wiggled his bare toes in the grass. "It's bloody cold out here. How do you stand not having your feet covered?"

"Hmph," I said. "Some Indian you are." And I smiled.

He shook his head.

"It feels good though, eh?" I asked, "the grass between your toes?"

"What toes," he laughed. "I cannot feel them anymore."

I rolled my eyes.

"Khalen," I said rather hesitantly.

"Hmm," he answered, donning his socks and shoes.

"Do you want to take another mate?"

He froze for a moment. "My brother has a big mouth."

I waited for him to answer my question.

"No," he finally said.

I nodded. The pang that rose from my gut constricted my chest and made it hard to breathe. Despite my efforts of not allowing my heart to bind with another, I failed. It was bound to Khalen, and now it felt betrayed. "I understand."

"But someone will claim you someday, and I cannot allow that either."

"Because your father wants us paired with each other?"

He shook his head. "No. Not entirely."

He crooked his finger under my chin and turned me to face him. His eyes shone like emeralds with specks of gold in the glare of the moon and stars. "You're like a fine bottle of wine, Skye, and that I don't want to share."

I looked at him questioningly. "Wine?"

"Yes," he said. "Rare and smooth with careful aging. A nectar to be savored slow and long."

"Uh huh," I said. "And when the bottle is drained of its fine juice, will you simply toss the spent container?"

"Perhaps," he said, curling the corners of his lips with mischief.

I shivered. "It's getting cold."

"Come," he said. "Let's go home."

"Home?"

"I moved your things back to my yurt. You will stay with me."

I stopped. "Why?"

"Because you are not safe alone, Skye. Traeger is out there and—"

"How long do you think you can protect me from him,

Khalen? It is not me he wants, it's you."

He laughed. "Is that what he told you?"

"Yes."

"Hmm, that sounds more like Damon's thoughts, not Traeger's." He thought for a moment. "No, Traeger wants the prize, I'm just the bonus."

"And if I choose to leave?"

He stiffened. "I won't allow it."

"You don't have a choice. I will not be used for bait, Khalen. So long as I am near you, I endanger you and the clan. If he learns that you are not interested in me, he will no longer want me."

He frowned. "I never said I wasn't interested in you."

I shook my head. "This feeling frightens me. I don't like it." I started to walk away.

"I won't let you go!" he roared. His hands gripped both my arms with such ferocity, Maiyun took notice. She released a low, soft growl.

Khalen ignored it. "Skye, you don't know what you ask of me." His grip did not soften. "I cannot let you go. Please don't be difficult."

"You're afraid," I said. "Just as afraid as I am."

He pulled me close to him and cradled my head to his chest. "Give me time, Skye," he whispered. "That's all I ask."

I breathed in his scent and held him tight. "I'll stay for as long as you'll have me," I said. "And not a minute longer." A warm tear fell down my cheek and soaked into his soft cotton blue shirt.

That evening, we spent time with Case and Eve by their fire. The sky was clear and the stars were magnificent. Case told stories of his father and their many adventures together. We laughed and shared a bottle of Madeira between the four of us. When the conversations died down, and the bottle was spent, it was time to retire. Case and Eve left first, leaving Khalen and I alone.

The fire crackled as he scattered the pieces of wood. "Come," he said. "Let's get some sleep." He took my hand and we made our way to his yurt.

He had been busy. The bed was covered in soft blankets, and my clothes had been put away in a new dresser. Apparently, he planned to keep me around for longer than I thought. Even Maiyun had a larger, fancier bed. He constructed a cedar frame and lined it with a soft bear skin and a fine collection of bones for her to gnaw on.

"The skin and the bones are new," I said, making a casual observance.

"Nothing goes to waste," he replied. "I figured it was fitting for her to have the prize, since she suffered the brunt of the attack."

I settled into bed and picked up my journal from the end table. There was much to write about this evening. As I scratched out my thoughts I occasionally glanced up at Khalen on the couch, reading a medical journal.

"Khalen?"

"Hmm?"

"Would you mind lying next to me?" I'm not sure where that came from, but I had a strange urge to feel him close.

He gathered his blankets and padded over to me in stocking feet. I closed my journal and waited for him to settle in before laying my head on his chest. The strong sound of his heart was like a lullaby to me.

So many questions swirled through my head regarding the past events; a lifetime could not possibly answer them all.

"What's on your mind?" he asked.

"How did Shanuk dispel my shield so easily?"

He laughed. "The older you are, Skye, the stronger you become. Your shield was nothing more than paper to him."

"Scary."

"I can still feel him," he said. "Like he's right here with us."

I breathed deep. "Perhaps he is."

He squeezed me tight and kissed the top of my head.

"He gifted me with the healing," I said. "In the hospital. He was the man I saw, the Reverend."

"No doubt," said Khalen.

"So, I'm not the legend people talk about."

"He believes you are or he would not have offered the gift."

"And what do you believe?" I asked.

He took a long breath and slowly exhaled. "I believe you are mine, and that is all that matters right now."

I looked up and felt his breath on my face. The sweet scent of Madeira lingered there. My heart raced and my body yearned for his touch. His lips, now less than an inch from mine, parted slightly. His thumb brushed against my cheek, while his other hand cradled the back of my head. I groaned with anticipation.

He gently pressed his lips to mine and held them there for a moment, as if I would break beneath him.

I reached up and touched his face, inviting him in. The soft stubble of his day-old beard tickled my palm.

His kiss deepened along with his breathing. Slowly he pulled back. His eyes were dark and liquid. "Good night, Skye," he said, guiding my head back down to his chest.

I would not be claimed tonight, but my heart certainly was. He wanted time, and I would give him as much as he needed. The ache in my body succumbed to the peace I found in his arms. I allowed the slow rhythmic beat of his heart to lull me to sleep.